DREAD

A Speculative Novel

Dread

Published by Per Bastet Publications LLC, P.O. Box 3023 Corydon, IN 47112

Starry Pines Background by Andrea Stöckel
Cover art by T. Lee Harris

ISBN 978-1-942166-90-0

Available in trade paperback and DRM-free ebook formats

DREAD

A Speculative Novel

PETER RUFER

Per Bastet

CHAPTER ONE

"It's the Draco, I told you. The Draco."

Steven's mouth formed words, but I was in a fog of confusion. My heart was going crazy in my chest. I couldn't catch my breath. Instructions to my body. *Breathe. In and out. In and out. Clear your head.* No matter how hard I tried, my breathing remained ragged. I glanced at the body in front of me and was almost overtaken with nausea. Steven wouldn't let me get down to help. What to do? I couldn't understand Steven no matter how I tried. He was still talking, but I got no meaning. I only heard . . . I don't know what I heard, but not words. Unintelligible sounds? Like the ones in cartoons — whah, whah, whah.

I looked down at the form on the pavement. The body bleeding out at my feet was Bob — MY Bob — and the pain I felt at first was now fighting with no feeling — numbness. Where was the calm I'd always taken for granted? Suddenly, tremors threatened to drain all energy from my legs — to make me crash to the ground. I staggered, dizzy. *No, no. You can't give into this. Not with the man standing next to you still holding the gun.* I was on the verge of crying. No, of sobbing. Of losing myself in grief and pain. I needed help.

I searched Steven's face for clues to help me understand. What I saw only laid on another layer of confusion. Finally, the sounds coming from him dissolved into meaning and still I was confused, "The Draco shot your wife? And Bob? The Draco shot Bob?" I peered both ways for retreating culprits. No one. Only Steven was standing there in front of me with the gun in his hand. Every time he said anything, he gestured with that gun. Every time the gun moved, I jerked out of fear. I croaked,

"You're the only one I see. The gun is in your hand. Where are the killers if it isn't you? No Draco around. How could they have killed Bob?" I looked down at my lover dying there on the sidewalk.

As my thinking cleared, a refrain danced through my mind, *dial 9-1-1 for help.* Maybe Bob could still be revived. By the EMS. Could they get here fast enough? Maybe? I might still be able to help him. I lifted my phone to dial.

Steven slapped the thing out of my hand and kicked it into the purple petunias lining the walk. Like a croquet ball, it stopped against the little flag put there last week to celebrate Labor Day. Was September second only a week ago? And now my phone was nestled against the little flag. My link to sanity was temporarily cut. I was alone with Steven. Steven and his gun, and perhaps the Draco. Again, I glanced in both directions in case they were still nearby and visible from where I stood in front of Helen's house. In this quiet suburban neighborhood. Quiet. We were alone, the three of us. Steven, Bob, and me. Oh, and his gun.

My breathing became raspy. I couldn't trust my voice. Blood roared through my ears. I couldn't tear my attention away from Bob's body. Mesmerized. *Get up, Bob. Oh, please get up. Please tell me it was all a joke, a prank. Please.*

Pleading did no good. He lay there — silent. Fluid congealing around inert body. Bob's life blood forming a glaze around him. I tried to scream for help, but the scream stuck in my throat.

Waves of panic and disgust threatened to overthrow me. And sadness. And grief. I wanted to sob out the pain starting to carve a cavern where my heart should have been, but that would have to wait until Steven was far away — far, far away. Steven and his gun.

Confusing emotions roiled inside me. The nausea returned, more strongly now. I wanted to throw up all over Steven. I wanted to slap the satisfied smile off his face. I wanted to run.

Run away from this man with the gun in his hand. Steven holding his gun, arm dangling at his side and then suddenly waving it around to emphasize a point. His gun could easily kill me. Still. Now. I didn't do anything. Immobilized. Not able to escape. Barely able to think.

Steven was irritated. I was too slow to understand. His words shot out like arrows. "I just *explained* this. Weren't you listening? *I* shot my wife and Bob. I shot them to protect the movement, the rebellion. I shot them because they were taken over by Draco. They were being used by the reptilians to stop us from fighting against them. I told you they live in tunnels below us. They're all around now, controlling too many. We want to get rid of them. We're fighting against the Draco and their human minions to save planet earth. I hate to think of what will happen if we don't win this war."

"Ah." What more could I say? I struggled to breathe deeply to slow my brain. I had to gain control of myself.

He gloated. "We've been planning and training for years. Now we're ready. Thousands are signed up and ready to fight the evil ones."

Again, he gestured with the gun. Only my logic could save me from the weapon waved in my face. Where did the current information fit into whatever history Steven had given me? We'd talked about this for years now. That story I'd believed to be the product of a fertile imagination fed by some conspiracy theory tripe on the Internet. He'd sent me emails and podcasts and videos about the aliens invading our airspace, but I hadn't taken it seriously. The narrators described the evil ones running our planet and how they enslaved the humans on the earth, especially focusing on the people in powerful positions. *Bob and Helen weren't in any powerful position. Why? Why?*

At the time I researched the truth, but any fact-checking I had done was denied by him and probably by his group of friends who absorbed the fantasies detailed in this closed loop of "experts."

3

Now, two real — flesh and blood — people were dead because of that dystopian tale. Imagination had become real. Very real. Blood and guts real.

I was standing next to a killer holding a gun. His wild eyes told me he was frenzied and on the edge. A killer who could shoot me if I didn't say the right thing. I racked my brain. What was the right thing? What?

No answer came. I stood like a statue bolted to the pavement beside a very dead Bob. And a crazy Steven. My mind instructed my legs to take me away from him. My legs wouldn't obey. Would I ever escape this dangerous man?

My awareness shifted. I felt heat radiating from the hot sidewalk. The smell of rust rose on currents of heat. The smell of iron in blood that had fed cells of my lover's body and now was escaping that body to spread on the sidewalk? Again, I gasped at the ferocious pain in my heart and felt the waterfall of tears nearing the surface.

Focus, Sylver. Bring your mind back from wherever it's hiding. Move, speak, do something. You cannot give in to the pain.

Distant sirens wailed their approach. Would they help? Bob no longer needed them, but I did. Would I get shot before police could rescue me? My thoughts were all over the place pinging inside my skull. Random words and phrases wouldn't stop long enough for me to see the sense. They wouldn't drop into patterns. I searched Steven's face for clues. Was he reminding himself I was a witness to his crime? Would he decide to get rid of all witnesses? To get rid of me? Oh, my God.

Steven shook his head. Was that an answer to my question/thought or was he expressing disappointment at my denseness? He sighed and then made a big show of masking his impatience with an exaggerated expression of patience. "I explained all this to you, Sylver. So many times. So very many times. The Draco are reptilians. Invaders from another planet. They live in tunnels underground. They operate by taking over human bodies to make people do whatever they want. They create all the evil in the world. Bob and my wife were possessed by the Draco. Both of them. They tried to stop me from completing my assignment . . . my mission. They threatened to tell people. Government officials. I had to kill them. I couldn't let them get in the way of the rebellion. Could I? They had to die for the greater good."

The greater good? How many times had that phrase been used as an excuse for bloody tyrants? There was no right answer for Steven. He would read into my answers whatever he wanted. *There is no way out!*

Shivers of panic rippled through my body. If I tried to run, would my cowardice be rewarded by a bullet in the back . . . front . . . side . . . or any place, for that matter? "Okay, then. Let's see if I understand what's going on. Millions or billions of years ago, a planet orbited the sun between Earth and Mars. It was named Tiamat. It was larger than the earth, but only by a little. Two species of aliens were battling it out for control of Tiamat."

"There were a number of different species fighting the Draco."

"Okay. A number of species. They fought with terrible weapons. Not only did they kill most of each other, but they blew the planet up. That explosion created the asteroid belt between Earth and Mars."

Steven's frown relaxed as he nodded. The faintest hint of a smile appeared on his lips.

I breathed deeper, steadier. So far, so good. Even so, I couldn't let my guard down. His gun remained at his side now. I finally convinced my legs to walk, to pace. Next, to run?

I smelled fear — my fear — mixed with the soft fragrance of flowers lining the sidewalk. Helen's flowers. I struggled to pull my consciousness back to searching for details of Steven's worldview in far reaches of my brain. Even though my life depended on it, I didn't come up with much. The retrieval mechanism was slowed by a wall of panic. "The Draco fought several other species, but they were meaner and lots more aggressive. They were merciless, willing to kill anything that got in their way."

Steven nodded. His fingers remained slack around the weapon. "Uh-hunh."

I calmed a bit.

Should I make Steven think I believed as he did? I went on, "No one really won. The war ended badly for both sides, because they blew up their home planet. During the destruction of Tiamat, the Draco escaped to Earth. Others established bases on the moon? Only a few of each managed to escape before their planet was destroyed. It's taken them all this time to grow their numbers to attack. Us. Here. Now."

Steven shrugged and his angry impatience returned. "No! I *explained* that the Draco took over the elite of this planet as soon as they arrived. They run the show here and now. From the time they arrived and to the current day. For thousands of years of human history, humans have been their slaves. We have. We are. Only some of us are breaking free. Waking up. Over time, we've learned more and have broken from their control. Some of us have. Not everyone. Some remain slaves. Unconscious. Like Helen and Bob. They were slaves . . . doing as commanded." His expression smoothed into smug. Triumphant. He glanced toward the sky. Waved his gun. "The other species fly ships around the planet. Sometimes they fly into our atmosphere and are reported as UFOs. They can only be seen when they aren't cloaked." The gun pointed to different places in the sky as if I should see the space ships.

I jerked in reaction to movements of the gun. I trembled, but fought my emotions to stay calm to think. There was something, some memory, in the back of my mind. Instinctively, I searched the sky again.

Steven practically spat out his next words. "You can't see them, Sylver. They remain cloaked and only let a few people see them and only on some occasions. The Draco are reptilians and live underground — in bases — on this planet. They live close so they can control leaders of the human race. They would attack the ships if they were visible. They feed on the energy of fear from people on the surface. So, they create trouble to generate fear. They create wars and natural catastrophes to generate more and more fear. It's like a soup of pain and anguish and fear that's their food. Fear."

I looked at my companion. I repeated what he had just said to appease him and then asked, "Is that why we have so many wars and so many natural catastrophes? To generate food for the Draco?"

The ploy worked, because he nodded, pleased I was finally catching onto his reality.

"And the good guys. They're in the sky? Right there above us? All the time? They hide — all the time? How do you know they're there? Or around here on the surface?" I waved my hand around to illustrate, but froze when my eyes crossed Bob's lifeless body. My Bob. I mourned that he was beyond help now. I mourned that the police hadn't arrived in time to make a difference for him.

Steven was getting frighteningly angry, as though my questions were an attack on him — a personal attack. "I know. I just know. I've seen them. Around Mount Shasta they power up to light up ships so seekers can see them. As evidence of their being here. To reassure us they'll help. Some land in bases in the mountain."

I remembered more, now that I was calmer. "So your evidence is those lights in the sky. Seeing them convinced you to join the rebellion to fight the Draco. I remember. How do you know the ships landing in the mountain bases are good guys? Could they have been Draco?"

He puffed up his chest triumphantly. "I told you, Sylver. I know. I just know. Someone must rid the planet of the Draco. Who better than me? You always spout off about taking personal responsibility. This is my responsibility. It's personal with me. I was put on this planet at this time to fight the Draco."

Damn!

My words were being used against me and what I considered sanity. "Who better than you? A retired military man. A crack shot, with medals and awards for your ability to hit targets at any range. Who better?" It reminded me I could not escape Steven's bullet if he decided I was possessed by bad guys. A crack shot. Keen eyes. Steady hand. Determined. I sighed and focused again on slowing my breathing and calming my brain. My brain was my only weapon here. My brain against his gun.

He looked toward the dead body on the sidewalk between us. "Bob must not have remembered I could shoot accurately from any distance. He must have thought he could outrun the round."

I shook my head but stood mesmerized by the sight of Bob's body. I whispered, "Big mistake on his part. Big mistake. Fatal, in fact."

I turned to study the man beside me. He didn't look like the member of a crack assault team with muscles ready to spring into action in hand-to-hand combat, kicking and punching to victory. Maybe that was a false image I got from watching too many action movies. Arnold, Sylvester, Dwayne? I shook my head to clear it. *What had Steven's military job been? An accountant? That's what he looked like. Besides, he could have been the lowest of the low for all I knew. Or a sniper.*

What I did know for certain is that for all the years since we met him, he'd spent hours at the shooting range. He won shooting matches and displayed dozens of trophies in a glass case in his den. Although he was tall — very tall — he was unusually thin. Whatever muscle he'd had looked gone. His thinness didn't look like a wiry strength. He was just plain skinny. For years he'd boasted that he didn't care to sweat himself into better physical condition. Leave that to others.

I had no desire to check that out. I might contract whatever madness he suffered.

I was lost in meaningless observations, meaningless guesses. I couldn't get my mind to focus on important things. It wandered all over the place. Random thoughts, random thoughts. Panic was growing again. *Stop it, stop it. Don't let it regain control. Where is the laser-sharp focus I've heard people say they experience during stress? Hadn't I heard that the clearest thinking occurs before the firing squad?*

Where was my ability to think my way out of strong emotions? Out of tough situations?

Steven's eyes seemed more intense. Brilliant blue. And now focused on me like lasers. Different. Did the act of killing increase focus? It must change a man. Just watching had changed me.

Was he looking for a Draco hiding inside my mild-mannered exterior? I look like the intellectual I am. Pacifist and reasonable. Not prone to violence. And right now frightened. Very frightened. Pretty much immobilized by panic.

My brain is my only weapon and I can't get control of it. Focus, Sylver, focus.

More than anything right now, I wanted to stay on Steven's good side. Actually, escape from the guy would be even better.

He stowed his gun under the tired jacket hanging in folds around his frame. Constriction around my chest eased several notches. I didn't much care where he put that gun as long as it was stowed and not close to his trigger finger.

I glanced at Bob's lifeless form and suddenly couldn't wait to get away from it. I blurted, "I have to get out of here. Can I leave now? Please let me leave."

Steven looked at me. "Where should we go?"

I shook my head. I didn't want to go with him. Not anywhere. Not any time. I didn't tell him because I didn't want to risk angering him. He might force me to stay. "Really, anywhere would be fine as long as there are no dead people. . . . No. Home. I want to go home."

He turned to look at Bob on the ground before us and nodded but didn't say anything. No remorse. No regret.

With all my heart, I wanted to go home. Alone. I wanted to curl up in my bed in a fetal position. Light years from revolution.

I tried to speak, but words only rasped out in a whisper. "Unless you have work to do — for the cause, I mean. I wouldn't want to keep you from it. We can meet later. Later. After you carry out your orders." I chided myself for sounding so nervous. I *was* nervous. No, I was terrified. And I didn't plan to visit him in prison when they caught up with him. I just hoped they would catch up with him soon.

Police sirens tore into my thoughts. Nearer. Almost here. Should I stay to explain what happened? I was a witness.

Steven decided for me. He jammed my phone into my hand and roughly shoved me toward my car. When did he pick the phone up from the flower bed? "Keep your cell phone close. And on. I'll call you soon, to let you know where we'll meet." His voice was conspiratorial, but also had an edge of command. I wanted to remind him that I didn't have anything — anything at all — to do with these killings. Only a witness after the fact.

I slid into my car, cranked the engine, and jerked it into motion. Where was I going? Was there some place to hide from Steven? Home? But that wasn't hiding.

I spoke to myself as I navigated the street, *Curiouser and curiouser. Who would have guessed when I got out of bed that this afternoon I would be a witness, an accomplice, to a crime? Not me. Certainly not Helen or Bob.*

And so much anger washed through me. Was this a part of the grieving process? *Of course, it is.*

Should I call the police? They were at the scene by now. How do I know if someone is a Draco? Not that I could do anything about it if I fell over one. Still, shouldn't I know?"

The scream of sirens stopped as I careened toward the corner. Police lights flashed in the rearview. I turned toward my condo. No looking back. Hopefully, my next call would be from a Steven in jail. Surely, he would be arrested. I hoped he would be arrested. I crossed all my fingers and prayed he would be arrested. A Steven in jail would mean a safe Sylver.

Should I have stayed to explain what happened? Should I go to the police station now? I could tell them what I'd seen. I was a witness — the only one other than Steven, and he had pulled the trigger. Or would he name me as the shooter? Leaving the scene of a crime certainly looked suspicious. I should. . . .

Images of Bob, dead, returned. I couldn't stop the tears. At the curb in front of my condo, I turned off the engine. In the car, I shook with sobs. My grief flowed out on a river of tears. My hands shook with such force that I couldn't work the handle to open the door. Finally, I managed to throw it open. I pulled myself out of the car, afraid of who might be out there. The zombie that was me staggered to the front door. Why couldn't I think of a place to hide?

CHAPTER TWO

My purse and keys landed on the table near the entry. I contemplated the phone in my hand as I moved it toward the table. I hesitated. Hadn't Steven told me to keep it close? What would he do if I didn't answer? How could he even call if he was in jail? Surely, they would lock him up on suspicion of murder. After all, he was the lone person at the scene of a crime. With the gun. . . . I shrugged. Confusion. I stashed the phone in my pocket, just in case. I didn't trust his impulses now. He'd become more violent or maybe I just hadn't seen the clues. He told me that his group had trained for years. Didn't that speak of violence? How could I miss that?

Familiar surroundings felt safer. The calm didn't last. Sitting on the sofa only gave my mind time to stoke the fires of fear. Pacing didn't help because I kept obsessing about — all that had happened and all that Steven hinted would happen.

I didn't want to talk with Steven. I didn't want to see him. But where could I hide?

In the den, I tried television. I thought the news might have something about Steven and the two killings, but the screen filled with images of rioting. One story after another showed violence — battles in other countries, riots here, peaceful protesters being attacked by men in military-style garb carrying assault weapons. The news commentators described what sounded like two armies set against each other. Was this Steven's rebellion? But peaceful protesters weren't evil. They weren't the Draco. Why attack them?

I surfed channels. Everything seemed to be about war and violence. Suddenly the scene was the one I just left. I turned up the volume. An outline of Bob's body was drawn on the pavement in front of Steven's house. The reporter talked over images of black militia in town to "demonstrate" because of violence against people of color. She conjectured that their rage had swelled to such a degree they had gone on a killing rampage to shoot two "innocent white people" in a lily-white, middle-class neighborhood. She didn't tell her audience their names — Helen and Bob. Were these two innocent people, she asked, in the wrong place at the wrong time? Was it retribution for deaths of people in neighborhoods in less advantaged sections of town? Law enforcement officials looked into the camera earnestly and pleaded with viewers to lock themselves in their homes until morning. "Be warned. It's not safe out there."

As I listened, I checked that deadbolts were thrown on doors and locks on windows. They were definitely locked, though I understood they provided only the barest of protections.

After the commentary, I turned the dial to off and peace. Only there was no peace in the turmoil of my thoughts. I paced around the room and around the condo. I forced all thoughts out of my mind to focus on the movement of my feet. Mindful walking. One step after another. Disruptive, out-of-control thoughts pushed away. At least a bit of calm returned. I had practiced these rituals for decades. Normally, they worked quickly, but this wasn't exactly a normal day.

I remembered the powerful sense of dread I'd felt down to the core of my being. It had started several days ago and notched up to panic level today. Was this the danger I'd sensed, or was this a new and improved crisis?

Perhaps reading the Tarot cards would help. I opened the ornate wooden box and pulled the silk-covered deck from its home. The copper dragon inlay on the top of the box drew my attention. The dragon is a symbol of warrior energy, of strength and ability to overcome. I laid my hand flat on the top of the box, willing myself to absorb some of that strength.

I shuffled the cards — slowly — concentrating on each move. The very act of handling the cards is calming. That, in itself, over the years has become a meditation. Serenity flowed from the cards into me as I cradled them in two hands. I inhaled deeply and exhaled slowly.

Home, again. And at peace in my practice.

I come from a long line of seers. The women in my father's family are strong in the spirit. We don't have the same cognitive make-up as others. That difference is encouraged by teachings — of philosophy and spiritual connection to the divine. It's from that connection to a higher power that strength comes. I must remember that. *I must remember that, especially now.* Especially in these times of trouble.

My aunt, my father's sister, taught me to read the cards when I was young. I learned from experience as I grew up to consult them whenever I was in a quandary. In time, I discovered them to be a remarkable source of answers . . . and of solace. Of guidance, when no human was ready to offer that help. The Tarot became my tool of choice, although I also know how to use other divinatory methods — the I-Ching, the runes, the pendulum among them.

As I shuffled, I remembered the warnings of the reading I last did, but so many past warnings had ended in nothing. Had that one foretold Bob's death and Steven's falling off the edge of sanity? Even if I had understood the message, what could I do? *Focus now, Sylver, to seek clarification.*

I did remember that in each of those recent readings, the Tower or the Death card played prominently. Both meant turmoil and challenge resulting in change, an overthrow of the status quo. Had the cards warned me, only for me to miss the signs? Death — Helen's and Bob's deaths?

I shuffled again, and the sound of card softly beating against card was like music, a rhythm for going within. The sound lulled me into a meditative state. Calm, breathing deeply. Another shuffle. With eyes closed and Tarot held against my heart, I repeated the familiar prayer. Never the same, but always with the same intention — to ask Archangels and Spirit for their help and protection. *Please send me information to guide me and help me guide others. From your vantage point, you can see so much more than I. Bring knowledge to me from the source of love and light.*

I divided the deck into three piles of cards moving from right to left and then I returned them to a single stack, again moving right to left. All movements tapped out a rhythm to slow my heartbeat. Slow my mind, open it to guidance soon to be revealed. I turned over the cards, one by one, and felt their wisdom.

The Magician was the first. A good beginning and perhaps he would help bring a good ending. His right hand reaches toward the sky and his left points toward the earth. He is a person bringing together the energies of Heaven and Earth to create good. The phrase repeated in my mind, "to create good." Comforting.

To his left, I laid the Queen of Wands. She's the good wife and mother. Always a sympathetic character in these plays sketched out in colorful cards on the wooden surface of my reading table.

To her left, the Fool. Prickles crawled along the nape of my neck and into my scalp. He's ready to set out on a path, but he must choose. The Fool signifies a person who faces several options and has the ability to select one from among them. He might choose wisely or not so wisely. In this reading, he might be influenced by the good intentions of the Queen of Wands. I hoped he would be.

The fourth card was the King of Swords. More prickles. Whoever this man was, a stranger or a friend, he could become violent. In this configuration, he seemed inclined toward violence. Was that feeling a part of the message? Or simply a reaction to the killings I'd seen earlier? I stopped to breathe deeply again to settle. I was struck by the odd turn my calm life had taken today.

The Tower was the final card. Two people pictured in a free fall from the heights of a tower. A zig-zag of lightning struck the tower from above. A catastrophe that would affect my own life and those of everyone around me. It would create great change. Would the King of Swords initiate this chaos? Was this Steven? Would he bring the downfall of the current way of life? He certainly had changed *my* life with one bullet. And his own with another. Perhaps the chaos would create greater enlightenment at the same time, but at what cost? Even more bullets taking even more lives? The seeker was being asked to relax into the change. I felt that as long as I rode the wave of change, I would not be hurt. The interim would be challenging. Very challenging, indeed. All affected would struggle to maintain their moral compass while falling into the new. By waiting, the outcome would bring more peace, more happiness. The tableau called for patience in the midst of turmoil.

Understanding comes to me, not from inside my own mind but from somewhere out there.

Oh, my! In this latest reading, the Queen of Wands must indicate Helen. Her biggest mistake was that she didn't agree with her husband and unwisely let him know. She probably didn't realize how dangerous he'd become. Neither had I. Not until today.

Steven fit the description of the King of Swords with his military background and skill with firearms. He certainly had a life and death influence over Bob and Helen. And me, too, I reminded myself. He had and did face decisions requiring consideration and careful weighing of options as the Fool would indicate. Had he weighed his options? From what I knew of the influences in his life, I wondered.

Or could the Fool mean me?

Who is the Magician? My head ached from going over and over the possibilities. Was meaning somewhere in this jumble of options, or had I missed it? Could I have used this information to help others? To save Bob's life or that of Helen? How could I use it to save my own life?

Had there been signs I ignored because I'm afraid? The Tower warned me not to ignore and not to fight it. Wait. Watch. Follow guidance. Wait, watch. Look for a new path.

The jangle of the telephone made me jump. *Steven.* I should change the ringtone I assigned to him to something that wouldn't startle me so badly. Could I let it ring until he gave up? He would never give up. Would he bring his gun to force me to his will? I glanced at the clock. I'd had a couple of hours to myself. I wanted more.

It was Steven on his cell phone. Unfortunately, he was not calling from jail.

Damn! A deep breath and I was ready to deal with this situation. I felt like I was riding a carnival ride into a tunnel filled with unknown dangers. The Tower card promised a safe landing ahead. More crossed fingers.

He greeted me just like it were any other day. Except, his voice practically buzzed with enthusiasm. Not even the tiniest touch of sorrow. "I'm on my way to pick you up. We can eat dinner and plan our next move."

I yawned for effect. "Steven, I'm exhausted. Today has been very emotional for me. How about lunch tomorrow instead?"

His voice was stronger and more demanding. "No, tonight. We have to talk. You need my protection."

My heart skipped a beat and then launched into rat-tat-tating in my chest. So much for staying in peace. "You didn't tell them about me?"

"Who?"

"The police. You didn't tell them I saw you kill two people, did you? That I'm a witness? Will they be knocking on my door tonight?"

He chuckled quietly. "Nah. Actually, you didn't see me pull the trigger. You arrived after all the fun. What difference would that make anyway?"

"The police didn't arrest you?"

"Not at all. The killer was already gone by the time you got there. I might have had my gun out to protect myself — and you — from the guy who did kill Helen and Bob."

"You had to protect yourself from marauding gangs with weapons and enough anger to pull the trigger. I was only a witness of the aftermath." Suddenly, I realized the ramifications of what Steven was saying. "The policemen are part of your rebellion? They gave you a pat on the back for eliminating two of the enemy? They told the news reporter it was probably a spill-over from riots in town." It was impossible to tell which team a person is on, regardless of his jersey.

Steven paused, and when he continued, his voice was strong, almost pedantic. "We've planned this for decades. It's finally happening. Waves of energy are flooding the earth. It's the goddess energy, Sylver. I told you about it. Well, it's here. Right now. Ripples of positive energy sparking greater enlightenment. More people are waking up. More people see the reality of our world, the truth about the Deep State. Soon we'll ascend to a different dimension so we can start on a different stage of our soul development. At least people who are becoming enlightened will. And it all started in 2012, when the goddess energy started pouring into our planet."

My pounding heart fell about three stories without a parachute. "A pretty picture. But what does enlightenment have to do with killing people on the street? With killing innocent protesters? Is rebelling against the government a sign of enlightenment? Just how widespread is this rebellion?"

He was silent for seconds before whispering, "We can't talk on the phone. We may have — company."

I lowered my own voice to a whisper. "People listen to private phone calls?"

"Uh-hunh. The Draco. The Cabal does their dirty work. I'm at your front door now. Come out."

What choice did I have? I didn't know how violent he could get, but still I hesitated before answering. "Be right out." After all, I didn't want for him to break through my door to drag me out by my hair.

I spent a few minutes cleaning up, then walked through the door and prayed for protection from this guy who might or might not be batshit crazy.

In truth, I preferred to think he is crazy and everything else in my world was still the same as yesterday. *If he's crazy, then maybe there's no rebellion. No other countries in full meltdown.*

When I opened his car door, the radio blared. He was tapping the steering wheel in time with soft rock. He was smiling slightly. The man looked absolutely happy.

All I could think to say was, "Hi."

He smiled his crooked smile and shifted the car into drive. "I smell mint. You brushed your teeth."

"Mint toothpaste. Yes, mint." Suddenly I was aware of the minty taste in my mouth. I sank back into my thoughts and listened for any warning of danger. After all, I was in the car with a killer. I could not forget that one little fact.

CHAPTER THREE

Steven wound through narrow roads in old neighborhoods. He dodged cars and grumbled about bicycles littering roads. I realized we were nearing the protests downtown by way of back streets. Television reporters warned viewers to stay well away from this area — tonight and in the near future. At least until this boiling pot cooled. As in nights past, hostilities could spill over into surrounding neighborhoods. A thought pinged — *You could still be shot today.*

Even with windows closed and the radio playing, the yelling and cracking reports grew louder.

Panic is non-productive. I continued with mindful breathing and positive self-talk and crossed my fingers. Yeah, it was the fingers I was betting on for the most help.

Steven stopped the car in the middle of the street, not bothering to park in a legal space. He motioned for me to come with him. With the doors open, noise from the gathering crowd of men was much louder. I saw a very few women, but there were some here and there, almost hidden in the gangs of men. I hurried to follow Steven as he skirted cars parked along the side of the street. His long legs carried him faster than mine could go. I jogged to keep up. Crowds of people in head-to-toe camouflage gathered in the cross street ahead. There were dozens of them, all dressed in similar uniforms. They fondled very big guns. AK-47s I guessed? Definitely must be called assault weapons. Scary.

I don't like guns. Not these. Not any. But these looked far more lethal than the little hand guns I'd handled up to this point.

"Your friends?" I threw a hand toward the people ahead of us. He nodded.

His expression was focused and determined. A man on a mission.

When we reached the edge of the gathering, the men pulled into a tighter knot to repulse us. They pushed us back and away until Steven held up an ID of some sort.

The guys parted to let him through. Parted like the Red Sea did for Moses. Their expressions screamed they were not joking. About anything.

I stayed close to my fearless leader. Who, in fact, seemed to be theirs as well. Cheerful greetings were shared, sometimes punctuated with man hugs and hard slaps on muscled backs. They spoke in low tones careful to hide conversations from me. After all, who was I, anyway? The only clues to the content of the exchanges were nods and glances toward knots of men in other "uniforms" down the street. They slapped weapons and dramatically pointed muzzles at antagonist militia. All the while they only indicated awareness of my presence by shooting furtive glances my way. Was this the calm before the clash of military action? Was there going to be war on the streets of my town, my home?

I tried to gather impressions of the participants. They were dressed similarly with their faces obscured by black goo. Their heads were covered by hats in a variety of styles. Mostly forest camo. Gunshots. Or was it fireworks? Sounds from further along the street. Other groups yelling some distance away. Men around me ducked their heads at every report as though they had experience dodging rounds.

In the middle of the crowd, Steven pulled a small package out of a pocket and pushed it at a big man during a man-hug. The other man nodded and smiled as he took the package. Then Steven suddenly turned and squeezed past me to retrace his steps through the mass of humanity. I followed through the blur of camouflage around me as though my life depended on it. As we jogged through the crowd, the men opened a path in front of us and closed quickly behind us. At this point we were moving so fast that I didn't have time to focus on any particular face. The result was that I could not have picked any of them out of a line-up of one.

Suddenly, we emerged from the mass of his buds to run smack into a cluster of reporters. My companion swore under his breath, but didn't slow his pace. He went faster — in a trot — leaving me in second place, well behind and struggling to keep up. I failed and was separated from him by reporters who closed ranks as he passed. Microphones appeared out of nowhere. They were jammed so close to my face that I was on the verge of an attack of claustrophobia. Questions came at me from every side and flashes blinded me. I couldn't move. Trapped. I pushed, but met something like a wall of news humanity.

And they bombarded me with more questions . . . faster . . . louder.

"Are these men going to shoot real bullets tonight or is this just for show?"

"Are these men members of a Neo-Nazi group or the Proud Boys? Who exactly are they associated with?"

"Who is the man you were with?"

"Is he the leader of this posse?"

"How do you know those men in camouflage?"

"The street is starting to look like a battlefield. How much of that is for show, and how much is really preparation for—"

I tried to plow through the mob of reporters but couldn't move. A hand grabbed my arm and yanked me through the people and equipment, essentially using my body to knock aside anything in my way. I raised my arm to shield my face, but it was frightening nonetheless. At the same time, two men from the armed group behind me stepped in to push reporters aside as I was being pulled through them. I heard some angry exchanges between the armed men and the media accompanied by flashing lights from cameras. By the time I finally emerged from the group, Steven pulled me along and we were running at a speed qualifying us for Olympic gold.

Steven yelled back at me, "You've got to move faster."

My face was hot with fury as I spat out, "I can't. They trapped me and I couldn't break through." I panted for breath and let my anger flow. "You left me. What was all that yakkity yak about protecting me?"

We raced to the car and as soon as he started the engine Steven sped away from the ruckus. I looked back to see flashes as the news people took photos of the car. Probably for the license. My companion seemed practiced at evading reporters. He was deep in thought. I didn't dare interrupt those thoughts, even to ask where we were going.

Besides, I was in the middle of my own emotional vortex.

After a half hour silently navigating more city streets — in and out and all around — we drove into the parking lot of Steven's favorite Ethiopian restaurant.

The overpowering smell of spice surrounded the establishment. My stomach practiced a few flips good enough for gymnastics competition. "I . . . I'm not sure I can handle Ethiopian tonight."

"Make this work. It'll probably be the last peaceful meal you have. Those vultures will find you and hound you, especially after tonight. Why did you let them photograph you?"

I blew out a furious breath. "Let them? Let them? You left me to those predators. They had me cornered — so penned in that I couldn't move. I hardly had room to breathe."

He eased into a parking space, turned off the engine, and turned to study me. When he finally spoke, his voice was calmer. "I guess you're not used to being in battle — or evading an attack. Takes a little getting used to. But I'm good with it now."

"Is this really my future? Something I'll have to get used to?"

No answer. He was lost in his own thoughts. "Because of you, they got my license number. We just landed right in the middle of their crosshairs in that one move. For all these years, I managed to stay below the radar. And now. . . ." He shook his head in dismay. Another glance in my direction to express his anger.

He appeared to be waiting for my response. At first, my voice wouldn't rise above a whisper, but as I spoke, I gathered more steam and my voice got stronger and louder and more strident. "No, I am not comfortable with seeing people die. Especially not people from my own life. Or even thinking about it. I'm not used to reporters getting in my face and hammering me with questions to which I have no answer. I am not involved in this war of yours and don't even want to see any of those men again. Never. I am not used to thinking that a war is being waged in my own backyard, so to speak. And I am definitely not interested in taking part in any battles. I want to go back to my peaceful and boring life."

He chuckled softly. "Not an option, Sylver. The people I kill are no longer your friends. The Draco invaded their bodies. They're the enemy. And those guys with the cameras have ended your boring life. That is no longer an option."

He sounded so sure that he spoke the truth. So convinced.

I heard only insanity. "Maybe I can talk myself out of this. . . . Besides, how do you know it was the Draco and not the other species? How do you know either way?"

"You know. You just know." He slammed his hand against the steering wheel, emphasizing his point. His other hand moved to the door handle.

"That's what you said before. It's just . . . just . . . well,

I'm having a tough time with all this. I do not see the Draco or even feel them around me. I know you explained the origins of this disagreement, but you didn't say that I would be — that I would be right in the middle of it. In the middle of a war. Of a civil war. You didn't tell me you would kill Bob. Although I don't think anything would prepare me for that kind of thing . . . even if you'd drawn a sketch of the scene." I was silenced by the memory of Bob's body bleeding out on the sidewalk.

My companion leaned back against his seat and closed his eyes, rubbing them so hard it was a wonder his eyeballs didn't pop out of their sockets. He turned slowly toward me. "You don't understand even yet, do you? Anyone living on this planet will be in the middle of the conflict. I told you the president signed a law creating the Space Force. He knows there are alien species out there. The government has lied to us for all these years. He set up the structure for our protection from an attack by those aliens."

I didn't want to step over — or even near the line of his beliefs, but I just had to ask. "I thought the president planned to put weapons on satellites in our skies. Isn't his goal to make it another domain for war, another theater of battle?"

Steven interrupted me. "Yeah. To fight the aliens."

"But those weapons are to be aimed toward the earth. Toward this planet. Toward us." I gestured around us.

He nodded vigorously. "To kill Draco on the ground."

I couldn't let it go even at my own peril. "But isn't that the way Tiamat was blown to bits? Isn't that why the aliens immigrated to this part of the solar system anyway? Didn't you tell me that? Isn't this a danger signal? A danger signal the inhabitants of Tiamat didn't take seriously?"

"Nah. Those satellites can pick out a specific person from face recognition. They can isolate an individual and kill just that specific person with a laser blast."

"Ah. Not making me feel any better." The problems with this plan were clear to me and I wondered why they weren't clear to Steven. "And you don't think the guys on Tiamat had better technology?"

He didn't hear one word I said. "Great, isn't it? Such precision."

Obviously, he wasn't open to any new point of view. Again, I felt like emptying my stomach on him — if there were anything in it. *Maybe later — after we eat.* I pushed aside much of what I was thinking and said the only safe thing in that jumble, "Scary."

Steven shook his head and turned to look at me again. "It's only scary if you're a bad guy."

I couldn't wrap my head around his logic. "Doesn't the definition of 'bad guy' depend on your position in the game? Aren't you the 'bad guy' to them? Suppose they decide you've overstepped your bounds or overstayed your welcome? Couldn't they classify you as *other* even though you haven't done anything against them directly? And you just told me that you've been neutralizing their guys."

He shrugged. "The people in charge of those weapons are on my side. But, yes, what you say could happen. But not to me."

I chuckled. Ah, yes, the I-am-special defense. OMG! How many times had that failed to protect? And then I realized he was telling me that he would have an important position in the new government. I shook my head. "Suppose the enemy takes control of that weapon. Aren't you in danger then, especially after you kill so many of their operatives? It should be easy for them since they're so much more advanced than we. Technologically, that is." By this time, I wasn't certain who I referred to as THEY. From my position in NO MAN'S LAND, it was difficult to tell. In fact, from where I stood, everyone else was THEY.

His voice mirrored the impatience on his face. "Sylver, why are you such a Doubting Thomas? All you think about is what could go wrong. Consider the good we're doing for the planet. We'll bring peace and happiness and freedom."

I marveled that the man didn't see the hypocrisy in what he said — and the incongruence between what he said and what he did. His expression was serious, deadly serious. He seemed to believe everything he was telling me with every fiber of his being.

I'd heard it before, and the result had never worked as the person imagined it would. Usually, there were horrible unintended consequences. At the present moment the better part of valor was to keep any doubts to myself. Hadn't that been Helen's mistake? She had tried to argue with this very same man. Look what happened to her.

My stomach growled to give me a detour away from the conversation. "I am hungry. That's the translation of that loud speech from my stomach."

"My stomach agrees."

I added a sing-song melody to my voice, "That makes it a chorus of two."

Steven opened his door without another word.

CHAPTER FOUR

When Steven opened the restaurant door, laughter and loud conversation crashed like a wave over us. The atmosphere was warm and heavy with the aroma of spices as foreign as the hostess' native garb. I felt as though I were entering another world. And still, the fear lurked very near.

The hostess greeted Steven by name and even asked about his wife — by name. He grinned at her and answered that Helen was in a far better place now. He made it sound as though she'd gone on a cruise. I was amazed at the sincere expression on his face. He seemed absolutely filled with joy and ready to party. I wasn't there myself.

Steven must have called from his car. As soon as he greeted the hostess, the young woman gathered two menus and led us along an invisible path zig-zagging toward a table on the far side of the room. My companion waved to someone seated in the corner and paused to exchange a few words with another man sitting at a table we passed. Several of the waitresses called to him and they exchanged words in some foreign language — Ethiopian, I guessed. He grinned and responded in the same language, but probably with slaughtered pronunciation. The waitresses giggled and continued in the same language. Steven shrugged his shoulders and mirrored their mirth.

Steven laughed as though he didn't have a care in the world as we walked around tables jammed into every inch of the room. Practically every one of them was occupied — people leaning over bowls of food or sipping drinks. Conversations bounced off bare walls.

Personally, not only did I not share his light-hearted spirit, but I was fighting off a very bad case of nervous jitters. Still, logically, if he hadn't killed me by now, he probably didn't intend to kill me. That thought was somewhat comforting. Regardless, I was emotionally drained and the contrast with my current surroundings was disorienting. It felt as if I had dropped into an alternate reality.

An alarming memory pinged in my brain. Years ago, Steven talked about what he and I could do if he were not married. At the time, I mildly discouraged him. Perhaps he thought I was inclined toward a personal relationship and was only denying it because of my loyalty to Helen? I should have told him, loudly and in well-enunciated phrases, that I wouldn't mate with him if he were the last human on the planet! But, at the time, I let him ramble on with only minor interruptions because I didn't want to hurt his feelings. He was, after all, my friend. And married to my best friend. Deluded perhaps, but still a friend. Was that an error?

Suppose he killed his wife in the mistaken belief that we would become romantic partners? Did he understand me so little? Didn't he realize the act of killing would be a turn-off for me, even if I had ever harbored romantic hopes? Which I never, ever had. Not for Steven. Not to mention that shooting Bob did not qualify him for my list of the world's sexiest men. *Not to mention* that in my humble estimation his worldview certified the man for admission to a loony bin. Not to mention. . . .

For years, I'd kept an open mind just in case Steven had access to information I did not. Perhaps he told me the truth — a truth I didn't have in my normal life. Right now I couldn't believe much of it. Still, I warned myself to not rile the guy. After today, I understood how truly unhinged he was.

I concentrated on spreading the napkin on my lap just so. *Which topics are safe?* For the hundredth time I asked myself why I was here with Steven. Probably because he'd been parked at my door with the means to "convince me." Maybe having dinner with the man was not so crazy after all, but rather self-protective. I did not trust his impulses after this afternoon.

29

But he did keep telling me of his intention to protect me. There was that.

We settled. Ordered. Drank wine. By the time the waitress refilled our glasses, I was almost relaxed enough to talk more intelligently. Read that, *somewhat anesthetized*.

I wanted to beg the waitress to leave the rest of the bottle on the table, so I sent telepathic messages to Steven to make that happen. He must not have heard my thoughts and the wine returned to the kitchen with the waitress. Too bad. I held onto my glass as though it were a life jacket in a turbulent sea. Right now, my life *was* a turbulent sea.

Food was brought to the table in communal serving dishes. Bite-sized chunks of meat and vegetables swam in a thick brown sauce. I could discern potatoes, but the rest was pretty much a mystery. The aroma of warm spices filled the air around us and when I closed my eyes I could imagine being in that far-away land. No individual plates. No eating utensils. Only a bowl of warm bread. Ethiopian food is to be eaten with fingers digging in the warm stew or by using a piece of bread to scoop it up. Their style of eating requires leaning close to the table and to your table mate. Probably another reason we came to this particular restaurant on this particular night. The first being the cover of noise. Actually, the first must have been because this was Steven's favorite food.

Conversation stopped while we leaned into the food, digging out meat and vegetables and beans and sauce and cramming them into our mouths. Not an elegant way to take a meal, but oh, so, effective. I always felt more like a toddler when we ate here.

Steven wiped hands on his napkin and leaned back to rub his belly. "Ahh — so good. Best food in the world. I ate too fast and need a short break."

"It is tasty." I breathed in the scent of spices. I savored the tastes mingling in my mouth. Wonderful. And here I'd thought I wouldn't be able to eat after the emotion of the day.

Suddenly, he leaned toward me and spoke in a hoarse whisper, "The rebellion has begun. What you saw today is nothing compared to what's coming. You'll hear about it on the news tomorrow. We're making our move all over the world in a coordinated action."

"Tonight?" My stomach flipped at the image of a world bursting into flame. There were already so many deaths due to new and old viruses swimming around the planet. Did we really need more from physical violence? From war?

He continued in a voice filled with excitement and pride, "It starts tonight, but we have plans for the future. Long term plans. There will be much killing. I know you're against killing, but it can't be helped. Collateral damage, you know. But if we can't convince the brainwashed masses. . . ." He shrugged in resignation. "Criminals in Congress and other government departments will be arrested. There are thousands, hundreds of thousands, of sealed indictments being opened and ready to be executed. Those people must be punished for their crimes. The rich people who use large corporations to steal money from all of us. The people who have stolen the wealth of the nations will be arrested, tried, executed."

I couldn't help but goad him. "Tortured?"

His smile became absolutely brilliant, "I wasn't going to mention that, but yes. They must be punished for their wrongdoing. We're planning more if the election doesn't go our way. By then we'll have a count of the people controlled by the Draco."

Chills shuddered down my spine. His determination frightened me. He was telling me that many others were joining together. They didn't like the way the country was being run and were determined to do something more about it than write their Congressman. Tonight. How many of them were out there?

Divergent facts zinged around my brain, but the focus became events leading up to and included in World War II. Did redistribution of wealth motivate actions of Nazis in Germany?

Or was this only an excuse used to cover the real reason art and gold were stolen to fill coffers of the elite rather than those of the state? Who is really behind this current power grab? This grab for the gold? Was someone using the fantasy of an alien race to cover their own — human — intentions?

His words echoed. *All over the world.* Ominous. Would there be any place to hide till it was all over? Would it ever be over? What would the world look like when this war ended? I watched with fascination as light danced in his eyes.

He grinned in delight, "We've been planning for decades. Planning and training. Our army is ready. The time is now. We're ready to end this mob rule. The Cabal feels our strength and has released these diseases as a defensive measure. From a lab in China. Here, but in Africa, too. All over the world, really."

That pronouncement stopped me mid-motion. "You're saying this new pandemic is the work of the bad guys? You're telling me that some group of people knowingly released a virus guaranteed to kill millions of their fellow human beings?"

My companion nodded. "They did the same thing years ago to start that last pandemic. We're getting stronger every day. They're fighting back any way they know how. Their desperation's resulted in this level of evil. I told you they're controlled by the Draco. And they feed on humans' fears. What better way to create more fear than the fear of death from diseases?"

I repeated more slowly to give myself time to catch up with these ideas. "They released a lethal virus into the population to create more fear to feed the Draco. You're telling me this virus is weaponized to kill the 'good guys', the people on your side of the battle."

"To strengthen their position and to feed the Draco. Yes."

I tried to understand the ramifications of this new information. "You say the intended victims are your supporters, but the people actually being killed are the very groups of people you've ranted against for years. How do you know this virus was not released by people fighting the Draco? People who think the way you think? People on YOUR side?"

He waved the argument aside. I wiped fingers on my napkin then lifted my glass to sip wine. The hand holding the glass was shaking slightly, making wine slosh around.

He ranted on and on about the evils of big corporations and the media that was brainwashing its audience. I drank wine. He listed all the groups of people with guns that would join the fight. I drank more wine. He listed all the people who would be imprisoned or tortured and killed. I drank even more wine. He talked about the money that would be released from the government coffers and given to the people. After all, it was taken from those citizens through an illegal income tax implemented by the Draco-controlled politicians for their own benefit. The waitress returned to refill my wine glass. I didn't think there was enough wine on the planet to help me deal with these new ideas. On and on, he laid his story out. He talked about using the water and air to ply the citizens with drugs to make them more compliant.

My hands were getting a bit twitchy and my lips were numb. Hmm. That's a bad sign. Given that I'd had about a hundred times my normal consumption of alcohol, I figured that I was headed for a doozy of a hangover. I gulped wine as I thought with disgust about the ramifications of Steven's predictions. I determined to never drink the water or eat the food. If I could help it, I would not breathe the air. Not ever again. Just in case! I dipped a piece of bread into the plate of coagulating, slimy meat gravy, doubt arising.

That's when I threw up . . . all over the table and the floor around us.

CHAPTER FIVE

I don't remember the ride home — only that it seemed to take forever. And that I did not feel well. Head spinning and stomach roiling, I laid on the back seat. Probably not the best idea. I threw up several more times into a bucket Steven had gotten from somewhere.

By the time the car pulled up to the curb in front of my home, I felt better. Not great, but not like throwing up again. There probably wasn't anything left to throw up.

He dropped me off without suggesting a nightcap. No surprise there. He didn't even walk me to the door. Hmm. Actually, I couldn't blame him. I probably reeked.

Mindlessly putting one foot in front of the other, the walk from the car to my stoop seemed to take years . . . and a gargantuan amount of effort. I opened the door and emptied my hands. Purse and keys landed in their homes on the table just inside the door. I carefully engaged the lock. Both locks. Hoping they would protect me from whatever was lurking outside my home. I inspected them and wondered if those flimsy hunks of metal would serve to shut the evil out. I was absolutely convinced there was evil out there. And then I wondered about the evil within.

Too tired to think, I shuffled through the living room. I barely noticed the European antique furniture I'd spent a lifetime collecting. Or the paintings. The other pretty things. What did material possessions matter when everything about the life I knew was threatened? In a daze, I moved across the hardwood floors and into my bedroom to fall into bed. My body was achy and tired from being sick, so I stretched out under the sheets fully clothed. I felt my body and my mind relax, starting to dive deeper for the sleep I craved. Suddenly, my mind snapped into high alert. *Oh, no. I am way too tired for this.*

Thoughts whirred around inside — running to some far-off place. I tried to fight it, but I only tossed and turned for a while. Soon, I realized sleep was light years away. I don't remember when I got up to shower and dress in clean pajamas. That felt better. On the way back to bed, I lit the diffuser filled with lavender essential oils. All the better to surround myself with the sights and sounds of sleep. It didn't work. I tossed for a while longer, watching numbers change on the digital clock.

Steven's words repeated over and over in my head. He talked blithely about killing billions of people. It seemed to me that the only ones who remained would be white males with enough women alive to . . . Just enough? In this world he envisioned, would women return to the role of chattel? What about all those others? This was a plot for a horror film.

Since sleep was a distant fantasy, I padded into the den to flip on the television. Maybe some mindless infomercial would be the tonic to induce sleep. Sadly, normal programming was preempted for news flashes documenting clashes in cities across the globe. So much violence. So many dead and still the fighting continued and more died. In Africa. In the Middle East. In eastern Europe. In South America. In the U.S. Right here in Kentucky.

What had started as "peaceful protest" in cities across the country and across the planet had morphed into what looked like the civil war Steven described. Was anyone winning? Was anyone keeping track of the death toll? Did anyone even care about how many people were being killed? Was police brutality being used as an excuse for war? Or was this season of protests concocted to cover a war carefully planned for decades? It was a chicken or egg kind of question. Were people on the streets militia or freedom fighters or innocent protesters or government "peace keepers"? It was hard to tell, regardless of the uniform. In fact, I wondered how they could tell each other apart. Who to shoot?

Other late-night "documentaries" described right wing groups. The narration painted pictures of real-life dystopian societies to follow the fall of democratic governments. There were also people fighting dictators for their freedom, protesting ballot boxes stuffed by the government even before the election began. The official answer was tear gas and bullets into the crowd.

One reporter talked over video of men in fatigues shooting at targets shaped like humans placed far down the range. Sharpshooters like Steven.

The narrator's voice was somber. "We have interviewed leaders of several groups of fighters who call themselves Neo-Nazis. They say many similar paramilitary groups are making a resurgence in countries around the world. We asked when the groups reassembled."

The scene changed to a close-up of a young man with very short hair dressed in camouflage pants and shirt and fondling an assault weapon. "We have not reassembled. We have remained strong and are getting stronger every day. We don't have to recruit men to join our group. We don't even have to ask them. Men by the dozens contact us asking how they can join our fight or any of the others around the country. They see the training videos and like what they see."

"Training videos?"

The young man nodded vigorously, grinning. "We teach how to make bombs and plan offensives."

The reporter moved her microphone closer. "Are you telling me that this movement isn't just getting started?"

The fighter smirked, "This movement has never been interrupted. We have been alive and well and gathering strength since the 1940s. We have training camps in locations spread across the country. Across the world. People join us because they don't like what they see happening in their countries."

The reporter leaned toward him, holding the microphone even closer. "You've stayed in business since the 1940s?"

The soldier smirked. "We post instructions about weapons and hand-to-hand combat all over the Internet. The reason you see us in so many cities now is because we're finally coming out into the light to let people know we're here and ready to fight for the rights of our fellow Americans. People are angry about being victims of debt enslavement, of working jobs they hate. They have reached their limits. Now is the time for us to make bids to come to power. There are too many people trying to destroy this country. It's time for us to defend it."

The reporter said nothing, but her expression spoke volumes.

According to other interviews in other groups, their goal was to get rid of all OTHERS in their countries. In Israel, they wanted to annihilate Arabs. "The lying, cheating, murderous Arabs." In Philadelphia, they wanted to eliminate the Jews. "Lying, cheating, murderous Jews." The definition of *other* was different depending on location and characteristic of the person speaking.

Isn't that what I asked Steven? In disgust, I clicked the remote to off and tossed it onto the coffee table. I watched, fascinated, as it slid to the far edge and stopped, balanced between safety and a nasty fall.

CHAPTER SIX

Was I balanced between safety and a nasty fall? *Careful, Sylver.* I stood to pace in my anxiety. In the kitchen I ate saltines and drank a glass of soda. I needed something in my stomach. Better.

I plopped down in the comfortable chair in my library, surrounded by books that had offered me solace for all my life. Now, they only prompted another line of fearful thinking. I chose many of them just because they introduced me to new ideas and to new threads of scientific exploration. Would they end up on a bonfire, burned in an effort to limit knowledge available to common man? Didn't Mao get rid of intellectuals during the Cultural Revolution? He didn't want them to threaten his message. Was I in danger for thinking too much? Is that why Steven said I needed protection? That, and the target painted on my back tonight.

Again, I paced to work off more of the jitters and then sat at my "card reading" table. I recited several Sanskrit chants to calm and to center. When that familiar wave of peace rolled over me, I automatically reached for the cards and shuffled. I rested them against my heart and asked to be protected from any evil and be given whatever information I needed. I asked to be shown how to use that information for the benefit of my fellow man. For a moment, I sat staring at the cards in my hand, immobilized by fear of what I might be shown. But then I laid them out in the familiar tableau.

The cards: The Hanged Man, Death, Tower, Magician, The Emperor. Nothing useful to work for good, for peace. More about turmoil and violence and radical change. The cards agreed with Steven's predictions for the near future. My, oh my.

My heart assured me the outcome would be beneficial. Unfortunately, the trip to peace required working through pain and suffering. Ah. Dread, again, stronger than before. Was I being warned that future peace would carry a hefty emotional and physical price? No hint came about who would turn up to help. Who was the Magician?

I stared at the tableau on the table before me. Too exhausted to function, my mind went blank. Pieces of the puzzle fit together, but it didn't seem complete.

Suddenly, it hit me — these cards were all Major Arcana. The more Major Arcana cards in a reading, the stronger they indicate control of a situation by invisible forces, by Spirit. Was I being told control of these world events was the expression of some plan by entities at a higher level? There was little I could do until the plan was in motion. Perhaps later I would be given a role. For now, it was above my pay grade.

For the time being, I was to watch. Watch and stay alive. Watch and wait.

I obsessed about it. Americans fighting Americans. Didn't they understand we're all brothers? We're members of the same tribe simply because we're all humans. And even more so because we're all Americans. Where was compromise, reconcile differences, work together? Where was the leader who could bring us together? Where was our Mandela who could use a game to heal a country? Or was that only the stuff of movies?

People using force or threat of force to acquire power were in ascendance on both sides, all over the planet, in countries on every continent. Details didn't matter, as long as they could force others to follow their plan. Any persons not willing to join with them were to die. People were already dying. Thousands of them. Hundreds of thousands. All over the planet. And then what would happen after they controlled their own countries?

Would they battle groups in other countries for the same reason?

What happened to "let's help others because it's the right thing to do"? The Partnership model? The belief that helping parts helps the whole? What happened to the predicted inflowing of the Feminine Ideal? Spiritual leaders predicted the flow of the Goddess Energy across the planet in 2012. Steven mentioned this. But not the way I understand it. The Goddess Energy was to blend with the masculine energy to level out emotions. It was to bring a softer and gentler approach to life. It was to tamp down the raw vitality of the patriarchy, that testosterone-drenched rule by men. I didn't see it in events of today regardless of what Steven said about its current tempering the violence. Would it form a part of the end state? Crossing fingers. Or perhaps this "war" was intended to rid the population of men willing to shoot first and talk later? Would there be more room for the Partnership Model? I could only hope. Again with the crossing fingers.

Stop, stop, stop! I willed my brain to stop going over and over these things. None of this news was set to a lullaby.

I don't know when I finally made it to my bed to fall asleep. The next time I saw the clock, it was seven in the morning. I had to fight a twist of sheets and blankets to drag myself out from under them. My night must have been filled with its own personal battles, but I didn't remember the dreams. And frankly, I didn't want to remember last night. I was still feeling the aftereffects of the wine. I pulled on some black yoga pants and a black tee-shirt, ready for a long walk. For exercise and calm. For recovery.

Coffee was the first thing on my agenda. Right alongside was the determination to call my friend Shelby.

For decades, he'd been a confidant with an amazing ability to ferret out truth in the jumble of my existence. In a former life, he had been the legal eagle who helped me through my divorce. From the first time I saw him, I thought he was very nice looking and a really great person. Too bad he wore a simple gold band on his left ring finger and on his heart. I didn't really get to know him until later, when I attended a friend's funeral. Some lousy drunk had drifted into her lane after hours of celebrating the finish of a job laying granite on the façade of an office building downtown. And now both the contractor and my friend ended up buried in front of big granite markers. She and I had played on the same tennis team for years, but I didn't discover that she was married to my attorney until I met her husband at her sending off party.

One of the other tennis players decided that we as a group should become a troupe of casserole ladies to feed the grieving widower. And so we set up a schedule to deliver food. I brought food for his soul (books that had helped me deal with the death of my marriage) along with food for his body. Our fearless leader worked her magic to bandage his heart and ended up in his bed. I guess her meatloaf was the best. From what I could tell, the affair lasted only slightly longer than the meatloaf.

Although Shelby and I had been close friends since then, we didn't ever seem to be without romantic partners at the same time. As a result, although I loved him, we had never crossed that great divide of the double bed. Maybe that was a good thing?

This man was the very personification of reason. Right now, I needed feedback from someone sane. Bob used to be my sounding board. Bob. . . .

My heart longed for Bob. I wanted to cry out my grief, but I couldn't. Not now. Not yet.

I crossed my fingers. I did a lot of that lately. Was it working?

I struggled to calm my voice and hide the growing panic. I worked for a perky inflection, but my voice sounded fake even to my own ears. After Shelby said his hello, I asked, "I'm dressed for a walk. Interested in joining me?"

"Sure. I'll pick you up. Or would you rather meet in the park?"

"No. 'Pick me up' would work better."

Shelby arrived twenty minutes later. By the time the car stopped, I was in and adjusting my seat belt. I wasn't anxious, was I?

My friend misread my excitement. "What? No kiss?"

I leaned over to place a hasty peck on his cheek.

He laughed. "That was the tiniest sort-of kiss you've ever given. Just raring to go, aren't you? You always were first on the court."

I nodded but concentrated on the cell phone in my hand as I motioned for him to go on. I was so focused on the phone that I didn't notice the trees and flowers around me or the sun already warming the air. I didn't take note of the brilliant blue of his eyes or his gentle, warm smile always there to calm me. All I saw was the signal strength indicator on my telephone. I concentrated on it, willing it to waver.

Although Shelby didn't say anything, I felt him glance at me from time to time. He was used to my eccentricities. Finally, the suspense must have gotten to him. "What are you doing? Willing someone to call?"

I glanced at him and then quickly returned my attention to the device in my hand. "No, I'm watching for variations in signal strength. Calls get dropped when people telephone from their cars. I'm looking for places where the signal is interrupted. Or weak."

He ran a hand through his hair, but said nothing. Probably because he didn't see the importance of having that information. Finally, he added, "I know some places between my house and yours. There aren't any around here or between your house and the park. At least none that I remember."

I nodded. "You're right. There aren't any dead zones, or even weak zones, between my house and the park. Not one so far. Amazing that I can't find one when I could actually use it."

He was attentive, listening, and seemed to relax into my weird ideas. They usually made sense — eventually. Often that sense was strange or unexpected. And I was certain he would judge the current situation to be the same. Shortly, he pulled into one of the last remaining parking spaces near Hogan's Fountain in Cherokee Park. From the looks of it, we weren't the only ones visiting the park this morning. We'd started walks from this spot hundreds of times, so it was the most likely place to leave the car.

I waved his hand away when he reached for his phone. "Leave it. I'm taking mine." I left my purse on the floor. My purse and the chip in my driver's license. Along with any of those other items Steven was so sure were used to track us. I shuddered at the fact that I was even thinking these paranoid thoughts.

Shelby withdrew his hand and shrugged his resignation. I guess he figured it was just another aspect of my current weirdness. While he closed up the car, I watched the children playing on the playground across the street. Some were enjoying the equipment and others were throwing balls or Frisbees to each other. The scene was filled with peace and laughter. Family stuff. The weather was still warm so the last fall flowers were still in bloom, but I could tell that they were at the end of their season. Fall colors in the leaves hadn't even thought of making a showing in this forest. Not yet, but they would in a month or so.

I turned to watch Shelby as he walked across the street to join me. I shook my head. Why hadn't I noticed the strands of gray laced through his dark hair? Note to self, *attend to your surroundings a bit better, Sylver.*

I returned my attention to the playground. Here, there was no sign of the "war" promised in my conversation with Steven last night. No bullets whizzed through the air and no screams of

43

hostility ripped through the peace. Just children playing while their parents talked to each other, smiling in enjoyment of their children's joy and their own moment of adult interaction. I loved watching this evidence of the normal activities in the calm of fall. I had to tear my attention away from the scene when Shelby reached my side.

Suddenly, images from the first scenes of the movie *Terminator* popped into my mind. In it, children were playing on a playground when bombs destroyed the area. Bombs deployed by AI that started out part of the defense system and ended up waging war against the humans it was designed to protect. Sometimes you can't tell the enemies from the allies. These children, like the ones in the movie, had no idea that men were shooting at each other in locations not far from this playground. I rubbed my eyes to banish the images. I sent a tiny prayer that those bullets would stay well away from these children. From all children. And then I remembered the wars going on in Africa. In the Middle East. On and on.

Shelby and I set off walking down the long circuit we usually took. We only got a few yards before our steps were synchronized. Our breathing, too. We fell into the comfortable patterns expressive of our long friendship. Comfortable and comforting.

Ancient walnut trees and tulip poplars towered over the path. Magnificent. Our surroundings were peaceful. My stress diminished, but hovered near my heart, ready to pounce. I glanced at my phone from time to time. We walked down the hill and then around the bottom of the circuit. At the lowest point, we hit a dead spot nestled between a stone road-cut and a creek deep within a wooded area. The creek ran through the forest where tree branches arched over water. Its natural beauty vied for control of my mind trying to push out the anxiety.

I motioned for my friend to follow me to a bench on the stone bridge and whispered, "This is a dead spot, but we should still be careful." Before I spoke again, I turned off my telephone and sat on the thing for good measure. I knew that speech creates vibrations in the body, but I couldn't do anything about that. Hopefully, they would be so weak the phone wouldn't pick up on them.

Thoughts repeated through my brain: *Oh God, you have become paranoid, Sylver. Paranoid.*

From his expression, I could tell that Shelby was growing more curious by the minute. "What the hell is going on, Sylver? Sometimes you act weird, but this is above and beyond."

I scooted closer and whispered, "I am totally outside my element here and need your insights. Tell me I'm crazy if you think I am. Otherwise. . . ."

"Tell me. Is it some guy?"

"You know Steven?"

Shelby jumped up and turned to lean over the railing of the bridge peering into the creek below. "Your friend Steven? I know more *of* him than I know him. But he's married. You're not. . . ?"

I ignored his implied question. "Good enough. We had dinner and a long talk last night — after he shot and killed his wife and Bob."

Shelby jerked upright and moved to stand in front of me, so close I could see every stitch of the logo on his shirt and feel heat radiating from his body. He raised his voice, but I motioned him to quiet. "What the hell? Are you telling me he actually killed two people? He killed Helen? He killed Bob? Or is this one of your quaint euphemisms?"

Last night, I had practiced putting the whole story into a very few simple sentences. I repeated those quickly, keeping my voice as low as I could and still be heard.

When I indicated that I had finished, Shelby asked, "Are you sure about this? Did you see it? Or did he tell you this fairy tale to frighten you?"

I nodded. "I definitely watched Bob bleed out on the sidewalk. He was about twelve inches away from me. Steven wouldn't let me call for help. No, this was very real. No ploy. No fairy tale. And later, Steven took me to dinner to explain."

"Did you actually go to dinner with him even though you knew he was a killer?"

"Had to. He was at my front door and I'm afraid of him. I am *really* afraid of him. I was afraid he'd break down the door and drag me out by my hair. If you'd seen him, you would understand. He was intense. Scary."

Shelby looked at his feet and nodded slowly. Then he looked toward the sky before turning back to me. I waited for my friend to think this thing through. Hearing something so fantastical this early in the morning would be unsettling to say the least. Actually, there is no time of day right for this conversation. None.

When he finally spoke, his voice was low, so low I had to strain to catch his words. "But you should at least have gone to the police to report the killings."

"The police were at the scene by the time I left it. Steven told me to go home and that he would explain the situation to them. Since he was the guy waving a gun around, I figured he was in charge. And that gun guaranteed my obedience."

"Okay? No question there. So why aren't you telling me that Steven is in jail?"

"Turns out the police officers were some of his buds. They were believers of the conspiracy theories and he told me they gave him a pat on the back for killing enemy agents."

"Bob and Helen? That's almost funny . . . if it weren't so frightening."

"Fine line, sometimes."

Shelby shrugged, but his stress was telegraphed by deep furrows in his brow and deepening lines around his mouth. "No wonder you were anxious to walk." He looked around us. "You wanted a place where we might avoid being heard. Makes sense." He motioned toward the seat. "You're acting as though you believe our phones are being monitored." He quirked his head and nodded. "You are definitely not playing according to any rules I know, but you were there, not me."

I shrugged as I shifted my weight, feeling the telephone under me. "Actually, I wanted to tell you all this in case something happens to me."

"You think something might?"

I shrugged. "I just don't know. Last night Steven told me the bad guys do monitor us. The 'bad guys' according to him. That started me down this paranoid path. I'm not sure of anything anymore. These devices are built for two-way communication, aren't they? Telephones, computers, tablets, smart watches? If it's true the 'bad guys' could monitor us, maybe the 'good guys' could, too. He could listen in and find out that I'm talking to you. I don't trust him."

CHAPTER SEVEN

Shelby nodded, and looked up again. Was he searching for another listening device? Maybe a long-distance microphone? A satellite? One of those lasers with pin-point precision? He lowered his voice and leaned closer, "Several whistle-blowers have come forward with evidence supporting exactly that. They say all communication is constantly being monitored, even when the devices are turned off. Mega-huge computers look for words or combinations of words in our emails, texts, telephone calls."

What he was saying agreed with Steven — on that point. I nodded. "Conspiracy theory or reality? Nothing you've said so far encourages me to be calm, but I am trying. The whistle-blower said they listen to our conversations?"

He nodded agreement.

The more nervous I got, the more I rambled, but I did explain the events of yesterday. Then I gave him the short version of Steven's view of life. And a lot of the other things Steven and I had discussed.

"My, but you have played an award-winning version of Little Mary Sunshine this morning, Sylver. Do you have anything else to challenge me?"

I shook my head. "Isn't that enough? Rebellion, martial law, takeover of the government, bombs that could end life as we know it? Isn't that frightening enough?" I hesitated. "Actually, there is more."

"I knew it. This must be the punch line."

I worked to arrange the information. "I used to hope that Steven was an armchair warrior, but it turns out that he's got a lot of buddies."

"Is that from programs you watched last night?'

I looked Shelby straight on. "No. From personal experience. There are lots of others. I don't know who all of them are, but I did meet some of them last night."

"You what?"

"You can see why I go along. I don't contradict him because I don't want him as an enemy. He's dangerous. And he is telling me about activities that are actually taking place. Now. Things I wouldn't know otherwise until I see them on the news. He is describing acts that are treason by any definition. Treason."

"They are, indeed. You're right. Steven would be a dangerous enemy." Shelby stood in front of me and held me, one hand on each shoulder. He asked slowly, enunciating every syllable. "What do you mean, you met some of them last night?"

Memories of last night flashed. "We went downtown. He was very friendly with guys dressed in camouflage clothes and toting very big guns. There must have been twenty or thirty of them and they greeted him like a long-lost brother. They shared man-hugs, even. There was a lot of weapon-waving and threatening looks at 'enemy' groups."

He studied my face. "Posturing. And you said the police didn't arrest him for the murders earlier in the day."

"They're paramilitary. He told me some police are part of this movement. Adds a lot of credence to the rest of the story, doesn't it? Still, I didn't actually hear him tell them how Bob died. I didn't see their reactions. I only heard his interpretation. In the news later, the killings were blamed on marauding Black Lives Matter militia. A convenient patsy."

Shelby's eyes took on an unfocused quality — deep in thought. When he spoke, it was almost as if he were having a conversation with himself. "Lots of groups throughout history wanted to take over the country. Some even organized, but this sounds larger, better-organized, and more serious than most. It

49

could only have been done with social media. I wonder. . . ." He looked toward the other side of the bridge. "What other good news do you have for me?"

I followed his gaze, but considered how to answer his question, "Well, the media may believe I'm involved in the camo group."

Shelby jerked his head around to look at me. "You, Sylver? How? Why?"

"When Steven took me downtown where they were gathering before the riot, he somehow managed to escape attention, but the media took lots of photos of me. They jammed microphones in my face to get me to comment. I wasn't thinking very well under the pressure of that assault, but later I remembered some of the faces in that mob. Reporters on the nightly news."

"No. No. No. That can't be good. They're always looking for new scandals."

I shook my head. "No, not good. I didn't say anything — nothing at all. I don't actually know anything. Maybe they've forgotten all about me after the protests turned bloody last night."

"Or not. Those people are looking for a leg up in the broadcast field. They want awards to help them climb the ladder to a post in New York or DC. They might be on camera right now blaming you for the killing."

"Oh, thanks. Now I really feel good."

A memory jiggled in my mental files. "I used to know a guy who had a black belt in some martial art. He lived surrounded by weapons of all sorts. This was decades ago. He was convinced the current system would soon fall and when it did the people with guns would take control. Eventually, they'd set up a whole new government. Meantime, order would be maintained by the guys with guns."

Shelby gasped. "Order?" He shook his head. "I really don't know the same people you do. Are these survivalists who stockpile food and ammo in case the sky falls?"

"I guess. Maybe so. I didn't ask questions. When he told me, I was too blown away to ask. But now, after hearing the same thing from other sources, my sense of reality has shifted. I do ask questions now. It feels a lot more serious to me. I'm worried. Really worried. And I guess he was telling me about this decades ago."

He shook his head. "I'm getting worried. You're the only one who has talked to me about these beliefs. Scary to think we have groups of true believers right here in our midst. Right here in the center of the country."

"I know, right?"

I stood to pace. Shelby handed me the phone and started down the path, obviously misreading my intentions. We walked in silence. I was mindlessly putting one foot in front of the other. All my attention was devoted to the question of where. Where could *we* find shelter? Would I have to start a whole new life in some country where I didn't speak the language? That sounded too much like the refugees streaming over our southern border. These were unsettling thoughts, but they might paint a fairly accurate picture of my future. That is, if what Steven described came to fruition.

When he spoke, the bright tone of Shelby's voice jerked me out of a morass of dark thoughts. "Hey, how'd you like that space weather website I told you about?"

I worked to match the energy in his voice with some of my own just in case our conversation was monitored. After all, I might be considered a confidant of a revolutionary. Certainly, I had become a person of interest regarding the paramilitary group called the Power Men now blamed for last night's killings. "Great site. Great information."

Shelby chuckled. "I hadn't known there were so many meteors out there. I mean, not so close. I heard one scientist describe these NEOs as death threats. We live in a shooting gallery, they said."

We walked past boys playing soccer in one of the fields. It was a pick-up game, or maybe a practice game, but the players were as serious about it as professionals on television. Several adults were on the sidelines yelling instructions. Probably coaches. Right now, the most important thing in their lives was this game. They probably weren't thinking of work or the honey-do list waiting at home or the bills due this week. They were absolutely focused on this group of young men kicking a ball around the grassy pitch.

I tore my mind away from the team of young players and struggled to wrap my mind around Shelby's new topic. Even it was about death and destruction that could put a permanent end to the game. "Oh, yeah. I would agree. How do they figure out the sizes of even small ones, less than ten meters wide?"

His voice sparkled with humor. "Must be someone out there with a measuring tape."

"I hope they're getting paid time and a half."

Shelby laughed. And then his expression became serious. "There might not be any safe place on this planet. If what they say is true, the entire world will be affected if one of those big rocks made direct contact with us. The extent of the damage would depend on the angle."

Although he mentioned the space rock, I thought he might be talking about something else. Threatened war or impact with a space rock? Either one could change the face of the entire planet. "I've been thinking about that. Wouldn't the most likely affected area of the planet be closer to the equator? Didn't the meteor that killed the dinosaurs hit in the Gulf of Mexico?"

He grinned. "You think we'd have the huge creatures living in our neighborhoods if they'd had astronomers to suggest moving to colder areas?"

"Could be?"

He walked in silence for a time. "That's a thought. Perhaps we should investigate countries in the southern hemisphere. Maybe we'll get enough of a warning this time."

Space rocks or rebellion? "But not too far south, just in case the earth's crust shifts to move the equator closer to one pole or the other."

He nodded. "Do we need a store of food?"

"Would that help?"

Our conversation of innuendos continued during the rest of the walk and in the car.

When we were stopped at the intersection near my home, I could see the mob of media people covering the green space around my condo. OOPS. They were surrounded by transmission trucks. Double OOPS!

I released my seatbelt and slid as far onto the floor as I could squeeze. Shelby drove slowly past the crowd and turned on the next street. He doubled back to his house and drove into the garage. I waited for the garage door to hit the floor before I emerged from my hiding place to get out of the car.

CHAPTER EIGHT

As soon as we got into his house, Shelby flipped on the television and tuned in one of the news stations transmitting from outside my home. News flashes repeatedly warned the audience. "A woman named Sylver is allegedly leader of Power Men, the local Neo-Nazi group taking part in the riots downtown. Cells of the national organization are said to be responsible for much of the violence in cities across the country, including attacks on peaceful protesters. According to our sources she may also head up their national organization. We are still working to confirm her involvement. Members of this group are thought to be responsible for deaths of hundreds of thousands across the country, mostly people of color. One of the stated goals of the group is essentially ethnic cleansing to bring America back to its original state. Sizable rewards are offered for information about her whereabouts. She is a person of interest and wanted for questioning by the authorities."

All this was said over images of me surrounded by reporters and then "escorted" by two members of the militia, the ones who had helped me get beyond those reporters. More images were of Steven and me running to the car and then driving away. I was not certain why his name was not mentioned, but there it was.

"No mention of the barricade of cameras surrounding me like a pack of hyenas. Those beasts stopped me from escaping. That's the only reason they got shots of me at the riots. They trapped me on the street to take those photos. No mention of the media lurking outside my home. Or that they're threatening me by making me look like the bad guy."

Shelby smirked. "No mention that this continent was

first inhabited by people of color and they were invaded and defeated by the white guy — and subjugated." Shelby laughed. "Sylver, you don't do it half way, do you? When you stir up trouble, you go full throttle forward."

"But I didn't do anything. I was just in the wrong place at the wrong time!"

My phone rang constantly — calls from "spam risk" and from media and from Steven. I didn't answer any of the calls and finally silenced the irritant.

News went on. The same stories were paraphrased on all channels. There was a stream of perky blond men and women — one after the other — reporting the story. Most told the same basic facts in a voice dripping with suggested menace. Each put a slightly different spin on it. Some bundled other events from around the world into the story of this woman, Sylver. Others skipped hinting at the connections.

There was an increase in gang violence — drug wars in the streets of the poorer neighborhoods and shootings throughout the night. People were killed while sitting at their dinner tables by bullets zinging through windows. Men, women, and children, innocents and guilty alike. Stray bullets don't discriminate.

Cities were on fire because of riots and looting — because of the virus — because of mass shootings, suicide bombers, and car bombs. The death toll surged ahead, the two causes racing to see which would amass the highest body count. Virus competed against human violence.

It had started. The war Steven described had started.

We basically hid in Shelby's house for the rest of the day. I stayed away from the windows and we kept the television tuned in to news programs — all day. There was coverage of the protests in cities across the country and around the world, with no end in sight. There was no more detail about the illusive Sylver, but she was mentioned.

Shelby made tuna salad sandwiches for lunch. I cooked up some Indian simmering sauce for dinner: chicken tikka masala.

I found some interesting things in his cabinets and managed to put together some coconut rice for the chicken. And vegetables from the freezer. I felt almost domestic even given the tense situation outside.

I used the small deck of cards I carry in my purse to do a Tarot reading for Shelby.

The cards presented a jumble of love and hate, of success and disappointment, giving no clear discernible message. Maybe my internal turmoil was too much to overcome in making the connection with Spirit. Or was the message that these next days would be confusing? I shrugged and returned the cards to their holder.

We played some card games until time for sleep. I changed into a pair of his sweat pants and a tee-shirt and stood at the window of his spare room searching the neighborhood for any sign of reporters or of the police. Who was backing whom? Were the police part of Steven's posse or were they really out there hoping to save the country from anyone who sought to create trouble? Did any of them really consider me a danger to society? So many questions.

Falling asleep took time because I had to stash the crises of the world behind some images of the beach on a sunny day. When I finally managed the feat, I slept hard.

I jerked out of bed at four in the morning, awakened by a loud banging in the back of the house. I arrived outside the kitchen just as Shelby opened the rear door a crack to find Steven on his doorstep. "Let me in. I have to get Sylver away from here. NOW."

Shelby shook his head and was probably about to tell him I wasn't there.

Steven raised his voice to a hoarse whisper. "I'm minutes ahead of the authorities. They're followed close behind by the media hounds. She'd better come with me quickly, or risk being arrested. Do you want that?"

I was hiding inside the next room and came into the kitchen just as Steven pushed his way into the kitchen. "How did you find me?"

He was furious. "Your cell phone. Anyone can do it."

"It's off."

"That makes tracking it difficult. Not impossible. I've been trying to reach you all day. Why didn't you answer?"

"It was ringing all day with numbers I didn't recognize and so I turned it off. . . . I'll get dressed." I was wearing Shelby's clothes and knew I'd feel more comfortable in my own things.

"No time. We'll find something for you to wear." He shoved his way through the room past the other man. He grabbed me roughly. In a rush, he pushed me toward the door. Shelby made to block our route, but I shook my head to tell him to let us through. I was afraid of Steven's reaction. I didn't want for Shelby to be hurt. As I passed the kitchen table, I retrieved the deck of cards left there after yesterday's reading.

Outside, Steven practically dragged me across the street and threw me into a car parked there. All I could tell is that it was a large, dark SUV and the headlights were off. The driver gunned the engine as the door slammed. We moved quickly, but only up to about the speed limit. One block. Two blocks. The headlights suddenly brightened the pavement.

The driver nodded toward the rear view mirror. "They're at the house. Your friend is taking his time answering the door."

Steven smirked, "Smart man."

Our driver peered through the mirror. "Where'd you leave the cell phone?"

"Plant beds in back."

"Hmm."

Several minutes later and blocks down the street, the driver spoke again. "Must've found it. They're leaving."

"Coming this way?"

Our driver glanced in the rear view. "Nope. Her buddy must have done a good job diverting them, but it won't be long before they're looking all over the city."

Steven twisted around to see the scene for himself. He nodded, a curious smile on his face, "Good for them. Let them look all over the city."

It wasn't long before I understood his derision of the search for me. Our car entered a ramp on I-64, heading toward horse country east of Louisville. We drove for about an hour before exiting the highway in the Lexington area. We rode on a four lane road and then on narrow twisty country roads.

Eventually we drove through a coded gate and onto a farm fronted with beautiful rolling pastures. No house in sight. Finally, the doors of a building opened and our driver drove into a barn, squeezing into a spot among vehicles already parked there.

Doors closed behind us, and a man in military-style dress, with bearing to match, opened the car door and roughly dragged me out. His hair was buzzed to within an inch of its life and his eyes almost matched the drab olive green of his clothes. "What's so damned important that you had to pick up this bitch?"

Steven said calmly, "They think she has information they want — she does, actually."

The other man grunted.

"I need to keep her away from the authorities until this is over. We don't need for them to question her."

The military guy pulled me close and looked into my face before he shoved me toward the middle of the barn. "Yeah. She was downtown before the battle. Was she the one caused all the flashes?"

Steven nodded.

"Stupid bitch. Don't you know to keep your head down?"

I figured the question was rhetorical, requiring no response, so there was none. It was all I could do to concentrate on keeping my balance as he pushed me forward.

"Why didn't you just neutralize her? We still could."

I had a really bad feeling about what he meant by this and determined to stay out of his way as much as possible. His expression told me that he was not joking about "neutralizing" me. I didn't think he could joke.

He shook his head. Resignation filled his voice. "Ah, crap, she's already here. Okay then, just keep her out of the way. I don't want her bothering the troops." He left us and strode quickly through the farther door to disappear into the bowels of the building. As he walked away, his words drifted back to me, "Besides, we might be able to use her. Maybe a distraction."

Steven led me into a room in the barn's interior. It must've originally served as a stable hand's quarters. Tiny, but it had a good bed, and I needed sleep. He handed me two zip-ties. "If we get raided, you put these on, both wrists and feet. Then act like you've been prisoner all along. It might save you if you can be convincing enough."

I inspected the strips of plastic before I laid them on a foot locker along with the small deck of cards from my pocket. They were my only personal possessions here. Wherever here was. I was hoping they'd be a source of comfort. No goodnight as he slammed the door. With it closed, I was left in total dark, black. I contemplated my current situation and considered the possibility of escape. But, to where? And how? We were obviously far from civilization here in this rustic barn.

For a short time, I listened to movement deeper in the building. Soon enough all movement ceased. Muffled snoring came from the same direction. *How many men were living here? Were these the men I'd seen just before the riots in town? It didn't sound as though there were many men in the part of the barn near this room. That meant no one guarding me. I should try to escape, but I was too tired to even reconnoiter the area tonight. Where the hell was I and what were they planning to do with me? Or to me?* As I was pulled into sleep by sheer exhaustion, I calmed myself with the idea that tomorrow would be soon enough to find answers to these questions. Only a couple of hours away.

CHAPTER NINE

The next day, I awoke when I felt light shine across the lids of my closed eyes. I felt disoriented. Smells of hay and horses filled the little room. Every part of my body ached and I was exhausted emotionally and physically. I really didn't want to wake up in the middle of the nightmare from last night. I wanted to find myself in my own bed, comfy and cozy. I wanted to listen to Bob's breathing for signs that he was awake. I wanted to shuffle my way into the kitchen to fix breakfast for the two of us. Maybe I would fix Eggs Benedict this morning. It was Bob's favorite. A special treat just to celebrate waking up in the arms of someone so dear to me. I wanted . . . I wanted. . . .

A deep breath. I opened my eyes to my current reality. *I am essentially a prisoner in a cell somewhere distant from my home. Bob is dead. He died in a puddle of blood at my feet and I couldn't even call for someone to help him. I was afraid to reach down to touch him, or hold him while he passed into that other place. I couldn't even tell him I love him. I hoped that he would tell me the same in return. But I was too afraid of joining him on his journey. Too busy trying to stay alive myself.*

To avoid being washed away by the tidal wave of grief, I inspected my shadowy surroundings. I wondered what surprises today would bring into my life, now become a string of constant surprises. I pulled myself into a sitting position on the edge of the thin mattress, not much more than a pallet on a wooden frame.

Slits of pale light streamed through thin cracks in the walls of my cell. Dust motes danced in those shafts of light, traveling on invisible currents of air. Laughter and conversation tramped past my door. Men on their way to meet some place and time.

What place? What time? Just more questions to be answered. And soon enough I would know these men and their destination. And my own.

Where am I? I was surrounded by strange sounds and patterns of light filtering through the walls and door. And then I remembered the fast ride through the night and past four-plank fences and through the gate into this field and into this barn. With distaste, I remembered the man dressed in army fatigues who had practically dragged me from the car and thrown me into this barn.

I slept in my clothes, or rather in Shelby's clothes, and so I had no need to get dressed. I was disconcerted by not having anything of my own here in this strange place. No clothes, no toiletries, no toothbrush. Coffee, however, was on my mind. Coffee and finding a toothbrush. And I was getting hungry. And more curious.

And so the next chapter of my life began as I searched for food and information.

There was no reception table or welcome committee, but by following the smell of strong brewed beans, I found a space set up as a dining area. There were tables and chairs and a grand coffee urn. I helped myself to a mug of thick brown liquid and to a couple of the donuts displayed on a large tray beside the urn. I vowed to intervene in the creation of the next urn of coffee to make the stuff more palatable. Reluctant to leave my second mug of coffee, I carried it while I explored my immediate surroundings.

A schedule posted on a cork board hanging from a wall nearby listed the many men guarding the barn and the surrounding fields. It turns out the barn was well guarded at all times of the day and night. I took away the knowledge that I was guarded too closely to escape; besides, I had no idea where this barn was located other than in the state of Kentucky and in the horse country not too very far east of Louisville. Although this was only my first day here, it was clear that the operation had been going on in this location for months. Here, I would stay for as long as Steven thought to keep me. Or that other guy.

The next several days were pretty much a blur. I explored the barn and learned where and when I could find the meals and the constant supply of strong coffee. I did take over brewing that coffee and it got better to my taste. Although some of the men complained that it was now too weak. So I compromised. After all, I am a reasonable woman.

I observed all of it, trying to make sense of the chaos. Groups of men came and went. And yet, I had no idea of how many people were living here. I learned the rhythm of their movements. I tried to remember faces, if not names. Sometimes a group of men would disappear into more remote areas of the barn for "briefings" or "strategy sessions" to which I was not invited. I realized that although they might use me to divert attention from the real leaders, I was not part of the group. Honestly, I wanted no part of it. It felt dangerous. *They* felt dangerous. Dangerous, even in this quiet barn in the middle of a peaceful pastoral setting. The troops' expressions telegraphed their suspicions when I was in the room. Who was I and why was I the only woman in this enclave of men?

At first, I spent as much time as possible apart from the rest of the inhabitants of the barn. The time alone gave me a chance to mourn the loss of my friends, but also to think of my immediate future. To escape or not to escape? From what into what? For the most part, I was left alone to my thoughts.

The primary exception — They called me in to enjoy any mention of my "leadership" by television news reporters. Stories got wilder and wilder with every reference to my involvement. From the stories on the news, one might think I had talents of a super-villain. Perhaps I could even move objects with my mind or leap tall buildings. And each reference to me hinted that perhaps I was able to become invisible at will. Was I an alien? That would definitely explain my disappearance. All this talk provided great entertainment for the men, encouraged by the violent military type I'd met on my first night here, Tadd.

Steven laughed and patted Tadd on the back, "Didn't I tell you she'd come in handy?"

It only frightened me. I was not amused. The world outside this compound slowly became a dangerous one in which everyone was searching for me. Not only would the media hound me, which was bad enough, but law enforcement might even torture me to extract a confession.

One night in the news overview, the announcer previewed a segment to discuss new discoveries about the military organization, the Power Men. "This Neo-Nazi paramilitary group is responsible for the deaths of thousands of peaceful protesters up to now with no hint of ending their rampage. The surprising fact is that the group of mostly men seems to be led by a woman. Hear more after the news summary."

"Our first story tonight is that the Space Force is again in the news. This sixth branch of the military was signed into law at the end of 2019. Establishment of the Space Force was part of a bill in effect doubling the amount of money for the military . . . to fund the new branch in addition to the other five.

A video replaced the reporter's image on the screen: the former president was on a dais addressing a large military audience. "I started talking about putting together a Space Force last year and people laughed at me. But here we are today. You saw me sign directives for a new military branch to take control of our skies. Truman was the last president to create a new branch — the Air Force in 1947. I'm the first President to do this since Truman. So much space up there. So much and we need to be able to take charge of it and to protect ourselves. From today on, we will see it as our newest war-fighting field. American superiority is absolutely essential for our national security. Right now, we are ahead of the rest, but not by enough. China is catching up. Russia is. India is. North Korea has great rockets and they will be ahead of the US soon.

This new branch will allow us to lead by a lot. It will enable us to defend our interests. It will help us deter aggression and control the ultimate theater of war. Our enemies are working very hard to build their strength and new technology. They are a threat to our national security."

The reporter came back into view. "That day the President changed what started out as material for late night comedians into a reality. . . ."

The rest of her comments were drowned out by cheering in the room around me.

I leaned closer to hear the reason the Space Force was again in the news, but didn't catch enough to get more than a hint that Congress was debating deployment of weapons into space.

Steven shouted over the din, "At least they're finally admitting that we're under attack by the Draco." Yelling in the room subsided somewhat to hear what he was saying. "It's time the government did something to protect us from those monsters. We know the secret space program has been in operation for decades. Decades. It's about time they admitted it."

Another voice yelled, "And told the rest of the country that aliens are out there."

"And in tunnels now controlling the president and Congress."

Again, the room erupted in noisy reaction.

After the summary of that story, reporters out in the streets in downtown Louisville described the Power Men and their activities during the previous nights. Suddenly, the room was quiet and all eyes and ears were trained on the television. New video footage was mixed with the footage taken days ago when I was led through the crowd by Steven. Descriptions of actual events were peppered with conjectures about this woman who could command men to kill so many people across the country.

The men around me laughed at the inaccuracies and missed details. They mumbled corrections that only their buddies could hear. The room dissolved into discussions among small groups of men. Many turned to glare in my direction from time to time. I couldn't understand most of what they said. Nor did I understand their obvious animosity. Or was it because they didn't want a woman to get any credit for anything?

Tadd fisted Steven on the shoulder. He thumbed in my direction. "This is working out better than I imagined. She can take the fall for us. At the very least, for the time being, she'll be a distraction from the real activities of the unit. I didn't guess we could turn that stupid mistake of letting her get in front of the cameras into a such a benefit. You were right to bring the bitch along."

He chuckled as he turned the television off. "Time to turn in. Morning comes early in paradise," he yelled into the crowd. Immediately, chairs scraped along the floor and men drifted out the door and toward the bowels of the barn.

The more I thought of the dangers awaiting me outside the confines of this group, the less I felt inclined to attempt escape. Louisville no longer felt like the center of peace and sanity it had once been. I would face law enforcement out there. Law enforcement in the form of the FBI, perhaps. And according to the reporter, they might not even give me a chance to explain myself before throwing me into a cell or shooting me. I would also face the mass of reporters and their entourage . . . even more frightening. Here, I felt safer. For now, this was a protected environment. That is, until they wanted for me to act as a human shield. I decided to put off thinking about that until later. I was trapped. Trapped here by elements of the world out there. Steven didn't help me at all. I guess this is what his protection looked like. Well, at least I wasn't in prison . . . yet.

The number of "reports" about the Power Men increased as the days went by. I was called in to hear every one of them. After a while, I lost track of all the places I had been spotted and all the crimes I was suspected of committing. The interpretations of my activities and my larger role were more and more extravagant. And my skills were now legend. This was the latest draw for the viewing audience. Did they realize they were being shown the same footage day after day? And every report ended with a prediction of more tragedy tomorrow. This paramilitary group was on a rampage. Tune in tomorrow for more death and dying. And for more tales of the superhuman Sylver.

I tried to dial in another channel one evening. What were other reporters on other stations saying about the war being fought on American streets? What were they saying about us? What were they saying about me? A tough military type stopped me before I could move the dial. I quickly discovered that we were permitted to watch only that one station. All reporters on show after show repeated the same story without adding material from what I regarded as more reliable sources.

At lunch one day I sat with Steven with the specific intention of interjecting some logic into our conversation. "I listen to reporters discussing the Space Force and there's never a mention of defending the planet from aliens or space rocks. In fact, I gathered that it was established as another step in our competition with other countries for dominance in the race to plunder minerals from the moon and from meteors."

Steven laughed heartily. "Of course not. They can't be open about what's been going on out there in space. Not at all. It would scare people. It would also let people know they've been lying for decades about aliens and the secret space program."

"Ah. It's all part of the cover-up?"

"Of course it is. What else would it be? You think this idea of making war above our heads is totally new? Of course not. They know how important it is because they've been waging war in space for decades. Ever since the first space shots. Landing on the moon. What do you think they found?"

"I don't know, except this Space Force is a frightening proposition, given the people involved. Wasn't this kind of thing stopped by the protests in the eighties? People at that time were smart enough to see the dangers of having weapons pointed at them in their homes."

"Times change. The dangers are worse. Besides, I told you a long time ago why that man was elected and why he will be again. The military chose him as their candidate. They backed him because he promised to bring out the fight that's been going on in space. He promised to make it all public."

I nodded. "He did give the military lots more money, and money is power. More room at the top. Easier promotions. Life is better for them now."

Steven laughed. His smug expression told me that he was delighted that at last I could see the light.

I murmured my thoughts. "They managed to keep it quiet until it was passed. They knew that once it was a fact, it would be hard to get rid of. Crafty."

Maybe I would have more luck reasoning with Steven later. But, I really wanted to talk with Shelby. He is so rational. And sane. He could help me figure out what is real and what is imaginary. Staying grounded is tough when you're surrounded by people telling only one story, people who don't bother with facts.

CHAPTER TEN

Steven laughed most heartily at descriptions of the actions of "our" group. He slapped my back and crowed, "You've become quite the celebrity, Sylver. Maybe I should get your autograph while I still can."

Tadd, on the other hand, scowled at me every chance he got. He was open about his intention to use me, but not include me in anything more than meals and watching the theater that was news on this station. In fact, he told Steven several times in my presence that he was not happy that I was living near *his* troops. Very proprietary. Someone told me he was second in command behind Steven. From the way he acted, he was actually in command of the men and only barely tolerated Steven. When he spoke, the men jumped. They didn't obey Steven like that.

I wondered if Tadd might not do Steven harm if he could. I pondered the wisdom of warning my "friend", but didn't. Besides, after the events of the past week, I wasn't sure that this man standing next to me was actually a friend and perhaps he was just as dangerous as Tadd only dressed in sheep's clothing. He'd always seemed like a mild-mannered guy to me, but obviously, I was wrong. Steven himself seemed totally unaware of Tadd's dislike of him and any potential danger those feelings might suggest. Tadd did look dangerous to me. Definitely not in sheep's clothing.

Most of the time Tadd was followed by Rick and Dereck, who were almost as nasty as Tadd. Almost. They always dressed in army drab as if the three of them consulted about wardrobe every morning. They were obviously his minions and did whatever he commanded. They always snapped to it when he gave them an order. They even scowled the way he did. I was amused to imagine Tadd stopping too quickly, causing the two of them to break their noses as they ran into his back.

Steven mostly stayed close to the installation, sometimes taking long walks around the farm. At other times he rode away in an SUV full of men. One time when he returned, he tossed a bag of new clothes in my direction — tee-shirts and jeans. Almost the right size.

Some of the guys goaded him into participating in what they called PT. Turns out the initials stood for physical training which involved a lot of running interspersed with calisthenics. I couldn't imagine what that might look like with his gangly arms and legs swinging all about. He returned from these adventures sweating and out of breath, but no more fit from what I could see.

A panting Steven saw me watching him after such a run and grumbled, "This war won't go on long enough for me to work up to running ten miles — at any pace."

I shook my head vigorously. "I didn't say anything." I hid my face and my grin with a hand, but could do nothing to hide the laughter in my eyes.

He was not amused by my failed attempts to stifle laughter. "You were looking. I don't see why you can't roam outside . . . as long as you stay within sight. Be a good girl and scurry inside if somebody, anybody, comes through that gate. We wouldn't want you recognized. There's a sizable reward for you and that should be plenty of motivation for some nosy nelly to snitch to the media."

I smiled. Was he really concerned about my safety or did he just like flexing his muscle with the little woman? Or, more to the point, had he actually told me more than was safe for this military operation? At any rate, I agreed with him. I didn't want to deal with the media. I had enough to manage with Steven. And Tadd. The two groups were neck to neck in the competition for the title of "most dangerous" and "annoying."

His smile was not a happy one as he looked around us, "There's no reason for you to be cooped up in here all the time. I'm trying to protect you, not hold you prisoner. Why don't you do some PT with the boys? That might get them to stop ragging on me."

I shrugged, but didn't say anything for fear I'd burst into peals of laughter.

He obviously didn't expect an answer because he went on without taking a breath, "Besides, I'm good with a gun. That's my contribution. I don't need big muscles to handle a weapon. And I do that better than any of these yo-yos." He turned on his heel and disappeared into the area occupied by the troops. I heard him yell several times about some infraction of the rules. Hmm, the person must have looked at him cross-eyed. I thought to myself, *Sorry for setting him up — or setting him off!*

Not your prisoner, Steven? Could have fooled me!

I was getting familiar with the inside of the barn. All except the area beyond the door that separated the troop's quarters from this more open space. So, maybe it was time to go outside.

When I finally did, I explored the field around the barn. The building itself was neat and in good condition. There were landscaping shrubs around it and some specimen trees protected with mulch around the base in the front on either end. It backed up to a tree line separating this field from the one behind it. Our new abode was on the edge of a pasture and another barn, its twin, was positioned facing this one in much the same orientation on the other side of this field. There were no horses in this pasture and the grass was about a foot tall. I could see horses on the other side of a fence that bordered this pasture to my left. Obviously, a real working horse farm. It really was a beautiful site, although I didn't imagine Steven chose the location for its natural beauty. The barn was nestled into the woods with roadways aplenty giving us a variety of exit.

I watched groups of men leaving the barn. They traveled in any of three directions, and down the road either way once outside the gate to the field. I wasn't certain whether for security or because their missions were in those directions.

A nice-looking young man came out and I decided to satisfy my curiosity. I'd seen him in the dining area. "Hey, Charlie, what's down that road through the trees?"

The young man shrugged. "More fields. More woods."

Suddenly a barrage of shots exploded from that direction. "Is that the training area?"

Charlie turned angry eyes toward me, "Look, lady, I don't know who you are. We're to protect you for some reason. We're not friends and I'm not going to chat with you like we are." He turned on his heel and disappeared into the barn.

That went well!

Minutes later another fuzz-faced boy walked out the door. He started to vape, strolling toward the left end of the building. Sometime later he appeared at the other end, the right end.

"Are you patrolling the perimeter?"

He grinned. "Nah, just walking."

"Mind if I walk with you?"

He quirked his shoulders. "Suit yourself. It's a free world."

We traveled around the structure in silence several times. Finally, he stopped to look at me and smiled, "I thought you'd try to pump me for information. You know, ask a lot of questions."

"Why would I do that?"

He shrugged. "As a test? Maybe you *are* the head honcho like the television says."

I giggled. Couldn't help myself. "Do I look like the leader of these fighting men?"

After some seconds with his forehead scrunched in thought he shook his head. He stuck his hand toward me in greeting. "Name's Buddy. And, yes, it is my real name. My Mom saw a show about Buddy Holly and fell in love with him."

"That's not a nickname?"

"Nope. It's on my birth certificate. Middle name Holley, spelled with a 'e' like his real name, not his stage name."

I grinned. "Sounds as though she has a wicked sense of humor, like my mom. Mom named me Sylver with a 'y' and I used to feel compelled to explain it to every person I met." I shrugged. "Now I just let them think what they want. *I* or *Y*. Does it really matter in the grand scheme of things?" I didn't mention I was proud of the name now, different, but not totally weird. Like its owner, I guess. And it did describe the color my hair had become over those years. I wondered if she could see this future when she hit upon that name.

I nodded my head in the direction of the end of the barn. "You in the mood for more walking? You do so much PT that you can't actually need the exercise. Moving keeps me more at peace these days."

We walked again. "Yep. There's a lot going on right now to make ya jittery."

"You can say that again. I seem to have landed right in the middle of a pot of stew."

Buddy grinned. "You surely did just that. How'd you manage to end up here in custody and on the run from those reporters? I heard the police are looking for you, too. That's what they said on the news. You're a person of interest. I always wanted to meet a *person of interest*. Ya know, just to see what one looked like." He laughed at his joke and that made me laugh. "Funny, but you look normal."

"I am normal. I didn't do anything. Wrong place. Wrong time. Went to visit a friend. When I got there I found she'd gotten herself shot by her husband. And then later, Steven took me to the protests. I didn't think to duck or dodge when reporters aimed cameras at me. All this is new to me. I've never been a person of interest. I wonder if I'll get better at it with practice."

"That's it?"

I nodded.

Buddy chuckled. "Good thing they weren't aiming guns at you. You wouldn't be here now, would ya?" He grinned at his joke. "That's it? Wrong place, wrong time?"

I nodded. *Wrong place. Wrong time.* Thinking about Helen and Bob made me sad, but thinking about being a refugee made me angry. That was Steven's fault. All of it was Steven's fault. "I'm a person of peace surrounded by all manner of turmoil."

Buddy patted me on the shoulder. "It'll be over soon and we'll have peace again. We'll also have freedom and prosperity. It'll be a lot better than it was."

I shook my head. "You wouldn't be the first person to underestimate the amount of time a campaign takes. That's one way leaders justify taking people out of their normal lives to fight. They lie about how little time the fight will last. Yeah, 'We guarantee you'll be back in your fields in a month.' Four years pass before you see home again."

Buddy looked at me thoughtfully and then we started walking in silence for the better part of a trip and a half around the barn. He looked sadder now. He tugged on my sleeve when we were at the back of the barn and led me silently through the tree line until we were stopped by a fence. He gestured to the field on the other side. "That's the kinda corn my pa grows. I worked on our farm until I felt the call of the big city."

We leaned against the fence, and Buddy breathed deeply. "Smells like home. I used to hate that farm. But now I'd be glad to be back there, back working that field of corn."

"You work in Louisville now?"

He nodded and was silent for a bit before he answered. "Work with the horses at Churchill. I got a degree from the Equine Industry Program from the University. It was my first job out of school. I hope I still have it after the war."

I left him to his thoughts. I took a thought trip of my own back to my own home.

Suddenly, he jerked toward me to whisper from inches away. "This revolution has been in the planning for years, maybe even decades. We're soldiers and we've been in physical training for years. Of course, I only just joined, but some of the guys have been involved all that time. First, in small groups and on the weekends and now at this camp. There's stuff on the Internet, too. There's a lot to learn. Detailed battle plans have been worked out by professional soldiers. They will work, but first we need to get rid of some men on the other side. To even up the numbers some. Then when we start the main offensive in the capitol, resistance will be too weak to stop us. Besides a lot more other people will join the fight. Then we'll be so big the other side will surrender right away. They'll be scared just seeing our numbers."

I considered what he was telling me. A traitorous offense by local standards. Why was he revealing so much? He was telling me, so it must be part of the plan — to attack the capitol. Which one? State or national?

I decided to avoid the thousand pound gorilla in the field. "Are you being paid for your service?"

"Nah, but part of what we'll be doing is to take back all the money that was stolen from the people. You know, by making us pay illegal taxes. By banksters charging high interest for mortgages and car loans. I got student debt for my college. That will be forgiven. All of it will. Pa paid a bunch to buy his farm and to build the house. All that will come back to us."

I nodded. This did sound a lot like what Steven promised. "What happens to these funds after they get confiscated by this army?"

"Given back to the people. It was made by them and only given to the government because of a fake income tax. We'll all get some, you know. What they call Prosperity Funds."

"Prosperity Funds? Have they told you anything about how all this will work?"

Buddy shook his head. "Like what?"

I reveled in a delightful thought. My mortgage would disappear — poof — according to this scenario. "Who's in charge of spreading this money around? Are you sure they're immune to the pull of great wealth? We're talking a bundle here. Are they honest enough to distribute it as promised? They might be as corrupt as the people who took it originally."

Buddy shrugged. "Hadn't thought of that. They probably already signed agreements."

I didn't hide the humor in my voice. "They certainly must be exemplary individuals lacking in the greed that afflicts normal humans."

Buddy looked thoughtful. He repeated, "They signed agreements."

As I spoke, I considered the papers throughout history signed, only to be ignored when it came time to deliver on promises. Treaties with the original inhabitants of this country were a perfect example — for starters. Many of them signed with absolutely no intention of fulfilling them. There was plenty of evidence that the human flaw of greed was plenty enough to make ink disappear from any piece of paper. But I didn't say any of this. Not yet. "I have actually heard of this before. How are you planning to use your Prosperity Funds?"

Buddy's broad grin revealed all his teeth. "My dad has worked hard all his life. I want to hire men to help on the farm. He says he wants to keep farming, but the work's hard on a man's body. He's got lots of bills and some days he could use a rest both from the physical labor and from the worry."

"Won't everyone get Prosperity Funds? Will they need to work? As I understand, with debt forgiveness, your dad's bills should disappear. Poof! At least he won't have that worry."

"Guess I'll have to find people who like that kind of work. People like my dad. If no one steps up, we won't have food to eat or to feed our animals."

Further out on that limb. "You're probably right. Have you heard of a model of working together called Partnership?"

Buddy shook his head no, but said, "Sort of. Maybe. I guess."

The vacant look in his eyes suggested that he had not, so I added, "It's a form of government and organizations of all kinds based on helping each other. One way to get power is to take it with force, or threat of force. The best way is to earn it by helping others be the best they can be. That sounds like what you're talking about. When everybody has plenty of money, people can help each other because it feels good. They can do work they enjoy."

Buddy grinned his full-faced grin. "You think there'll be people to help my dad?"

I looked out into the corn field. "There would be now, if leaders didn't acquire power by hurting people, by dominating them, or by killing them. If people were encouraged to work together for the common good instead of being used to kill people the leaders don't agree with." I backed off to let the seed I'd planted sprout.

I startled. Several men crashed through the trees and shrubs behind us.

The guy in the lead barked at me, "What in the hell are you doing out here?"

"Buddy was showing me this field."

Buddy looked shaken. At my answer, he calmed. "Yep. It's like the fields my Pa works back home. I was sharing a moment, thinking about when I was a boy."

I smiled sweetly at the men, "Yes, Buddy painted a lovely picture of growing up on a farm. It seems you don't miss things until you no longer have them."

One of the guys grabbed my arm roughly and pulled me toward the barn. "Stay in sight."

I looked him in the eye, smiling as sweetly as I could with his fingers digging into my flesh. "We've walked a lot already. I'm ready for a cup of tea. Would you mind fixing me one?"

The guy looked as though I had three heads. Suddenly, he dropped my arm and moved away. He pointed a threatening finger at me with a straight arm. He glanced at Buddy and pointed toward him. I smiled even more sweetly. At least I hoped it was sweetly as he turned toward the barn.

After the boredom of the first days, I decided there must be some reason I was here in this place and now — during this time of high energy and crisis.

Why not make friends with some of the guys hanging around the barn? Buddy was the first, but there were others. I'd start talking about the weather and later ease into talking about differences between Partnership and Dominator models of relating. During the first conversations, I discovered I had to adopt a different vocabulary and a different focus. The message was more acceptable when we talked about work and romantic relationships or friendships, rather than government.

Apparently, they had been instructed not to share personal information. I operated within those rules as well — for a while. It took some time to sort out the safe areas of discourse.

CHAPTER ELEVEN

A flash of insight hit me. Maybe men would warm up to me for more conversation if I did simple Tarot readings for them. Isn't that what Shelby might suggest?

Even for people who don't believe in the Tarot as in the possibility of communicating with "the beyond," dabbling with the occult is intriguing. Like people who watch a magician to discover his tricks so they can debunk magic, there are people who go to a psychic with the goal of proving that it's fake. So, readings should open the door to believers and nonbelievers alike.

One morning after breakfast clean-up, I set up on a table in the kitchen where it was relatively quiet. My intention was to attract men to my table one by one. Only half the space in this room was used to prepare meals and to clean dishes afterward. I dragged the table used for prep work to the middle of the open space and put chairs from the dining area on either side of it. No candles. No crystals. Just the cards and me. Then I sat in the quiet to think. And to find the peace within that enabled me to reach beyond the veil for answers.

Without my usual Tarot deck, I had to use the small travel cards I normally carried in my purse. Although it didn't really fit my hand and was more difficult to shuffle, it worked just fine in offering information.

I shuffled cards, focusing on my intentions. One by one, guys slipped into the room and stood against the walls. I heard movement rather than actually seeing them. Curious. The word must have been spreading through the troop because I hadn't actually told anyone. At the end, there was quite an audience. The space was not intended to accommodate a dozen men and so there was a fair amount of crowding. There was a lot of whispering — murmuring about what I was all about.

For starters, I did a couple of general readings. I explained each thing I did as I went through my ritual. I named the cards as I laid them on the surface and interpreted the tableau out loud for my audience. During the reading I looked for reactions in the men around me. They seemed interested. Actually, they seemed intrigued.

More gathered as I continued. I looked around the room to find there were so many watching that some had to remain outside the room peering at me through the door. I asked who would like to ask the cards a question. More murmuring. None sat for a reading when I motioned them to the chair. In fact, they seemed to press even more firmly against the wall.

I motioned for Charlie to take the chair. "Wouldn't you like for the cards to tell you if that beautiful blond will dance with you next time you're out?"

He looked embarrassed and shook his head vigorously. Had I actually guessed his question? "No ma'am. The Bible says not to ask fortune tellers anything."

Walt laughed hysterically. "It was talking about gypsies, not nice women from Louisville."

I grinned. "How about you, then? Is there a question you want to ask? Just for fun?"

He shook his head, "Nope. I don't like to play games. I know it's fake and I don't waste my time with nonsense."

I laughed, "How else do you plan to spend the next few minutes? Got a hot date?"

He laughed and so did the men around him. Their reactions morphed into raucous laughter and rude, teasing comments.

Walt shrugged and moved out of my sight. He remained behind a group of guys, but didn't leave the room. He was probably curious about this "game" I offered. Curious and wanting to have a reading himself, but too reserved to be the first. And not wanting to provide a show for all the other men in the room. I saw that battle of desire and fear played out in most of the men standing around my little table. Just about this time, Steven walked through the door to get a soda. His first reaction was surprise. Then, he nodded and smiled at me and glanced around at my audience.

"Steven, why don't you show them how it's done? You've sat for readings with me before. Many times, in fact. And you haven't melted into a puddle of salt water." He hesitated and looked at the men leaning against the walls, curious, but not courageous.

He shrugged in resignation and took the seat on the opposite side of the table. Was he concerned about appearances? Slowly, he stretched his hand for the deck of cards and cradled them against his heart with eyes closed. Yes, he knew how it was done. Handing the deck to me, he gulped from the can of soda as I went through my ritual.

Again, at each step in the process, I described what I was doing. When I laid out the five cards, the first was the Knight of Pentacles. The remaining four were cards of success and material gain.

I looked at Steven and cocked my head. "Why, Steven you asked who would win a horse race!"

"Yeah, so?"

I laughed. "Good enough. It will be a black horse with knight in the name."

He stood and walked to the radio on the counter, turned it to the race at Keeneland, and two races later, a long shot named Knight's Bridge won the third race. The horse was raven black with a white blaze between his eyes.

Whoops sounded from around the room.

Buddy was the loudest, "Too bad you didn't get a reading before the race. You could have won a bunch." Steven smiled enigmatically and walked out of the room.

The guys lined up for readings after that.

That first day, most questions had to do with horse races and ball games. They checked the accuracy of my predictions by listening to the radio later. I could hear whoops of appreciation as I left the room. Proof of the accuracy of the cards. At least I got some things right.

I approached Steven later as I walked toward the barn door for some time under the canopy of stars. "You looked too pleased with yourself to just have called the race accurately. I'd wager you did place a bet on Knight's Bridge earlier."

He grinned broadly. "Ya got me! I don't spend all my days in planning sessions or physical training."

I looked him up and down. "I can tell that."

"We're on a horse farm, Sylver. Where better to get race tips? Guys working in the stables know the stock. They know how horses have done in practice runs against each other and during training and time trials in the privacy of their home tracks. I put bets on the sure things, the horses absolutely certain to finish in the money."

"How has that worked for you?"

Steven's grin spread across his entire face. "Well. Very well, indeed. Actually, I've made a ton of money." His expression suddenly turned serious. "I give the stable hands a percentage of my wins, too. So they can feel a part of the game."

"This war has been a financial success even for you, an upper-level manager!" I had thought to call him a foot soldier. Steven didn't see himself on the first line, but rather as a general close to the apex of the pyramid. Recognition of his status and his win appeared to please him. He walked off, seemingly intoxicated by the heady air of self-aggrandizement.

The next day, I set my table up in a more private location, hoping to encourage more personal questions. It worked. Tucked away in a corner of the area of the barn used for hiding the cars, I got more questions about romantic relationships as well as other personal relationships. And, yes, would that blonde beauty dance with me the next time I run into her?

A reading was interrupted by a call from the television room. "Sylver, you're on the news again."

We ran to catch the newest sighting of the elusive Sylver, the woman riding on the white stallion at the head of the invading hordes. The room was filled with guffaws and snorting laughter.

One deep voice called out, "How can she be there when she's really been here all this time?"

"None of those people know anything about you. Do they? They're shooting in the dark. They're trying to get more people to tune in to their show."

I shook my head. "How did you figure that out?"

He laughed, "It's obvious to us and we've only known you for a couple of weeks."

The others joined in the nods and laughter.

Buddy laughed along with them. "You're much more the thinker. I see how upset you get during reports of deaths during attacks, or actually from any cause. If they'd taken any time at all to research anything about you, they'd realize you would not lead people into situations to kill or be killed."

There was a chorus of agreement from every corner of the room. "You're a lover, not a fighter," came a voice from somewhere behind me. The room was filled with a roar of laughter.

I looked around me. "Well — I just don't understand why we can't all live together in peace."

"And cooperation." Came from another voice in front of me. It was answered by hoots of laughter.

"Some of you were afraid of me when I first came into the barn. Now you see how harmless I am. You learned that by spending time with me. What would you learn about Muslims or people of color if you spent time with them?"

Another, angry voice answered me — Tadd. "I think you become more dangerous by the day."

"Because I'm a person of peace?"

No answer.

I was on a roll. There was no stopping me now. "Domination is not the only way to garner power. Cooperation and working together gets more for the whole than fighting over the crumbs the group already has. You get more flies with honey than with vinegar."

I stood to look at the earnest faces around me. There was murderous fury in Tadd's eyes. "You train every day. You work hard. You fight and risk your lives, but who claims the booty? Aren't the guys calling the shots from DC getting more?"

A familiar voice answered. "Maybe now, but we'll get our share when it's over."

I shook my head, "You're talking about the spoils of victory? How has that worked so far? Haven't these men been in power for years? During those years how much has trickled down to you? If they get more power, won't they keep more of the spoils like dictators in other countries? They may start out poor, but they end up billionaires. Citizens of the country remain poor or get even poorer."

"That's why we have to get rid of this system. So the little guy can get his share."

I shrugged at their reluctance to see the reality around them and walked out of the room to return to my corner of the garage. I might be able to make some small changes here — one by one. But seeing the totality made me feel the enormity of the problem. This was a problem so big that anything I did would only be a drop in the bucket. I felt the energy seep out of me. The energy and the hope.

A seeker asked about the outcome of this rebellion and whether Prosperity Funds would actually come through. At last, we were beginning to get somewhere. Of course, the answer was the Tower. The remaining four cards indicated no sign of material gain. The subject of the reading walked away disappointed. Later I heard him telling someone I was no good at telling the future because I didn't get that right.

For several days after that incident, no one came to consult the cards. At mealtime the men quieted as I passed a table. Were they discussing my inability to see all the great things their leaders were promising? Who, then, had they decided to believe? That pacifist woman reading the Tarot cards or their leaders pushing them to be stronger and fight harder and telling them that killing the other was patriotic?

Eddie came to my table several days later. When I picked up the deck, he shook his head and pushed my hand and cards I was holding toward the table.

"You don't want to consult the cards?"

"Nope. No cards. I'm here to ask why you're so against this holy war to reclaim our country?"

"Does your definition of holy include following the Ten Commandments or just the two proclaimed by Jesus?"

Eddie looked confused.

"You know: 'Thou shalt not kill?' Or the ones that tell you to love your neighbor, no exceptions?"

Red hot fury climbed up his neck. "People coming across our southern border are taking over our country. They're criminals and putting us into debt because they go right into the welfare system. They're a blight on this beautiful land of ours. We need to get rid of all of them."

"Ah-h-h. Sounds as though your beef is with people who immigrate here from other countries and taking our jobs. Have you met the stable hands training horses and mucking stalls in the barn across the field? Do you lust after their jobs? Are they the jobs being stolen from you?"

Eddie didn't have an answer. He shook his head and seemed taken aback that the mild-mannered gypsy could get angry.

I let a bit of that anger flow. "They came here for a better life and end up taking jobs that people here don't want. One way of putting it might be that if you send the new immigrants back you must agree to take the job they left here. How about that?"

No answer, but the skin of his neck was blood red and his eyes looked as though they would pop out of their sockets.

"Must mean you want white people to leave and return the land to its original inhabitants, Native Americans?"

He looked angrier still, if that was possible. "My family is from this state. We've got generations in the ground right here."

I tilted my head and tried to look confused. "You don't look Indian. Where did your people come from? Originally? Ireland, isn't it? You've got the freckles."

He stopped to think. "Yes, Ireland. Cork, my ma told me."

I nodded and hoped he could see the irony of what he was saying. The stubborn expression on his face told me he was blinded to any version of truth different from his own. "If your family is from Ireland, you're not Native American. That means that your family took land from the Indians who originally owned it."

This time, he shook his head violently in answer. "What difference does that make? We came over from Ireland soon after the land was discovered."

I went on because I was angry and wanted to force this man to see the truth of what he was saying. "Since this land was settled by millions of Native Americans, they discovered it. Put that way, weren't the first illegal aliens the English? Or the Spanish and Portuguese? Later came waves of French and German and Polish. People came from countries all over the world. Each successive wave of pilgrims took more land that belonged to people of color who were here first, the first to claim the land here. They're called Native Americans because they were here before any of the other people who are now called American."

"Well, well. . . ."

"Eddie, you just told me that your family originally came from Ireland. When large waves of Irish finally got here to escape the potato famine, they were discriminated against horribly. Was that good? Are you telling me that you want to repeat history, only the victims would be some other ethnic group? Not the Irish this time, but the people from South America, say?"

His voice became belligerent, with tones of self-righteousness. "I want to help make America great again."

"That's a great idea. How exactly do you propose to do it?"

"Get rid of all the aliens stealing from us."

"So, you plan to kick out all the people from England and Spain and all those other countries, including Ireland, to return the land to its original owners — the American Indians."

"I'm an American and a Christian. . . ."

"Thou shalt not kill or love thy neighbor?"

Eddie stood so quickly he knocked his chair to the ground. He almost sprinted out of my sphere of influence to return to his friends, the people who made him feel better because they thought the same way he did. Would he ever answer the question about which kind of Christian he is? It was important for him to figure it out for himself.

As I lay in bed later that night, I pondered Tadd's accusation I was becoming more of a threat. Not if I treated many guys as I had Eddie. I was sorry for that, but he got on my last nerve. Or maybe being confined to this barn with these men was getting on my last nerve. Being able to watch only slanted reports of events from around the world? Or maybe feeling so damned helpless was getting on my last nerve. Whatever it was, I needed to deal with it.

I was here against my will, originally. Now I stayed even though I might have slipped away while no one was watching me. I was not being guarded now. At least not so's you'd notice.

Conversely, I didn't want the wrong people to find me, either. The television reporters could make my life miserable, not to mention the police who wanted to question me about all the killings I ordered. The very thought was laughable.

Passage of the days was marked only by the announcement of dates on the nightly news. What had I done with this month of my life? It was November already and I had not read a book or created anything. — except new relationships. Then again, perhaps those relationships were the most important things for me in this moment.

I didn't treat everyone with hostility. When I came out of peace, I was more of a threat. *Remember, Sylver, you get more flies with honey than with vinegar*! Was this a lesson for me? Did the readings and our conversations encourage men to think? I crossed my fingers and toes they did. And did I think more clearly about the things we were talking about? Or about the men with whom I had these conversations? I asked Spirit for help. The key to my success in this battle for the minds of men is that I was known to be "a lover, not a fighter". I should apologize to Eddie.

Wasn't I right about coming to appreciate people with whom you spend more time? Perhaps I, too, would appreciate the Eddies by getting to know them better — and sending more honey in their direction. Perhaps I could learn to understand the way they think. Perhaps I would see the value in them and their commitment to their ideals?

CHAPTER TWELVE

Buddy was a natural leader, looked up to by his comrades. Whenever I could, I joined him for walks around the barn. He didn't need exercise. His group of men disappeared into fields and woods beyond the barn and jogged back hours later, sweaty and out of breath. He must have gotten plenty of exercise during physical training and during demanding field maneuvers. From what I understood, they stood or laid on their bellies for practice on the shooting range so audible from my favored position at the barn door. I brought a chair so I could sit there any time.

Our walks around the barn were more about conversation than exercise.

"What did you say to Eddie during his reading? He was really angry with you and threatened to use your head for target practice the minute he could."

I stopped in my tracks. "Really? That angry? I'd better be on my guard."

Buddy grinned. "Nah. You're fine. I straightened him out." He grinned more broadly. Was he remembering something?

"Well, let me ask you how you feel about immigrants."

"What? Is this a quiz?"

"No quiz. I'm just curious."

He walked in silence before answering. "I'm the descendant of immigrants so I can't say anything against people coming to America for a better life. Everyone deserves a good life as long as they work for it and don't steal part of another's. Here, we're told to get rid of specific groups because they don't contribute."

I had a tough time waiting for Buddy's punchline.

He didn't disappoint me. "I've worked side by side with Mexicans at the stables. They're the best workers. They tell me how much they appreciate their new lives. How great America is compared to where they came from. They want to work hard so they can get even better. I'd rather work with any of them than with guys who think two hours is a day's work."

"Interesting insight. That's the issue I brought up with Eddie. We white guys are all immigrants and don't have any greater claim to a better life here than any other person. He didn't like my saying he had less right to this country than the Native Americans whom we have used and abused through the years and continue to mistreat even today. Isn't the white man the illegal alien who stole the land from the first Americans?"

He nodded. "That's about what he said, only you put it nicer. I don't think we should support people who don't work or contribute to our country."

I smiled. "I agree, but with a few exceptions. I also asked Eddie what kind of Christian he is. "Thou shalt not kill" or "love thy neighbor"? He didn't like that question either."

Steven burst through the nearby door. "Where in the bloody hell have you been? I've been looking all over for you. Change your clothes. We're going to a rally." He held new clothes out to me, gesturing with his chin.

"I thought you didn't want me to be visible."

He snorted and acted as though he would toss the clothes at me. "Becoming visible was your stupid mistake. Since you made it, we've decided to use the situation to our advantage. I've decided you're going to be our mascot!"

I groaned. "You're going to put me on the front line so any stray or not-so-stray bullet will land in my soft body, rather than in one of the hard, trained military types. Thanks."

Buddy laughed. "She has a point, you know."

I couldn't help myself, "What he said. What he said. I'd rather stay here in the safety of the barn. It might be rustic, but it is safe."

Steven wasn't hearing any of it and dragged me into the barn. He threw clothes at me and pointed to the door of my room. "Your new uniform. Change."

Yet again, I had no choice. I was to wear black pants and a long-sleeve camo tee-shirt. Great. Now I looked the part.

As soon as I exited my room and saw Steven standing where I had left him, I said angrily, "The first new clothes I've gotten in months and you couldn't get me something more elegant or even pretty?"

He inspected the outfit. "I'll get a smaller shirt next time."

"Are you serious? If it were smaller, it would cut off my circulation or stop my heart from beating."

He practically threw me into an SUV. The door slammed, and the driver accelerated to fifty miles per hour — to parts unknown. As soon as we turned onto a decent road, we traveled at speeds well above the limit.

The "rally" was a political gathering held in a park. American flags and red-white-and-blue bunting were hung all around a gazebo serving as a stage and draped in nearby trees. The open space in front of the stage was filled with people of all ages. Most were dressed in tee-shirts and shorts or jeans. Everyone was fanning himself in the unusual heat and humidity of this fall evening. Tables offering free bottles of water were positioned around the outside of the audience. Several food trucks were operating in the parking area along the edge of the field. In the distance I could see sports fields. A soccer game was being played in one, but the others were empty.

Our caravan of SUVs rushed into the parking area and then into spaces fairly close to the stage. There were stanchions claiming the spaces for "security." We didn't get shooed away so I guessed we were security. The doors opened and all of us tumbled out into the parking area and marched toward the stage.

We arrived as one of the candidates railed against evils of illegal immigrants, the welfare state, and the evils of letting a woman kill the baby in her body just because she no longer wanted it. He didn't talk about the latter in terms of women's right to make choices for their own bodies. It was murder, period. And he didn't consider the times when terminating the pregnancy was to save the life of the mother. He didn't mention the employment of so many foreigners in the horse industry and as house cleaners right here in this county. The audience was wildly enthusiastic and yelled in agreement as the speaker went through his list of "nevers." I didn't hear a promise to introduce new programs for the good of the citizens, but maybe that was covered earlier. I gave the speaker the benefit of the doubt.

The roar was tremendous as the speaker paused after each point. "We are being held back by the evil ones. We have to defeat them so we can take control of Congress and of state government." On and on. Spewing mountains of hate. Like lava from a volcano, it spread throughout the audience to touch every member in it. They lapped it up and threw their fisted arms in the air to show their agreement with a need to defeat the OTHER. Was it my imagination or did his country twang become more pronounced the longer he spoke? Never mind that his definition of OTHER was not the same as that in other parts of the country and there was no mention of compromise in those cases of great difference.

The candidate reminded his audience "Election Day is only days away. The only way we will take back our country is for each and every one of you to go out to round up ten votes. On Election Day, you get those people in your car or march them down the street to the polling place. You get them to mark their ballot for the real patriots. WE are the real patriots. We are the people who will work to pass laws to restore our republic."

My companions and I waited for a lull in the speech to slip onto the stage to stand behind the group of people ready to take their times at the podium. A muscled guy stood on either side of me. Minutes later, Tadd replaced one of them. I wondered if they were guards to make certain I didn't disappear into the crowd. Or were they here to play the role of bodyguards for the esteemed organization leader? Either way, I was screwed. Musclebound men had me penned in.

So-o-o screwed.

I looked around for anyone I might recognize, but saw no one. The audience must all be local, not one person I knew from "the big city."

I knew the minute the media noticed me. Flashes came from every camera in the crowd.

Great! Screwed.

I was developing a very personal understanding of the media's bad reputation. At least I was experiencing up close and personal the *modus operandi* of reporters from the only station permitted on our television. My presence would be interpreted in whatever way they needed for the cohesion of their story. Not for the sake of truth. Every tale would be illustrated with photos of Sylver, the fearless leader of this patriotic paramilitary protecting America from mobs attacking our southern border. The Power Men, ready to defend the rights of citizens of our great country against evil hordes.

Yay. The news would have a field day with this new sighting of the illusive silver-haired woman, the leader of the Power Men. Oh, well, what could I do about it anyway? I stood there to watch the crowd getting more animated by each new point made by the speaker. There were yells and screams and fist bumps to indicate their agreement.

Steven stood at the edge of the stage, positioned like a toady ready to do duty. I followed his gaze to different places in the crowd. Clusters of men with military bearing were positioned at regular intervals. They kept their eyes on Steven most of the time. They were the loudest as the audience cheered the speakers. They started chants about the rigged election of the past and the need to take back our country.

If we lose it's because this election was rigged.
They cheat, those candidates on the other side.
They're evil.

Each chant was in response to a signal from Steven. Every time they repeated the scripted words, people around them joined in. Noise increased in volume until the entire audience screamed in unison.

Members of the press corps would get the chant on video. Cameras pointed at them encouraged people to join the chant, but more loudly than others. Each person in the audience jockeyed for center stage in this spectacle. Steven and the media working in concert made the rally into a roaring success. The average guy in the audience was being played by the best.

Smile for the camera!

Steven mimicked an orchestra director whenever noise was needed to punctuate a statement or underscore an accusation. After the last speaker ended, the military guys surged toward the stage to form a gauntlet for me — and my bodyguards — to pass through to our vehicles.

Along the way to our parked transport, they made certain that cameras flashed in my direction but didn't allow anyone to talk with me. Yell questions, yes, but not get answers from me.

Answers were provided by my "protectors." I was too busy trying to keep up with the men pushing me along. Besides, I didn't actually know anything about what was being called "my operation."

The rally was a marvel of precision. Beautifully orchestrated. Had Steven planned it? I considered his strengths and weaknesses. Probably not. This kind of organization didn't fit what I knew of him. Not part of his skillset, but he did play his part to perfection. In fact, I doubted the idea of using me as "mascot" was his. An image flashed in my memory of Tadd's satisfied grin as he got into the vehicle in front of ours. Was he the architect of this plan to manipulate patriotic citizens? And generally, to manipulate the entire rally?

Later, I was invited to watch the news coverage. It was very well done. The event was orchestrated so I got more air time than the politicians. After all, they were known quantities and I was a woman of mystery. Reporters seemed to dismiss the fact their questions were answered in male voices and not in a woman's. I heard Steven tell them I was modest and didn't like to be center stage. *Good ad lib, Steven!* Or had Tadd provided him with that line?

The entire room erupted in cheers and applause at the end of the segment. Absolutely the best theater I'd seen in a long time! The performance deserved an Oscar for both directing and acting.

Only Buddy looked at me with questioning eyes. I quirked my shoulders in response. We would talk later. But as he had said, he and some of his friends knew more about me now and all this didn't fit with the image of me in their minds.

The benefit to me of this charade was the men in this unit became more open with me. *Maybe I* was *the head of this serpent.* After all, what would the fearless leader do to hurt them? And didn't she already know anything they might want to discuss with her? She probably planned it anyway, no? The men who had not spent time with me personally must not have considered the inconsistency of this display of militancy with my words of peace and partnership.

CHAPTER THIRTEEN

Steven banged on my door in the morning. "Rise and shine. Time for you to inspect your operation."

I rolled over, wondering what in the bloody hell he meant by "my operation"? It was very early in the morning, not even light out yet. "No, no, no. You've got the wrong room. Go find someone else to torture at this ungodly hour."

Steven's voice was smiling. "You've been hidden away for long enough, Sylver. We need to bring you more out in the open. The men will be cheered to see their fearless leader taking an interest in them and in their training."

It took all the energy I had to raise my voice above a mumble. "I am an unwilling mascot for a cause with which I do not agree. Leave me alone. In fact, find someone else to be your damned mascot. I resign." And I rolled back over intending to return to dreamland.

The next knock was louder and more violent and the voice belonged to someone else. Tadd. "Up and at 'em or I'll break down the door."

Tadd sounded serious and so I started pulling myself out of bed. "Will you huff and puff. . . ."

"One, two. . . ."

"Damn! Where's you sense of humor? Okay. Okay. I'm on my way. Give me just a few minutes to put clothes on."

As I walked out my door, Steven pointed to the other guy, "Tadd. This is his idea. If you're in the mood to yell, yell at him."

One look at the fierce determination on Tadd's face and I decided against fighting back. In any way.

Tadd was supposedly second in command of this "army," but it looked to me that he had taken charge of rousting me. And much else in the barn. He didn't nod or recognize me in any way before he walked double time to the barn door. I trotted to keep up. I was delighted to see Steven trotting, too. *Bastard.* He was already breathing hard while Tadd didn't have a hair out of place. I was panting.

The thick-necked goon finally said something to me, "I had to answer a lot of reporters' questions yesterday. Eventually, you should be able to give answers yourself."

I huffed out my response, "You forget, this is not my operation and in fact, I am here as a prisoner, essentially. I don't want anything to do with this fight — nothing. In fact, I resign *post haste* from the rare honor of representing you as mascot!"

Tadd stopped so suddenly and without a signal that I ran right into his back. It was so muscled that running into it felt fairly much like running into a brick wall.

He turned to look directly, and too intimately, into my eyes — my eyes that are so dreamy and hazel ran right up against his drab green piercing ones. *Oops.*

I backed up a couple of steps. Steven was standing too close and I bumped into him as I was trying to get away from Tadd. *Trapped.*

"We are at war here and everyone needs to pull his — *or her* — weight. Only someone who is not a patriot would refuse service when his — *or her* — country needs him — *or her*. Are you that non-patriot? We have punishments for that kind of behavior."

In the glare of his intensity, I felt like I was actually in front of a firing squad. I would have backed up a few more paces if I hadn't felt Steven's breath rustling the hair on top of my head. The only thought that ran through my mind was, *I am screwed. I am royally screwed here. This guy is nuts and violent. And too close.*

Tadd stood waiting for an answer I didn't have. The longer his eyes bored into me, the farther away the answer moved. I obviously do not do well under pressure. Especially not the pressure of being squeezed between two men, one of whom wanted nothing more than to skewer me.

Finally, words came to me from somewhere and they spilled out into the air between Tadd and myself, "My country t'is of thee. I am a patriot and love the Constitution. I believe in loving my neighbor as Jesus told me. And I believe we can always reach an agreement in any situation — an agreement that doesn't involve violence of any kind." Once I put the period on the tumble of words, I fairly melted from the heat coming from front and back — and the morning was chilly still.

Tadd looked past me to Steven and then back at me. Then he laughed and, in the end, laughed so hard I thought he would lose it. With the release of tension, I finally took a breath. I was guessing I passed his test. Good thing, because I was about to pass out from lack of oxygen.

Steven smiled wanly as he backed away several paces, "I told you she was smart."

Tadd grabbed my arm strongly enough to create yet another bruise. He pushed me out the door and then into and through the woods to an open field. This was the source of all the noise. There was a shooting range and a field in which soldiers did exercises. Not only was there the constant pop of weapons firing, but there was also an undercurrent of male grunting from the exertion of jumping jacks. Beyond that exercise area, there was an expanse of woods in which some men played at shooting humanoid figures. A different version of field maneuvers.

I looked at everything around me, but my mind was busy doing the end zone dance. I was still alive. My actual feet were working to keep my body moving along to keep pace with Tadd as we trotted long the rutted path. Moving that fast made me keep my backbone ramrod straight. I hoped Tadd saw patriotism in that backbone.

Tadd explained the different weapons being used in the practice range. Not one word of that explanation found a permanent home in my brain. He might as well have been whistling in the wind. He explained the uses for each of these weapons and how many men were practicing with each of them. I looked around and didn't see half that many people practicing. Was this man psychotic, delusional, or just lousy at math?

I shook my head. "Wow! It's so complicated. I just thought they were all used to kill your fellow men, any members of the human tribe you didn't like."

Steven gasped sharply behind me, but he didn't say anything. I guessed he was warning that although I survived the first test, there could be others. Perhaps the message was that every bit of interchange was a test of some kind. Although Tadd still had his gun holstered, he could easily pull it out to use on me. Still, he knew I rarely hid my opinions, especially if they differed from those of people around me. By now, everyone knew that about me. Still, I was not so dumb that I was blind to how dangerous Tadd was. He was a killer, not a diplomat. A doer, not a thinker. From what I could see, he would rather shoot you than shake your hand. Yes, Tadd was dangerous in the bullet-in-the-belly kind of way.

On the far side of the shooting range was the field in which men doing callisthenic exercises were already sweating in the morning chill. I was impressed by the strength and stamina displayed by the members of "our" unit. I began to appreciate what it took to perform the antics of the soldiers I'd seen portrayed in the movies.

"You set this up?"

Tadd stood a bit straighter and puffed up his chest. He smiled with pride. "I did. We've been training here for months. This is the base for our forays into the local communities. For our raids."

Steven added from behind me, "Actually, for years. We've been training for years, but here for only months. This is the final push to get ready for the attack on the capitol in case the president doesn't get reelected."

If Tadd ratcheted up the intensity of his stare just a bit, he would have drilled holes straight through the man standing next to me. I planned an escape out of the way of his searing glare — in case Steven suddenly exploded from the intensity. Tadd didn't have to say one word to express his lack of respect and general dislike of this man who was supposedly his superior. Well, he probably hated Steven, to be exact. All that was evident in his expression and in the strength of his gaze.

Steven obviously noticed he had displeased the man and started stuttering. "I-I-I thought we were going to tell her everything."

Tadd winced. "There is 'everything' and there is 'everything.'"

Steven missed the nuance, but I didn't. They planned operations for years that were soon to get very real and personal. They probably didn't want for me to know the end goal just in case I actually escaped and reached someone who could take countermeasures to stop them. From here on out I expected to be more closely watched. Just when I thought I'd gained at least a modicum of Tadd's trust, Steven ruined it all.

Everywhere I went that morning the men looked at me, curious and with just a touch of hero worship. After all, I had suddenly catapulted into fame as the fearless leader of their national organization, a group intent on bringing down a powerful oligarchy running a powerful country! And me, just a little woman, after all. And obviously not so buff as they.

All I could think, *I am screwed. I am so screwed!* Note to self: be on guard for snipers — always and everywhere — front and back. Wish I had another set of eyes in the back of my head.

"Tadd, who pays for all this ammunition? It's expensive,

isn't it, and you seem to have an endless supply."

He shrugged his shoulders. "Donors. Lots of donors."

"Donors who support overthrowing the government under which they managed to make so much money? They must expect to get far more if you're successful."

Steven hissed behind me, but Tadd only grunted without a word. "We have to go to the speeches in the capitol this afternoon. Maybe we should be on our way?"

Was this the real thing? Are we on our way to Washington this afternoon? I didn't dare ask that question. Maybe we weren't going to DC after all.

Finally, whatever big event they'd hinted about was going to take place. No more waiting and wondering. But, then again, maybe not.

Tadd nodded and turned toward the barn. He seemed to march double time. Did he ever just walk or even saunter? I didn't think he did.

I thought, S*how's over. At least this show is over and we're on to the next where they will probably try to make me the star! Splat!*

"Tadd, what rank did you achieve in the military?"

"Sergeant."

I nodded. This information answered a lot. Tadd had been a grunt. Maybe a drill sergeant. I hoped he hadn't taken any higher level schooling in the military. No classes in military history or battlefield analysis. "Are you still in the military, Tadd?"

No answer. I didn't think he was. Maybe he quit so he could devote his full attention to this revolution.

I put on my new uniform and was pleasantly surprised to discover Steven had not shrunk the shirt for me. With wear, this one was stretching out a bit. Still, it was tighter than I preferred. To show my muscles, I wondered?

Tadd and Steven again pushed me into a vehicle and we tore out of the farm gate like we were being chased by a posse of sheriff's deputies. This time the event was an indoor program of speeches, including one by a candidate for a national office. We arrived early enough to position ourselves at the back of the stage as we had the day before. Tadd and I along with another muscled military guy, Rick.

The room was full. People in the audience were in tee-shirts and jeans mostly, but there were more people in business suits here, sitting in temporary bleachers that lined the walls. From the way they talked among themselves in small clusters, I guessed they were members of the staffs of various departments in state government. I wondered if they were in this audience by command or by personal preference. From where I was standing, that was difficult to discern. The atmosphere was party-like, but that could have been because they were getting time off from work to attend. When the speakers came through a side door to get to the stage, members of the audience stopped talking to take notice. And when the candidate for Senate joined us on the stage the entire audience stood to applaud.

Yup! True believers all.

Steven was positioned by the stage to play director as he was the day before. I noticed the small clusters of our unit scattered in the audience. For now, they were talking among themselves, but glanced in our direction from time to time. Ready to play their roles.

There was a huge difference from the event yesterday. Since a Senatorial candidate was there, we were surrounded by a much larger security detail and there was a larger crowd surrounding the stage. In addition, more security and a larger press corps preceded the candidate into the room to take up much of the space close to the stage.

The head of the state party welcomed the audience and ended with a pitch for our side. *Get the vote out and we will overcome.* Several of the local candidates spoke first. Their speeches were much like those I heard the day before. Then the woman running for Senate was introduced. Now, this is

Kentucky and I didn't feel she had much of a chance of being elected until she started her prepared remarks. She hugged the local candidates and told the audience how they would help to improve the daily lives of the citizens of the state. *But they can only help you if you get the vote out to assure their election.*

First, she greeted the crowd and got them excited by complimenting them— "This Is your year. This is the year you will win big, Kentucky. You will win in the state with my fellow candidates on this stage. And you will win with me as your Senator from the grand Commonwealth of Kentucky."

I thought about the voting history of this state. She was pretty much guaranteed of being right.

"It is within your power to take back the control of our state and national governments. After all, you are the people the Constitution means by 'for the people.' I am also mentioned in that document in the phrase, 'by the people.' I am your people and will work for you in Washington. I won't work for the special interest groups who control the majority of our politicians. I will never sell out to the special interests."

She was a cheerleader getting football fans ready to see the game, except she was also the game. And yet, I wondered who was paying for her very successful campaign. Were they part of the "special interests"?

I had seen the woman speak at televised events, but never in person. She was good. She was definitely good at working the audience, at mesmerizing them. And then she started repeating the message mastered over the last couple of months, the message I'd seen in videos about the Cabal and how they controlled the country and enslaved the people. Only she spoke in veiled terms about taking the control of our country back from that other party. Radicals that wanted to destroy it.

"We have indictments and we're going to get these criminals out of government and out of the country. We need more laws with sharper teeth for enforcement. We have a problem. There are people stealing our lives. I promise that when you send me to Congress, I will make sure that our defenses are stronger and our borders are better protected.

"I'll work with people already in office to take back our country. I speak for the people and if I don't win, it's because this election is rigged. If I don't win, the election was stolen from me. From us. From you."

As she went through her rant, listing all the bad people, the bad groups, I looked around and at the men on either side of me. Heads nodded in agreement. Expressions were ecstatic. These fat cats in Congress and their wealthy supporters were the criminals holding her people back, keeping them from the prosperity that was their due. They were the thieves. If they don't go peacefully, we will neutralize them some other way. We have to get rid of them. Jail them.

The crowd interrupted her periodically with enthusiastic cheering. Steven was the instigator of most of this cheering and the loudest voices were the men in uniform who lived in the barn with us. Whenever they started the rousing expressions of their admiration, they were joined by the people around them. Great job, Steven!

She went on, "I promise you right here and today I will introduce bills to restrict voting to only educated people. We don't need the uneducated to tell us what to do. They will want to spend our federal money on give-aways to people who don't want to work, who don't want to contribute to making this country great again.

"Let's not waste our hard-earned money on people who don't want to help re-build the country. That money should be spent on programs to build America. I will give all of you a break from the high taxes when you send me to DC. I will introduce a bill to end income tax and the IRS. Instead, we should have a national sales tax that everyone will pay. I will introduce a bill to end the payroll tax." She didn't mention the tiny fact that so much more benefit from tax cuts went to the billionaires than to the lower earners. She didn't mention that Social Security is funded by the payroll tax . . . which is different from income tax. She didn't mention that changes to the tax code can only come from the House of Representatives . . . and she was running for a Senate seat.

On and on, she described the new world she single-handedly would create. "Let's get rid of those candidates and officials who want to turn this country into a socialist country. Do you want to live in a socialist country?"

The roar of her listeners answered that question in the negative.

"Why do we need to pay for college for every citizen? Or to institute universal Medicare? That is socialism pure and simple. And we don't want this country to become a socialist dictatorship."

I noticed the grand leap of logic, but no one else seemed to. The audience loved her message. Mouths grinned in appreciation of her carefully painted picture of Nirvana. How lucky they were to have such a woman on their side. Not to mention how horrible her opponent was — a man willing to sell their children as sex slaves and bring black drug dealers into their neighborhoods. A man who will let gangs take over their cities. Not to mention the waves of foreign criminals flooding across our southern borders.

Whoa. What a huge leap of logic.

When she turned to compliment the Power Men for their contributions during the protests, the applause was deafening. She pointed at me in particular as a woman with great power. Now I was the head of a band of demi-gods! Never mind that hundreds of thousands of innocents had already been killed by these men and goons like them. I was disgusted. The crowd was screaming their heads off in support of the new way things would be done soon — very soon. Only days until the election. Members of the audience were entreated to do their parts by helping get new voters to the polls on election day. "Do the work now so that we can work for you when we're in positions of responsibility and power. If we do this right, we only have to do it once."

She brought the other candidates to the front of the stage and they held hands raised above their heads in a sign of unity and the victory soon to come. Yelling from the audience morphed into an organized victory chant. That was probably Steven's work.

The show was over — for today.

One advantage of sharing the stage with such a mesmerizing force is the media didn't look twice at me. Oh, there were a couple of cameras flashing in my direction, especially when she focused the light of her gaze on me, but when we left the stage we were not followed. She moved like a tornado through the crowd, pulling the reporters in her wake. Members of the audience followed the light of her sun.

We slipped out the side door and were probably back at our refuge in the country before the media realized we were off the stage. My companions were talking about the candidates as though they were direct disciples of Jesus, the Christ. They ignored the fact that Jesus didn't advocate the wholesale slaughter of his opponents. Just as we negotiated the gates to the farm, the conversation entered the how-can-we-kill-more-people chapter. EEWWW! I could not wait to get away from these men.

CHAPTER FOURTEEN

During the evening news, local anchors covered the political rally extensively. The cameras panned the audience while the narrator described it as huge and wildly enthusiastic. Some of the reporters who attended posted details of the event complete with interviews of candidates and of some supporters. Snippets of all speeches were shown for the benefit of viewers who could not attend. Most of the Senatorial candidate's speech was aired. After watching her speech, the talking heads interpreted her words for the television audience. Their interpretations focused on the rosy outcome she envisioned, but didn't mention the violence implied to reach that outcome.

The room around me was filled with whoops of approval after every point she made. When she focused her attention on the Power Men — and me — this testosterone-filled room erupted into a roar of support. Here was their candidate, a leader in the fight against the enemy. And here were their leaders right there on the stage with their candidate. They were being honored by the next Senator from Kentucky and would probably be admitted to the august halls of government when she took them over. What could be better?

Loud conversations popped up in the room around me. There was mention of martial law and units dispatched to round up anyone who didn't agree with the new government. Tanks rolling through neighborhoods would communicate our intention to turn this country into a god-fearing place that didn't condone lawlessness. We would help to change the country into a more unified society. If the dissenters didn't respond to "retraining" then they would be neutralized in other ways.

We would punish government officials who participated in the abuse of children and other forms of sex trafficking.

When the station played a short video of the opposing point of view, there were calls to shoot the SOB at any mention of programs he would support if he were elected. He supported helping the young avoid starting their lives with so much student debt and described several options to make that real. From their reactions, I could tell that no one bothered to listen to him before condemning every idea he advanced, every word he uttered. They booed him even when he told his audience he supported the laws being introduced by his opponent.

"Draco! Draco!"

The next news segment showed fighting in all corners of the world. Others showed mass graves filled with victims of ethnic cleansing — hundreds of thousands of men, women, children of one religious sect killed by members of another sect. The men around me yelled their disapproval.

"People who kill so freely should all be killed. They're no better than animals. Draco!"

"Let's do another raid in the south of Louisville where immigrants have taken over. I know the location of a mosque with a large membership! They should be neutralized before they can bring this kind of violence to our country."

THEY are not as smart as we are. THEY don't want to work. THEY are criminals. THEY want to take over the world.

As I listened, I looked around the room at the strong emotions in their faces and realized they would kill those others right now if they thought they could get away with it. There is power in numbers and anonymity when you hide in a crowd of faces. And yelling in a room with other like-minded people is easy.

Our friendly news reporter brought our attention back to killings across the planet. Dictators and their proxies sent death squads to arrest opponents in the name of reestablishing order. Some of the protesters in places like Hong Kong went into retraining centers never to be seen or heard from again.

In fact, protesters in Hong Kong were being killed outright as Government forces increased the strength of responses to quell even peaceful protests. There, any protest against the state is deemed a violent attack. Never mind that the government now in charge refused to honor the promises made to the citizens and to the British colonialists who had ruled for decades before transfer of the territory to China — the promise of continued freedom. In the eyes of my companions, this was terrible and "We should go help them. But only after we've straightened out the situation here."

Men around me didn't seem to understand that if rights of the OTHER could be limited so, too, could their own.

The final blast of death and destruction was the large number of deaths due to the growing pandemic. Part of that segment were the people speaking passionately against another lock-down to prevent more infections. That resulted in damaging the country last time. It took too long to recover. Plants and factories were closed, resulting in an interruption of the supply chain at all levels. Empty shelves in grocery stores were shown with dire warnings about horrors still to come.

Again, my buddies decried the infringement of our freedoms. There were calls to kill anyone who suggested an interruption or even a pause in life as we know it.

A gruff voice called out, "I thought they were going to use martial law to control this? When will they shut down our country?"

Now that shocked me. It seemed that shutting down the country was only good if "our side" did it. If anyone else shut down the country, it was a limitation of our freedoms and punishable by death — if they could get away with it, that is.

Some of this was yelled as reporters encouraged people to stay at home to avoid infection. In fact, they informed their viewers of the potential of a government-mandated curfew and mask-wearing in public places. The response from the men around me, "Our freedoms are being taken away." "Why should we be forced to wear those stupid masks or stay away from restaurants and bars? What right do they have to take away our rights?"

"I plan to refuse. That's my right."

And yet, as I looked around the room, most of these men were dressed just alike. Did that mean they all had the same taste in clothes or did someone tell them how to dress and when? Where was this call for freedom when Tadd ordered them around all day?

I was drowning in this testosterone-drenched room. I had to get out. I needed air. I turned back at the door to say, "I thought you wanted a lock-down with martial law. Isn't this the same thing?"

The yelling hesitated, but not for long. Did they even hear me?

I shook my head. Were these men making "raids" in city neighborhoods? Were some of the deaths blamed on drug wars actually committed by these troops? Had they become a vigilante group killing innocents just because they were different? I wondered, but really I didn't think I actually wanted to know.

Minutes later, Tadd found me just outside the barn door looking up at the stars. "Why are you trying to confuse the men?"

"I don't know what you're talking about. A lock-down due to a pandemic is perhaps a more palatable way of instituting martial law, isn't it? The reason given is medical rather than military force. The effect is the same. People are stuck in their homes rather than moving freely around town. What's the difference? Or is it only bad because you didn't start it?"

Tadd practically yelled at me. His entire body tensed. His hand balled into a fist. I was preparing for a blow. "We will dominate. We must take over this country by force. Nothing you can say will stop this movement." He fell into a sudden silence and turned his eyes toward the night sky.

I could not let it go. "I've been watching for weeks — and listening. It seems any act is good if your side does it, but bad if someone else does it. You can limit the freedoms of other people, but don't want anyone to limit your own freedoms even a little. Seems hypocritical to me."

He said nothing, but I could hear him shifting on his feet. A faint growl came from his direction.

Just then the space station came into view as it cleared the tops of the trees to our west.

Tadd's voice picked up a notch and he moved nervously several paces into the field. "Is that a space ship? It moves slower than an airplane. It's a lot bigger."

I chuckled. "I'd bet if you checked on the computer, you'd find the space station is scheduled to pass over us tonight."

He watched for a while. The man was agitated and nervously paced in the clearing, and then moved under the shelter of the trees. He kept looking toward the sky. Suddenly, he turned to enter the barn. Would he check out the schedule for the ISS?

Not more than half hour later Buddy walked through the door behind me. "Been looking for you."

"Want a reading?"

Buddy chuckled. "No, but I could probably do a pretty good reading for you right now."

I grinned, "What would the cards tell me?"

Buddy laughed, "I don't know what the cards would tell you, but I tell you to be careful what you say."

"Am I in danger of getting a bullet between my shoulder blades?"

He hesitated, "Maybe. More likely your movements would be restricted."

I turned to look into my friend's eyes. "How could that be? I'm already essentially a prisoner here. They only take me out when I can be of use. And in fact, that use is probably putting my life in danger."

He said nothing for a few minutes, probably weighing the truth of what I said. I thanked him in my mind for actually thinking. I gave him the space he needed and turned again to watch the space station. He followed my eyes and grinned. "The space station."

I laughed. "You certain it's not an alien space ship? I think that's what Tadd thinks it is."

"Hmmm."

He spoke slowly when he finally spoke. "When we win this revolution, because you're with us you'll be safe. Otherwise, I'm not certain what could happen."

"Are you so convinced you'll win?"

"Yep. Just look at the numbers. Most of the NRA members are on our side. And retired military with all their guns. Half the current military. The majority of the weapons in this country are raised in rebellion. A lot of politicians are just waiting for the balance to shift more in our favor before they step up to take control."

Logical. But I wasn't buying it. "Why? Why would they back a rebellion? Any of them? Wouldn't that be risking a lot? This is treason, you know."

"The military take an oath to serve and protect the Constitution. We are all about reinstating the Constitution. That's our goal. So, joining us would be in service to the oath they took."

I nodded and then said slowly, "You're reinstating the guarantees of several freedoms by killing and incarcerating people who are exercising those very freedoms? Have you ever read that esteemed document? Do you know what it says? Do you know what rights it guarantees?"

He looked at me, but didn't answer.

I was tired of having empty words bandied about. "Read it, before you say you're reinstating it. Read it, because I think you're engaging in activities that are in opposition to the Constitution." I waved to take in the camp. "Most of what's done and talked about here is a total rejection of the rights guaranteed by the Constitution. Most of what I hear in this camp is total falsehood, created by people to manipulate uninformed men who want to play army. An elaborate game of bang-bang, shoot 'em up. Do you believe because you want to believe or because you're ignorant?"

He was quiet for about fifteen minutes and then whispered, "Just be careful." In minutes, I was alone in the growing chill of the night. Alone in more ways than one. I was sorry I had fought with my only friend in this friendless place. This dangerous place. More dangerous without friends.

CHAPTER FIFTEEN

Again — the news. The election. Threats of the new pandemic of infection by the virus and controversy over the new vaccination. Protests all around the world, peaceful and violent. The growing tally of the dead. The news was depressing. The only station the television in the common room seemed to receive was one not known for its fair and balanced reporting. I wanted to stay away from those awful shows to avoid depression that was lurking just around the corner. That's what I should do.

Instead, I watched the news whenever it was aired, mostly to watch my comrades' reactions. I wanted to learn how they thought and why they thought. To my horror I saw men who treated me — and everyone else — kindly most of the time turn nasty and violent when urged forward by the news anchor and Tadd. This must be what brainwashing is. The men were worn out from all the training and then inundated with this negative interpretation of current events, complete with a bit of liquor from time to time.

Normally I don't drink much liquor, but alcohol is truth serum in the average man or woman. When they brought out the bourbon during the six o'clock news, I reached for a glass like everyone else. I wanted to see what would come out in these men. And I could use a bit of anesthetic myself.

A lovely woman stood in front of the camera with scenes of destruction behind her — temporary shelters laying in ruins on the ground, billowing smoke obscuring the images from time to time. "Today there was an explosion in a refugee camp on a Greek island in the Mediterranean." Under the reporter's words there was a stream of video showing different views of the camp and the damage. Some men were cheering with fists raised above their heads. The reporter continued, "There is some question about whether the bomb was set off to kill refugees living in the camp. Some locals are advancing the suggestion that residents themselves destroyed part of the camp so they would be moved to better neighborhoods on the island . . . or ferried across the water to other communities from which they could escape into the countryside."

Comments came from all around me, "Kill the @#$ rag heads." "We don't need any more of those bastards flooding the rest of the world." "If they can't manage their own country, why should they be allowed to destroy ours?"

The bourbon loosened my tongue, too. "Do you think they destroyed their own homes or did some group of men overdosed with testosterone kill and maim their family members? And bomb their homes? And chase them out of their own country with a threat of death?"

The guy sitting next to me turned to look at me menacingly. But I answered his glare, "Do you think those women carrying babies did the fighting?"

Buddy was sitting on the other side of me and jabbed an elbow into my ribs. When I turned to complain, he said under his breath, "Careful."

As usual, I couldn't let it go and I turned to the middle of the room. "Do you see any women with babies here — in this camp? In fact, do you see many women? Isn't battle mostly waged by men to dominate other men?"

I could sense Buddy shake his head again in warning. His voice was soft, but strong, "Careful."

The commercial ended and another reporter was standing near a group of protesters in Hong Kong. They were angry that the Chinese-run government passed a law making it illegal to protest their restrictive laws. The young people who were interviewed told reporters, "We were promised we would still be free under Chinese rule, but every year the noose tightens."

The room erupted into calls for invading Hong Kong to help those people fighting for their freedoms. "As soon as we finish here, we'll be sent there to fight by your side."

Before I could add my two cents, the focus of the news show returned to the transmission from Hong Kong. The reporter on the scene was interviewing a protester who asked, "Where is the western support we were promised? Why did we see the candidate for American president smiling and friendly with Chinese officials instead of demanding protections for us? Shaking hands and he promised more generous trade deals with our oppressors? We've been sold out. The Americans have sold us out."

I looked around the room and saw blank faces staring at the television. Ah, now where was the support for the freedoms of others?

The New Virus Mutation. The segment led off with development of a vaccine for this new virus and then doctors urging the viewers to wear masks and stay home as much as possible. The camera cut to the anchors of the show shaking their heads in disagreement. "Wearing masks only hurts the person wearing the mask. It limits the amount of oxygen you can get into your lungs and can encourage infection, not discourage it."

Where did they get that information? I read research that contradicted everything the anchors were saying. Everything. All around me were murmurs of agreement and vows to disobey anyone trying to limit their freedom by making them wear masks.

"I'll be damned if they're going to take away my freedom of choice like that. It's Communist."

"Nah. It's the Cabal taking control any way they can. . . ."

"Aren't they the ones that spread the virus in the first place?"

I was about to open my mouth when Buddy squeezed my arm with great force and pulled me out of my seat and toward the door. He didn't stop until we were outside the barn under the stars. When he spoke, it was in a hoarse whisper, "You might have information from other sources, but you need to keep it to yourself."

By this time, I was angry. "Are you telling me that the men here are too stupid to understand the science of it? Or are they too brain-washed by the intelligent people who are pulling their strings? Is it so bad to make people wear masks, but great to make women have babies they don't want by denying them contraceptives?"

He looked furious, but didn't say anything. He stormed toward the barn.

It was a good thing that he didn't argue his point because I was ready to unload on him, with all my ammunition powered by the seething anger built up during the time I'd been held prisoner in this camp of men whose only aim was the one looking down the barrel of a gun. I wanted to ask where my freedoms were, like my freedom of speech.

I was certain Buddy was right that my only protection in the case of an all-out rebellion was to be protected by the guys with guns on the winning side. But I just didn't think any armed rebellion would be successful. At least, I hoped and prayed that it wouldn't be. Maybe I could help stop it.

I looked around me. No one was guarding me now. I was free to walk through that gate, or over the fence. By the time they realized I was gone, I could be miles away. I could inform the authorities of where they were and what they were doing and what their plans were.

Images of reporters crowding in my face were suddenly projected on the screen in my mind. I shook my head. No one would believe me since all those false stories about me had taken hold. I would be an easy target to blame and who knows where that would lead. Out there, beyond the fence around this farm, I had no one to protect me. Here, at least, they would protect me as long as they had a use for me.

Who could I trust? How many law enforcement and military were aligned with this rebellion? They were hidden in the shadows and would stay there until they were no longer needed in the shadows. They would join the fight when it was safe for them to take a more active role out in the open. That's the story I'd been told. I didn't know what was true and what was a lie. Not here in this bubble of hate. At least I knew this bubble of hate . . . I might not like it, but it was familiar.

My heart was on a dangerous slide toward despair. Despair and the temptation of giving up. Maybe it would be smarter, and definitely safer, to keep my mouth shut and smile for the camera. Later, I could say, like Patty Hearst, I was brain-washed by my captors.

In the dark, alone, the answer came to me. I am here at this time with these people for some reason. By following my heart, I would surely see a path to saving myself, at least. Perhaps I could change some other minds along the way? I couldn't answer their illogic with logic. I couldn't directly fight the hold that the evil ones had over them. I had to be smarter than that. I had to answer their emotion with emotion. Their feelings of powerlessness with visions of a path to power, even if it was only personal power.

I thought about their reactions to news reports. They were looking for a leader, someone who was sure what path to follow, someone who would plan the actions to take and coach them forward. Or yell obscenities to batter them into submission . . . the Dominator Model. Now the people they were following planned to use these men with honorable intentions to achieve their own personal dishonorable ends. Overthrow the current government so that they would have more power . . . more authority . . . end this government to replace it with something made in their own image. Every dictator who had replaced a bloody tyrant to *save his people* over time became an even bloodier tyrant himself. I could see these men were not ready to hear history. Unfortunately, I was afraid they were reliving that very history.

I watched the stars, hoping to see an alien ship to indicate support. Or even a shooting star to show that Spirit was on my side and would help with this gargantuan task. Nothing. Well, nothing but the stars and galaxies in the universe beyond my own solar system.

Buddy! Buddy was a natural leader. I wondered if he would help bring peace in the end. He did seem leaning in the direction of saving me from myself. . . . But had I shut him out?

I studied the stars and felt the awe of being so small in this huge universe. And here, I was alone now . . . and small. Where was Shelby when you needed his counsel?

CHAPTER SIXTEEN

Buddy jogged back with the rest of his unit, sweaty and obviously tired from the morning's workout. He disappeared into the area of the barn reserved for the "troops." As soon as he emerged again, I corralled him for a walk around the barn. I couldn't wait to put my new plans into practice. I had considered what topic to talk about and rejected anything modern, including religion, that might get his dander up.

"I'm sorry I was so testy last night, but the stress of the situation is getting to me. I'm a pacifist, and to watch so much fighting and killing stresses my constitution. It seems to be the topic of choice here."

His expression was curious and cautious. It looked as though he suspected a new plan on my part. Perceptive of him!

Be careful, Sylver, be careful. "Did you ever wonder why I read the cards? Or how information comes through them?"

"Or how you sometimes know what I'm going to say before I say it?"

I laughed. "I do?"

He nodded. "Yep. You sometimes say exactly what I'm thinking. Use the very words I'm thinking. In fact, you do it more lately."

I nodded. "All that."

He nodded. "I have been curious."

I pointed to my head. "My thoughts are really chemical and electrical flows, vibrations, whirling around inside my skull." I knew that the truth was more complicated than that, but I didn't want to hit him with too much outside the realm of his current understanding.

He nodded, waiting for me to continue. "I went to college."

I pointed to his head. "The same is true of the activity inside your skull."

Another nod of understanding.

Then I waved in the air between us. "This might look empty to you, but it's actually filled with lots of molecules carrying vibrations. And if you're sensitive to them when the vibrations travel from one person's head to yours, you can tune into and interpret them."

I gave this tidbit a moment or two to sink in.

Buddy looked at me closely. "You're telling me you can read minds?"

"That's part of it, but only a part. It is actually only a tiny part. The bigger picture is that there's information traveling through the universe all the time and like the television waves around us here, they're invisible until they're picked up by a receiver."

"You're a receiver."

I smiled. "You might say that. Everything, living and not living, has a vibration and as in some movies lately, we're actually all connected in one huge — gargantuan — whole."

He didn't look convinced. "How does this relate to your being able to get answers from a deck of cards?"

"I don't actually get the information from the cards. I get the answers from all that energy — information — flowing in the universe around us. It organizes the cards in specific ways."

Buddy waved all around. "You're telling me the answers to all the questions in the world are right here, available for anyone who's a receiver."

"Sort of. It's more complicated than that, actually. And not every receiver can access every bit of information. Plus, I think some of the answers are hidden from us because we aren't to know it at the time. Sort of like the answers to a quiz we're taking. The teacher wouldn't want for us to have access to those answers because if we had them, the test wouldn't be a true assessment of our knowledge, our level of development."

He looked far off into the sky. "Yup. I'd say this is way above my pay grade."

By this time, we were at the back of the barn near the tree line. "I have an idea. We could try to teach you to feel the energy of the trees."

"You could? Why would I want to feel a plant's energy? If it even has such a thing."

"That would be the first step to feeling people's energy."

This time, Buddy seemed to retreat into himself for a bit. Then he looked directly into my eyes. "Just how would you do that?"

"First of all, you have to know the tree's energy is felt strongest under the canopy of leaves. So, you can start to feel it more strongly at the edge of that space. That would be like running your hand through a shower. Outside the stream of water there are some drops, but when your hand gets into the stream, you feel the water strongly. It's at the edge that you can sense the beginning of the flow."

"So, it's like a shower?"

I shook my head. "Not exactly. That was just an analogy."

I stepped back from the tree line until I was about a foot away from where the leaves floated on the branches above me. I held my hand out with my palm toward the tree and stopped when I sensed the edge of the plant's energy. I motioned for Buddy to copy my motions. He moved quickly through the area, hand parallel to the tree trunk.

He shook his head. "No, nothing."

I motioned him back to the starting place. "Okay, this time, close your eyes and move slowly through the space. Very slowly. And feel the air brushing against the skin on your palm."

He did as instructed, and when he reached the drip line, he stopped and his eyes snapped open. Very wide open. Very. After he moved his hand back and forth through the area several more times, he looked at me. "Oh, my God. I feel it. I feel something, I mean. I don't know exactly what it is, but I do feel something."

I laughed. "Great!'

Just then several of the guys rounded the corner of the barn on the run.

I whispered to Buddy, "Lesson's over."

We both turned to face them, "What's up?"

The first man spoke. "Tadd's looking for you, Buddy. He's giving out assignments and going over tactics for the next offensive." Then he seemed to notice my presence. "Private meeting, so you can stay out here if you want."

"Ah. You're telling me I don't have the proper security clearance to be a part of the meeting." From their confused looks I could tell that they didn't at all get my joke.

Buddy laughed. Then he leaned closer to me to whisper, "Be careful."

I put my finger to my temple and closed my eyes. "Hmmm."

The other men only looked more confused, but Buddy laughed heartily as he and the group jogged around the end of the barn. He turned to look at me just before he rounded the corner and I could tell that he was still laughing.

I hugged the tree and felt its energy grow stronger. "Thank you for helping with Buddy's first lesson. I was wondering what to do and you helped me with the answer."

As I stood there looking at the trees separating this field from the one on the other side, I was filled with a joy that I couldn't explain. I was energized by the feeling that I was part of a much larger whole. I wasn't alone. I was joined with so many others. I loved thinking about the idea that this boundary between fields was only illusory. Yes, there was a fence separating the two areas, but I could get into the next field by hopping over the barrier. It was like the boundaries between people. Illusory. The borders between countries. Illusory. All put in place by the will of men.

I wanted to explain to Buddy that we, all of us, everything in and on the planet, were a part of the planet, but that discussion would have to wait. Perhaps if he understood the interconnectedness of all, he would come to understand why I didn't like killing.

I grinned. Buddy was a natural leader. Tadd had seen his strengths. He would be assigned to a leadership position, I just felt it in my bones. Then what? I didn't know, but things would fall into place, hopefully before the entire world exploded in flames. I didn't want to think about the problems. I didn't want to feel the despair I'd felt earlier. I wanted to stay in this euphoria of hope for the future.

CHAPTER SEVENTEEN

The new "offensive" must have been really important. Buddy's new role must also have been more demanding. Maybe it required more planning or more training. Whatever was the cause, the result was I didn't see Buddy hanging around for several days. Any time I did see him, he seemed to be running off to somewhere or returning from somewhere. Usually in a rush. Always distracted. Sometimes he would nod in my direction, but most of the time his attention seemed to be focused like a laser on his goal. He seemed to spend his time half in the training fields and half in the meeting rooms. Some days there seemed to be almost constant "meetings."

From my vantage point, it seemed as though he was leading the group. As they jogged out to the training area, Buddy jogged in front. Often, he called cadence. In groups of men around the barn, the other men seemed to pay Buddy more respect. Yes, indeed, things had changed. I'd have to wait to learn how. I could tell that something was up. And soon there would be more excitement.

My life changed, too. Suddenly, more guys asked for readings. Most questions were about romance and relationships. After readings, conversations often morphed into discussions about the meaning of life and aspects of relationships their mamas didn't teach them. I sensed I had gained respect as "the grandmother." That was just fine with me. I was the older woman whose years of experience endowed her with answers to important questions of life. Since I wasn't actually related to them, I was free of the complications of family ties. So, they probably asked me questions they wouldn't feel comfortable asking Mama or any other relation.

These conversations gave me opportunities to talk about the necessity of showing others respect. All others. "It works wonders to strengthen a relationship if you tell the other person what a good job they did from time to time. Especially after you've known the person for a long time. They still need to hear that you like them, and love them, and value their opinions."

One of my visitors asked, "Well, suppose I know what they like and how they feel about things? Do I still need to sit through them telling me again?"

"Ask yourself if you want her to ask you for your opinion when you're talking."

He blurted out his answer, "She doesn't have to ask. I tell her."

"And you like it when she listens intently to your answer."

He nodded.

I went through a list of situations in an effort to get my visitors to see it from the other's point of view. "Do you want for your preferences to be considered when you're planning an outing? Would it feel good for her to always assume she knew what you want? Wouldn't you want for her to hear you out?"

A nod. "I reckon I would. But mostly, I do the talking with her."

"Do you ever ask her what she's thinking? Or what she wants in a situation? Or what she wants to do?"

He shrugged, confused.

I wondered if he'd ever thought of his girlfriend as a real person. "Do you wait in silence? Listening to her opinions?"

He blurted his answer, "Mostly, I already know."

I didn't let it go because I knew this was an important concept to understand. "Does she feel free to contribute — for her vote to count?"

"I tell her I want to know what she thinks."

I smiled. "That is excellent. And then do you listen without interrupting? Even when you think you know what she's saying?"

"I . . . I . . . think I do. Maybe. I'll have to think about this."

I smiled. Thinking was at least a beginning. Solving a problem starts with awareness. "Do you do what she wants on a date sometimes?" I got the feeling he was beginning to get the idea.

He shook his head in confusion. "Ahhh. . . . Sometimes?"

I wanted to introduce the idea that listening to the other's opinion was only the beginning. "Is it really freedom when you can't do what you want? At least some of the time?"

"If you could . . . I mean you have freedom if you could do that thing . . . well, I guess it doesn't feel like it if you never get to actually do what you want to do."

"How can a person feel respected, if you don't listen to them and show how you understand? Oh, you could repeat back to them what they say or ask for clarification from them. That would show your understanding."

He was quiet for a few minutes. "But I guess doing what they want to do would really tell them in a big way that you got it. I wonder if that's why she wants to be with her girlfriends a lot."

I grinned at this epiphany. "Doing what she suggests is a much more powerful way to tell her how important she is. Doesn't that show her she has some control over the relationship with you? Would that work for you? Look at it from her point of view — how would you like to be treated? What makes you feel important?"

Of course, these talks sometimes lasted into the night to give them time to figure things out for themselves. Slowly. Slowly.

As they left my reading table, I could almost hear the wheels turning in some brains. Some of the same guys would come back for repeat "readings." During the second or third meeting the guy would often show he saw the situation from his family's point of view. Then we would talk about the rest of the world . . . and of course, I would extend the idea of Partnership and feeling a part of a very big whole. "That movie *Avatar* actually got a lot right. Just think of what the natives on Pandora believed. What did they feel? A connection with the planet and with everything on the planet. Everything. Even with animals that attacked. They apologized for killing those animals."

At every meeting, I laid out a tableau of cards, but most of our time was spent discussing relationships and what freedom really meant. Or we might talk about the Native American shaman and energy healing or how they felt a part of the land. How they joined with the planet to combine energies to meet some end. Like bringing the rain. I introduced the two ways of acquiring power over another person: Partnership or Dominator model. Working together so all were satisfied versus forcing your will on the other person.

It was a delight to see the light go on in their eyes as they talked about parents, brothers and sisters, and girlfriends. I was patting myself on the back for preventing a lot of future divorces. I was helping lay the framework for healthy relationships. And always I crossed my fingers as they walked away from my table, hoping for a bright future for these earnest young men.

At night in bed, I wondered how to use a bit of that love to neutralize the antagonism swirling all around me. According to the news, hate was erupting in cities and countries all across the planet. So much anger was expressed by the men sitting around the television. It was a reflection of what they were hearing, echoing that hate. I was having an effect on their emotions within personal relations, but how to move that loving approach to things less personal?

One night before dinner a loud male voice sounded through the barn: "Cancel all your dates for tonight!" That order was answered by a lot of rude comments not appropriate for the refined ear. "Tonight's movie night. Everybody reports to the common room after dinner." I wondered if I was included.

Once the room filled with disgruntled males, Steven stood at the front of the room with his chest puffed up. "I have a compilation of speeches by the candidate for Senate we "guarded" a couple of days ago. I can't tell you who to mark on your ballot. It's a free country. She would be my choice for the office and she should be yours." He pushed the play button and a harsh female voice raged on and on about how we had to fight back the enemy and once we did, we would arrest members of the Cabal and they would end up executed for their crimes. Stop the stealing and the abduction of our children. On and on. Accusations without evidence.

Several deep male voices around me whispered, "Dominator Model."

I laughed inside, but was afraid to break the spell by acknowledging the label.

The female diatribe ended and Steven held forth for another half hour. He pretty much repeated the same stuff. "This great citizen has laid out the reasons we're here. These are the reasons we fight. We're here to save our country from people who want to destroy it. Most of the people now serving in Congress should be taken out and shot. They are not working for us. We want to put people in their places who will work for us. This should motivate you to improve your performance at the shooting range and at the obstacle course. Work and work harder so you can do your part to save our country during this fight to the finish."

My heart sank. It all sounded ominous. I looked for reactions on the faces around me, but saw only blank stares.

Steven took the DVD out of the player and Buddy stepped up to take his place at the machine. He inserted a disk and pushed the play button. As the video was starting, he turned to the audience. "This is a film for your entertainment and requires no introduction.'

Avatar came on the screen and the room was filled with cheers.

As the story unfolded, I thought I heard the words "Partnership" and "Dominator" whispered at appropriate times to describe action just then on the screen. I couldn't help it, but my heart swelled. Perhaps I taught some of the guys something at least. Even if they had only an intellectual understanding, perhaps a true understanding would follow. Perhaps they would understand it in their hearts one day. Their future wives should thank me.

From time to time, I glanced at Steven to see if he understood what the comments meant — or even if he heard them. Apparently not. His eyes were on the screen at first but then they fluttered closed.

At the end of the show, the applause was deafening. Comments of "great show" and "what a great idea" peppered the room. Buddy glowed at such approval. As he ejected the DVD, he said, "Maybe we should just have some fun from time to time? You heard the meme about all work and no play. . . ."

Cheers filled the room as it emptied. The men dispersed to their own diversions, return to their rooms or walk in the fields.

Buddy caught up with me on my way to visit the stars and wonder where Pandora might be in that star-dotted sky above me. "You like the movie?"

I grinned, "Great choice."

"Got it out of the library so we didn't have to use up any more of the earth's resources. I also took some books out, some of the ones you've mentioned. That way we don't have to cut down any more trees." His eyes sparkled as he said this and I definitely felt a slight tug on my leg. "I also read the Constitution while I was there. It's not very long, really."

"Good thinking. All around good thinking."

He laughed. "Now that I have a command position, I

get to make suggestions. This was one — a weekly night of entertainment. Just for fun."

I grinned. "Yes, very good idea to have a night devoted to fun."

"But once I suggested it, Steven had to insert his propaganda video. From their comments, Tadd didn't think it would be good to stray from the constant propaganda stream they control. Steven's video was the compromise."

I patted Buddy on the shoulder. "The whole evening worked out very well. Very well, indeed. Even including the propaganda video. All in all, I think the guys paid more attention to the movie and less to the Senator's speech."

He nodded. "I believe it did turn out well." He was clearly pleased with himself. "I've already researched a movie for next week."

"Will you give me a hint or is that information above my security clearance?"

"*Invictus*."

"I love that movie."

Buddy laughed, "I thought you would."

I stood in front of my friend looking him over, head to foot. "Where is your new uniform to match your new position?"

He shook his head. "We don't have distinctions like that here. Much more democratic, I think." He took his time before going on. "I probably have you to thank for the promotion."

"Me? But why? How?" I turned back to search the sky for Pandora.

"One of the guys who saw you for readings was Tadd's second in command. Apparently, you and he were talking about his girlfriend back home and he figured out that being with her was more important than anything we could possibly do here and so he left. After all, he wanted for her to be there for him when this is all over. He talked to me before he walked away. Part of why he left is we've been here too long and only done minor things. They seemed more an irritation and killing of people not even involved in the war. Raids, really. He didn't like what he was being asked to do for the cause."

"Kill innocents?"

"Some of them were drug dealers and killers in the poor neighborhood and so that seemed like a service to the community. He said he saw it as being a vigilante for the people who couldn't protect themselves. Their problems got worse because of protests demanding to defund the police. And they still haven't gotten back to before."

"Has anything?"

Buddy shook his head. "The police stopped spending as much time patrolling those neighborhoods. After seeing what goes on there after dark, I don't blame them really — and so when we were doing that, he felt we were doing a good deed. Like the Boy Scouts. He watched the news and found out that a lot of innocents got in the way of those bullets. He was close to the top and told me he didn't see any real plan. They only know about winning on the battlefield, not about putting different battlefield plans together into a whole."

"Was he suggesting they don't have planning skills to win the war?"

He nodded. "Didn't say it in those words, but he hinted at it."

I smiled. "He had a good heart, it seems. He also was smart enough to see the truth of his surroundings. I am more hopeful for the future when I see young people with that much intelligence."

"Yes, a good heart. He joined the group because he watched a lot of videos on the Internet and they offered a great story about the need for help to get rid of the crooked politicians and to heal our country. He wanted to do his part. Besides, playing army is great for a while. Only, he said by now he's spent too much time away from his family and his girlfriend. He missed her birthday and he didn't want to miss Thanksgiving and Christmas. He's only hoping he can find another job. He lost his when he joined up. According to the news, there seem to be a lot more new jobs though."

I grinned. "You're now Tadd's second?"

Buddy nodded. "Well, second in command of troops. Those two other goons have been with him forever and will always have more power than I ever could."

"Dereck and Rick?"

He nodded. "Steven doesn't like Tadd taking so much control of the unit, but Tadd keeps telling Steven the three of them are here on orders of high command."

"Do you know where this high command is located?"

"Nope. Never hear much about that, just about the numbers of men being prepared. Not where they are or how all of us will be united into a fighting force."

If I could find out about the plan from higher up, it might be worth escaping to inform the authorities. I would wait and perhaps one of these days Buddy would bring me that information.

Buddy almost giggled. "Maybe I can have some real influence now. I've got a sense for the way a war should be run. . . ."

I felt a sinking in the middle of my chest, but hid my disappointment. "From books or videos?"

He shook his head. "Nah. I've done a bunch of gaming. I'm good at putting together a winning strategy. Maybe I can help with the bigger picture, too."

I wasn't hearing that he would argue against the war and killing. "But you know these are real people who die when they're shot. They are mothers and fathers, children. They don't get up once they've been shot down."

"Yeah, I know. This is not a game."

"And the whole will miss their parts. Just like on Pandora."

He nodded and turned his head toward the sky. "I wonder if we could ever call a UFO down here to visit us? Don't they communicate telepathically? You should be able to link up with them. I think you're that strong."

"Good question, my friend. Should I do a mind-link with the space ships to ask for help?"

Our laughter helped break the tension.

CHAPTER EIGHTEEN

Days passed. The news was just more about the predicted pandemic. The rising body count. Progress on a new vaccine. Riots all over the world. The rising body count. Civil wars in which brother fought brother. Ethnic cleansing. The rising body count. The killing that resulted when the US Army pulled out of any war. The rising body count. The election and the leaders' horrible verbal attacks on the other guy— any other guy. Mass killings aimed at some group of OTHER. The rising body count. And now we were fast approaching a billion dead from all causes. Would we eventually reach the level of seven billion dead? That was the number Steven predicted. I certainly hoped not.

This "military unit" cheered as the death toll climbed. "Isn't our side killing most of these people? Fewer that we have to neutralize! But we need to neutralize the Cabal soon. Before they kill too many on our side. When are we going to get to the really big battle?"

I guess Steven hadn't told them about the potential death of seven billion of their fellow men? And women and children?

The guys who watched the news every night spent the next hours complaining or ranting about whatever was reported. There was no attempt to check facts or to question in any way what they were told. They repeated the stories over and over to each other and to the men who stayed away from the television. As they retold stories, their belief became more solid with each telling. The listener would think the "facts" of the story had come down from some mountain carved on stone tablets.

One night after the news broadcast, I stopped Steven just outside the common room. "Steven, who is winning? Really? Who?"

"We are, of course."

"So, your people are killing more people than the Cabal are?"

He looked at me as though I had two heads. "They're the killers, murderers. We're the soldiers fighting for our country."

"Semantics. You both kill. I don't see any difference between the two."

He shook his head. "They brought this virus into the country so they're responsible for all the deaths from the illness. And now they're behind the vaccinations. There are nanorobots in the vaccine and when they get into your body, they implant themselves in your brain. Any time the Cabal pushes a button, the nanorobots release a poison into your body to kill you. So soon people will be dropping like flies. Just you wait to see."

Really? Steven had a talent for turning anything into conspiracy and some sort of attack on the good people of the planet. I shook my head. "Really? You said these were nanorobots."

He nodded. "Developed by the Cabal. They plan to use the vaccine to reduce the population of the planet to a manageable number of people. Few enough to be easier to control."

"Nanorobots are microscopic, Steven. You just said they travel through blood vessels. Think how small they would have to be to accomplish that. Where would they have room for a reservoir of poison?"

He shook his head, "I don't know the science, but that's the way it is." He turned on his heel and rushed away to end the conversation. He said over his shoulder as he left, "I just know that the vaccine is poison and we're told not to take it."

Again, I shook my head in confusion. "If the Cabal is in control now, why would they mess up a good thing by killing the people who're making money for them? Why would they kill the golden goose, as they say?"

He turned to take a few steps toward me. "They have all

136

the money they could ever possibly need and now they want to tighten their control on the people of the planet. That would make them more powerful."

"I personally don't understand why they would do that . . . It is not logical. You're suggesting they're using the pandemic that started so very many months ago to 'cull the herd' so to speak?"

He nodded in agreement. He looked eager to pounce on any flaw in my logic. "They're also behind this new pandemic. It's a way to get more of us to take the vaccine."

"Ditto for the protests going on for years now? They're an excuse to kill more of the people who don't agree with them?"

Another nod.

"What I don't understand is why you're helping kill people who are protesting inequality. Isn't that killing the people who want the freedoms you say you're defending? That would seem to be in service of the Cabal and not in service of humanity."

Steven's face got red with fury. "You've accused me of working for the Draco before. That's enough. You are so stupid that you can't understand what's really going on. It's complicated, more complicated than a woman can understand." He turned his back to me and almost jogged toward the sleeping quarters in the other end of the barn.

That was it. The last straw. Fury welled up and I couldn't stop it from boiling over into the air around me. I shouted down the hallway to his retreating back. "Just think about what you're doing. Think of the ramifications, of what these actions will lead to. Don't just accept what you're told, think for yourself. Open your eyes. Steven, you're helping the repressive regimes of the world cement their stranglehold on the people, both here and in countries across the planet. Are you working for the Cabal? That's a good question. I've watched the candidates you support and they're for repressing large groups of people in this country. Are you for an oligarchy with a tight control of anyone who isn't white male? Or are you for a republic based on freedom for all? Frankly, I'm confused."

He suddenly stopped and turned. He looked as though he wanted to fly through the space separating us to hit me — or worse. He looked as though he would have done anything to shut me up. I had really hammered a nerve this time. He only glared hate at me and then continued on his way to his sleeping quarters.

That night I dreamed Steven and I were walking in a field, probably the field outside the barn. We were walking and talking as we went.

I asked, "Steven, do you want me here to tell your story? Am I the witness of your glory and power?"

He continued to walk but turned slightly toward me, "Can't I just want you here? Not for any specific purpose, but just because I like having you around? You add feminine sparkle."

"Is that what women are best for? Sparkle? Surely there's another reason for me to be here? Some role I'm to play? Do you like for me to confront you with the truth? Do I make you think when I present a different point of view?"

"I just want you near." Steven morphed into a reptilian.

I awoke when he attacked me. I felt he meant to kill me — perhaps to eat me. In the dream, that is, not in the barn in real waking life. But I wondered if there wasn't something of a desire to consume me in him? Was it my ideals, my energy? There was something he wanted, but he wouldn't tell me what that was. At least, not yet.

At breakfast the next morning, I searched his face for signs of scales or for slanted eyes with slitted irises. I was spooked any time I was around him all day, spooked so badly that my skin crawled and I got duck flesh. Did my dream warn that Steven was the enemy? After all, he had killed two people who were good, and he did it right in front of me, so he didn't care that I knew. Every time I thought of Steven that day, I saw the image of Bob on the sidewalk with his blood congealed around him. Bob, who was my friend and confidant. Instead of having Bob to talk with, I had to look at Steven and hope he wouldn't kill me someday. Still, he wasn't as scary as that first day after I watched Bob die. When I feared that he planned to kill me right away.

Finally, election day arrived. Activities of the day went on as usual with a rhythmic flow of men from the barn to the training fields. But at night, the news was turned on during dinner so we could watch results of the voting as they came in. (I might add that I was not allowed out to vote.) At first the tallies barely moved, but as the night wore on, the numbers moved more rapidly. Each time one of "our" candidates moved ahead, the men cheered. Each time one from the other party moved ahead, the men booed.

The process of counting seemed to take forever. All the while one side surged ahead and hoped for victory and then the other side surged ahead, hoping for victory. Like a roller coaster — complete with the stomach break-dancing.

Commentary and predictions and explanations by the talking heads took up far more broadcast time than the actual tally. Tadd announced that due to this important bit of history going on tonight, training would start in the afternoon tomorrow. He stressed that he expected most of the men to watch the election results and so this might be considered a part of training. The cheers in response to that announcement were almost deafening. It was almost a holiday for the men. In fact, some of the men got cards from their quarters and games popped up all over the room with an audience of on-lookers gathering around certain of the games. They remained in the room, but their attention was divided from that point on.

Still, each move of the election tally was met by cheers . . . or boos. From what I heard, conversations were about almost every subject, but rarely about the election. Although I did hear a few comments about how rigged this election was turning out to be. Those were more plentiful whenever "our" candidate was falling behind that of OTHER.

Late at night, with the majority of the votes counted, the results were still mixed. At the state level, a mix of candidates won, ours and the others'. In each speech, the winner reiterated some of his goals for this term. Of course, it sounded as though they were setting out to save the planet. "Thanks for giving me the opportunity."

At the highest levels on the ballots, the results were disappointing to the audience around me. Personally, my faith in humanity was a bit shored up by the choices our national voters were making. Most had not fallen for the string of lies and the hyperbole of "our" guy. The winning candidate was the one who had promised intelligent moderation, but he won by an unimpressive margin.

The voters' choices seemed to indicate that they were more discriminating than I'd been convinced they'd be. I wondered what happened to the hordes of supporters "our" candidate and true believers like Steven had predicted. They took turns, Steven and Tadd, standing next to the television declaring that this result was absolute proof of the corrupt system of governance in this country. Evidence of rigged elections. There was no mention of the fact that many of "our" candidates won down-ballot even while the top of the ticket did not.

Election night did, in fact, end late for the unit, but the common room cleared out before all the votes were counted. The next morning the margins were a bit wider than when we left the common room. The general trend had not changed — "our" candidate lost. Throughout that day, I heard Tadd and Steven use that loss to motivate the guys to do better. Work longer. Work harder. Work stronger. HMMM? For what, I wondered.

CHAPTER NINETEEN

The news the next day was filled with more about the election and the stunning losses of "our" side. Expert after expert suggested irregularities. Given the polls, there was no way "our" candidate could have lost. . . . Talking heads railed on and on.

And now the viral infections were designated a pandemic because the numbers affected were so large. Not just in the US, but around the world. Authorities were discussing the merits of another lock-down.

Even reporters on our approved television channel talked about a new vaccine to fight the new virus. It was soon to be available for the general population, but they warned against taking it. They practically said that if we take it, we die! Components of the jab were to blame for all sorts of physical problems from nervous tics to infertility to death. They talked about herd immunity, but said the best way to develop it was for people to allow themselves to get the virus. Like the measles parties of the past, perhaps we should have virus parties now. When talking about the growing death rate, they blamed all those deaths on the vaccines developed for that last pandemic and not on infection by the new virus . . . or the last virus du jour. Ehhh! And where, I wondered, was the fact-checking here? Did no one understand that millions of people were saved by the vaccine to fight the last virus? And so, the cries of "Cabal" were raised again in our little television room. From time to time, the din was so loud that it drowned out everything else.

During one of these rants, Steven jabbed me in the ribs with his elbow. "I told you that stuff is meant to kill us."

I rolled my eyes and returned my attention to the inaccurate science being reported by the pretty woman on the screen. I knew enough about medicine to be certain she was lying through her teeth. She smiled and looked earnestly into the camera. The expression on her face asked the viewer, "Would I lie to you?" And being the resident Doubting Thomas, I wondered who was paying her for the performance. Yes, I was beginning to see conspiracy around me, but the bad guys were not the people Steven blamed for all the evils of the world.

Later that night, I walked beside Steven in the chill of the fall evening under starlit skies. "Steven, you keep telling me that the bad guys plan to kill a large percentage of the population with these shots, but you told me that your own goal is to eliminate most of the people on this planet. So, are both of you working toward the same goal? What's the difference?"

Steven harrumphed.

He didn't stop me so I continued, "Yet the candidates you support are talking about banning abortions and contraceptives. The long-term effect of those measures should be to increase the number of babies born. In speeches, they say that those children are needed to energize our economic growth. Which way is it? Reduce population or have lots more babies?"

I felt the emotional steam rising in my companion, but I continued still, "And yet they want to stop the flow of immigrants who actually take the jobs now. Babies born today won't be able to do those jobs for twenty years. So which way is it? Are we going to have to wait for this generation of corporate slaves to grow up so that we don't have a recession? Very confusing. Or perhaps child labor will be *de rigueur* again?"

Steven stuttered for a few minutes and finally spat out, "You don't understand the way these programs fit together."

I took a deep breath and answered slowly and calmly, "That's precisely why I ask. I only seek an explanation. I was hoping for you to clear up my confusion."

Without another word, he turned on his heel and returned to the barn. No answer. Never an answer.

The new vaccine was released. The first in line to get the shot in the arm were the nurses and doctors. I wondered if they were falling on their swords for the cause or if they really believed they would be saved by the drug. After all, they saw the ravages of the disease up close every day. Many who were interviewed said they really didn't want to be infected with the virus. They felt helpless as they watched patients die, in pain and terrified and alone. I couldn't imagine those people committing suicide. It didn't fit with what I know about human nature in general. Neither did it fit with what I knew about the kinds of people who generally become nurses and doctors.

I asked Steven and he answered without giving the question much thought. "They must be political prisoners who were forced in some way to sacrifice themselves. Maybe to protect their families?"

Irrefutable. Hmmm. I wondered.

With the elections being over, conversations around the camp were now about pros and cons of getting jabbed. "Well, if it's so good, why do they say we'll have to wear masks and stay away from people? Even after we get the vaccination? Doesn't make sense to me."

Mostly, I was not involved in these arguments, but they were all around me and I was getting really pissed by the inaccuracies presented as truths. Finally, my anger boiled over — again — and I started snapping at anyone who crossed my path, especially if I heard them repeating lies. This was so unlike me. I needed a vacation — to escape this situation for a short time at least.

I interrupted yet another of Steven's rants to ask, "Why are you railing against the vaccination to me when you keep me holed up here where I couldn't possibly get a shot in the first place? Are you trying to convince yourself?" I wondered if I had developed a death wish. Why else would I confront the man who had killed Bob and Helen? Why? *Must* be a death wish.

He looked as though he wanted to throttle me. His face was red with fury and his hands were balled into fists, but with great control he turned away from me to disappear into the troops' quarters. I thought I heard him yelling at some poor slob who just happened to get in his way . . . or tied his laces wrong . . . or breathed wrong. I shook my head. Was I cruising for a bruising? Why didn't I follow Buddy's admonition to be careful, to keep my opinion to myself?

Others were getting testy in these close quarters. Fist fights broke out between men for no apparent reason. With the constant diet of negative information about the events of the world, it was difficult to feel anything but fear, anger, frustration, suspicion, and despair.

In the late news show, a pretty man stood in front of the camera to repeat much of what we had already heard several times that day. For a couple of minutes, I was lost in a reverie about the "pretty face school" all of these television reporters must attend, especially the anchors who remained in the studio to receive reports from the guys in the field. They must practice how to smile and how to tilt their heads *just so* in order to appear more authentic and accurate. It's more difficult to keep yourself neat during a gale-force wind, so the reporters on location are not so schooled in the pretty face movements. They were more focused on staying upright and on the planet and without bullet holes.

I was suddenly brought back to reality when the man stationed in Paris started his report. "Although the authoritarian countries like China and Russia are essentially closed to the outside world, more and more information is leaking out. It was revealed today to both government officials and to a number of reporters with connections in those countries that the infection rates are spiking in both of them. China has tightened controls in order to keep people from infecting others or from being infected. These edicts are followed to the letter because what the government tells the people to do *has* to be followed to the letter. Do or die. No word is available regarding the Russian response to the rise in cases of the fever. It is said that labs in both countries are working on their own versions of a vaccine."

Discussion of the pandemic was followed by example after example of the repression of humans in countries all over the planet. People were jailed, tortured, killed for voicing their opinions. For their religious beliefs. For their attempts to make decisions about their own lives.

Terrible nightmares kept me awake. Every time I started to doze off, another nightmare assaulted me. For hours, I stared at the ceiling. I thought longingly of standing in the field outside, under the stars. Would I still be safe in the field or would I be attacked by someone filled with hate? Wasn't I surrounded by those people now? I loved being under the stars, the stars with no hidden agenda. Or was I now trapped in this tiny room? Over and over, I asked what I could do to stop the killing. The questions repeated themselves in different forms until I was sick of hearing them. No answer. What more could I do to teach people that working together is better? Would I be seen as THE OTHER if I tried to reach them with logic and morality?

Odd thoughts — killing the opponent was pretty damned effective, wasn't it? Shooting the person who disagreed with you permanently ended the disagreement. NO risk of a repeat. It did not require much in the way of soul searching or fact-checking. You didn't have to waste time finding a middle ground where both people could be comfortable. It was short and to the point. It was a strategy leaving only people who think the same and have the same goals. I remembered some movies about dystopian worlds remaining after the repressive ruling class takes over. There were always some freedom-fighters who escaped being "neutralized." They remained to continue the fight; after all, without that struggle why would you stay to see the rest of the movie?

I don't remember going to sleep. I must have, because I was aware of waking up to the sounds of troops coming awake.

CHAPTER TWENTY

That next day, I awoke happy, convinced everything would be just fine. For minutes I lay there in my small bed, eyes closed, listening to sounds of the morning. The shrill chirping of birds in the trees around the barn got louder every time the door opened. Mixed with those sounds of nature were the tramping of heavy shoes, the boots of soldiers, passing my door. Male voices in a variety of volumes and cadences rising and falling in the hallway. I could follow their journey to and through the door to join those calling birds in the field. I wondered how many of those men were aware of the birds, or of anything other than the training that would fill their morning. And would they see the bright leaves, changing color by the day? Thoughts of the beauty of our planet in the morning brought peace to me. More peace than I thought I could ever feel here in this place of my imprisonment. These were the sounds of my morning and the meanderings of my mind.

A surge of calm and peace flowed over me. The answer to my questions: It is as it is meant to be. I am here for a reason, a good reason even if I don't know what it is. Problems would resolve. Everything would turn out if I followed the nudges from my higher self. That's all. Simple. The Tower card indicated that long ago, so long ago. Why hadn't I believed? Why do I now believe?

Suddenly the aroma of coffee mixed with the other sensations. My growling stomach pushed me to discover what was on the tray of breakfast foods placed next to the coffee urn. Or perhaps I could cook myself eggs if there weren't any out today.

After eating and the morning dose of death and destruction delivered by the television in the common room, I went to my favorite place outside the barn door. A unit of men jogged to the training fields, but this morning they looked tired. Buddy was leading and even he didn't have the old spring in his step. He didn't even glance in my direction, but I was used to being invisible now. I missed the wonderful talks we used to have. His new position was serious and he seemed intent on doing his best. In truth, I was disappointed he bought into the rhetoric.

I stood in the sunny field for several hours, breathing in the clean air and enjoying the warmth on my body. During that time, guys sought me out to talk about their relationships. Some confessed they hadn't left their parents on good terms, with peace in their hearts. They were concerned they wouldn't get the chance to say things they wanted to get off their minds, off their consciences. They feared something might happen to their parents or to themselves during this conflict. If anything unspeakable were to happen, they would have left so much unresolved.

As they spoke of their fears, I became more concerned about what was brewing in this stew of male hormones. Others talked about girlfriends. A very few confessed they were no longer certain what we were doing. These latter spoke in whispers and looked around furtively like criminals afraid of being undone.

"I don't know how much you know about the raids we've been making on the big drug dealers. Some of those raids have actually started wars over territory among the dealers. To my way of thinking that's good, because a lot of criminals are killed and that must protect the people in the neighborhood."

Even though I don't like violence, these raids didn't seem all that bad to me either. Not as long as they played the game of "Let's you and him fight." Honestly, I wasn't certain that was the goal. "I've heard some about the raids, but not much in the way of detail."

The young man's buzz cut head bobbed. "That doesn't bother me; it's like I'm doing the people some good. Sort of like a private peacekeeper, you know, but. . . . When Tadd talks about invading the government buildings here or in DC, I get nervous."

Shock, but he didn't notice my reaction. I must have covered it well.

He glanced beyond me toward the training fields. "A lot of the guys are totally in for the attacks, but I'm not sure. If we use guns and violence to change our government, aren't we the same as all those violent military coups? Like the one that took over Myanmar? Tadd tells us the people in the government are not legitimate representatives of the people. But that's the same story told by the military in that country and the leaders they replaced were elected like ours." He shrugged thoughtfully. "The story in a lot of the videos Steven shows us says our elections, the ones that put those people into office, were rigged. But I don't know how that could be. Isn't all that talk against our Constitution? I thought we were here to protect and defend the Constitution."

I felt a jolt of hope almost knock me off my feet. "Authors of the Constitution enumerated rights in the Bill of Rights to avoid that kind of armed conflict at every change of elected officials. By giving people the right to protest against what they see as injustices, they let the government know their desires. After all, our government is of, by, and for the citizens, all the citizens, and not just for a small minority."

He nodded. "So, the right to riot was okay with the founding fathers?"

"Not riot, but march or demonstrate." I explained my understanding of our form of government and the meaning of the Constitution and he listened intently, nodding at points in the discussion.

He inspected the hands in his lap. "You mentioned

rebellions to replace governments in other countries. Were the replacements any better than the one they kicked out?"

I searched the old memory bank for any evidence about the subject of his question. "No, I honestly don't think they were. At least not from what I've heard." I tried to remember more history. "All over the planet, whenever the military takes over a country, things don't seem to go so well after that. Not for the majority of people living there, anyway."

He looked all around us. "I guess fighting men are good at defending the people of a country, but not so good at running the government of that country."

His military-cut hair bobbed again. "This has been helpful, very helpful. I mean, I wouldn't be telling you this but you seem to be tight with Steven and Tadd. I figure you must hear something about our actions. I need to talk with someone who is intelligent and has a different way of thinking. You obviously do. We hear a little about it when you and Steven fight. It's plain you don't mind telling him what you think. You don't get shot for it so you must be tight with him. Like a marriage where the fighting is a part of the marriage, you know?"

I chuckled. "I hadn't thought of it like that, but you might be right."

He smiled in answer. "You also seem to know a lot about how government is supposed to work, too. They're always telling us we're here to stop a small group of people from ruling the rest of us. But from what I see around here, they don't know how to run this little group. And I haven't seen any hint that there's better leadership anywhere higher up. My dad had his own plumbing business and he was a very good manager before he retired. I learned a lot from my old man." His expression was wistful as he remembered. "I shoulda listened to him about this, too." He waved around us.

I grinned at the pride in his smile at the mention of his father. "Doesn't it seem as though this is the small group of people trying to take control of the entire country?" I waved my hand to encompass the whole camp. "I don't see a lot of residents of this area coming to join up."

He nodded and stood silent beside me for a long while. That was our last conversation, and I didn't find out if it changed his mind in the least. I could only cross my fingers. But I did know that he loved his family very much and perhaps he recognized that in himself during our conversation.

Soon these men were jogging to the practice fields to grunt and sweat through afternoon training.

~*~

Our nightly news show was definitely more indoctrination than information. The men around me nodded and punctuated the reporters' comments with fists slammed on chair arms or tables. There were lots of angry conversations after the television turned to replays of NASCAR races. And yet, I thought I heard some grumbles of dissent, too. Some men who had actually read the Constitution and were discussing how that information fit in with the image of the world given by the news commentators.

Tonight, the handsome reporter spoke into the camera with a very serious expression warning of awful news. "There was an 8.2 earthquake in Chile. Thousands are dead and more are still missing. In Japan there was another earthquake in the ocean floor off the island. It created a tsunami of colossal proportions that killed hundreds of thousands. Closer to home, a 7.5 earthquake was set in the middle of the United States. The epicenter was in Memphis and tremors were felt all the way to New York City. Fortunately, the death toll was only in the hundreds, but many buildings collapsed and hundreds are missing in the rubble."

The woman on the other end of the table from him started reading her gruesome news from the teleprompter. She had the good grace to wear a serious expression rather than her pretty-face smile. "Thousands were killed by floods in western Germany and in other western European countries because of record-breaking rainfall. The rain often topped seven inches in a twenty-four-hour period. A tornado tore through the Midwest today laying waste to a large swath of land and killing hundreds. More are without homes tonight as they survey the destruction." Snippets of video illustrated these stories. Scenes of wide-spread destruction. The body count continued to rise, but this time from natural catastrophes.

I looked around, hoping to see some kind of human reaction, but the faces around me were blank. Had they heard so much about death and destruction they forgot these victims were people like their parents and grandparents? *They are real flesh and blood people suffering.*

~*~

The monotony of my life in prison was broken up a bit the next day. After breakfast I was surrounded by a great rush of activity and noise. When the hubbub died down, the barn seemed empty of people. I stepped outside to see what was going on and was unceremoniously thrown into the back seat of an SUV. I wasn't even settled in the seat before the vehicle peeled out at the head of a long convoy which must have been carrying our entire cadre. I was squeezed between two big men and I could almost feel the buzz of excitement all around me. I didn't bother to ask for information because they wouldn't tell me anyway. From the road signs, I could tell we were heading toward Frankfort, the state capitol.

This could not be good! I asked anyone who would answer, "Am I to play the mascot again?"

No answer. But as we neared the state buildings, I heard the clicking of a magazine being checked for rounds.

My heart started its rat-a-tat-tat and my blood pressure went into the fight or flight zone. Except I was so pinned in, no response was possible.

The cars and vans parked in a lot across the street from the state capitol building. Men tumbled out of vehicles. Excitement and nervous energy rolled across the open space of the lot like a tsunami. Tadd motioned and the rest of us followed him across the street and entered the stately building. I was pushed forward by a rough hand squeezing my upper arm so tightly I felt the circulation being cut off. Damn! I was tired of being manhandled.

No people were visible as we moved through the building. No sounds of business as usual. Strange. We trooped up the stairs toward the governor's office complex while the rest of the men fanned out to search other offices. Where were the occupants? Tadd was hoarsely whispering instructions regarding how and where we were planning on holding the Governor and how we would notify the rest of the unit to evacuate the building.

As we entered the suite of rooms used by the top guy, the only person we met was a woman sitting at the secretary's desk. My handler roughly pushed me into a chair, all the better to guard me, I guess. He made his point by jabbing a finger into my chest. I looked up to see the woman glance at me quizzically.

The woman at the desk had brown hair piled on top of her head in a messy knot and wore big blue glasses. "May I help you? I'm sorry, but the governor has been called away. I'm a temp and I didn't know to cancel your appointment." She smiled sincerely and warmly, only doing her job.

Steven was almost yelling now. "Where is everyone?"

"Pardon?" She was unflappable and remained extremely helpful. All smiles and nods.

He calmed slightly, but was still agitated. "No one is working in any of the offices? You're the only person we've found."

She looked shocked. "Well, as you've heard, a woman's work is never done. I'm just the secretary and I really don't know where anybody is. You mean, they aren't in offices upstairs?"

"Not upstairs. Not downstairs. We've checked all rooms on every floor."

The pretty woman smiled broadly and I realized that I recognized her, but determined to keep my own counsel. She pointed to the schedule on her computer to show that the Governor's schedule was clear for the day. As the men all leaned to read it, she looked at me and mouthed the word, *Hostage?* I nodded slightly and primly folded my hands in my lap.

Now I did remember her.

She stood quickly and moved to open the door of the inner office as evidence that the big man was not here. As my companions crowded to see, she made a step closer to me and mouthed, "Need help?"

I looked at Tadd and quirked my shoulder. For a moment I considered asking to be extracted from my prison, but decided that I was perhaps making a difference in some small way. I shook my head in a slight gesture of no. I shrugged and mouthed, "Better not."

Tadd must have seen her checking me out and decided to make the best of it. "This is our leader. She calls all the shots. Great at planning military actions."

Boy, that must've threatened to bust his gut to give a woman credit for anything, anything military, especially.

She looked in my direction and I closed my eyes and shook my head again slightly.

She laughed, "It's nice to see that you have a woman as a leader. Most men don't much like to follow the orders of a woman."

I watched Tadd jerk in response and could see the yearning in his eyes to claim all honor for himself. He was stopped by Steven who added, "Yes, she is truly remarkable, our fearless leader."

"Since my boss is out of the office, would you like for me to show you around?"

Steven nodded his agreement. Tadd looked as though he would have rejected her offer, but grudgingly went along. He growled all the way.

She stood before the group as though she was used to giving tours. "First of all, I'd like to point out all the security in the building. There are cameras in practically every corner of every room. If we were attacked, security doors would shut down to lock our attackers in the building or in a particular part of the building. They were added after 9/11 as an added measure of security."

She smiled sweetly and motioned to the firearms in the hands of the men. "You know it's against the law to bring weapons into this building? You could all be arrested for the offense, but since we're the only people here, I won't mention it if you don't."

There was a mixture of fear and belligerence on the men's faces when they considered the ramifications of this news . . . of all this news. Only Tadd's expression grew more bellicose. And he grunted and growled practically with every breath.

She waved around the suite. "This is the executive office. Offices of the second in command, the Lieutenant Governor, are down the hall. The mezzanine is pretty much like an art museum with sculptures and paintings of famous people from the state. If you'll follow me, I can point out. . . ."

Instead of following her, I was roughly pushed out the door and down the stairs in the middle of the crowd of men. We joined the rest of the unit waiting on the first floor.

To her credit, the woman continued her portrayal of the civil servant at the service of citizens of the Commonwealth. But as we reached the bottom of the steps, I glanced up to see her smiling. She nodded to me, a knowing smile. Ah, perhaps this woman would be able to defend me when I needed it. I nodded in response and felt some kind of kinship with her even though I had never met her before. I promised myself to vote for her the next time she ran for office. She's the woman! Nerves of titanium.

We jogged back to the vehicles which were now surrounded by police cars and men in uniform. The first line of our men stopped so suddenly I ran right into the back of the muscled man in front of me. Someone ran into my back. I smiled in appreciation of the ploy. She was taking her time, keeping us there so the police could block us in and prepare to arrest us. Crafty. I had to say it was an excellent plan that worked as intended.

We turned to run in the opposite direction, but were stopped by men who appeared from everywhere behind us. Trapped.

Steven and Tadd swaggered toward the officer who looked like he was in charge. "Hello, Officer, we were just taking a tour of the building over there. You can check with the nice secretary in the governor's office."

I could barely keep myself from falling down laughing. All I could think was that those stupid men had been played by a very intelligent woman and I wondered if they realized it even yet. The hand around my arm tightened and when I looked into his face I realized that he totally misread my reaction. Rick. There is no accounting for stupidity. Or was it arrogance?

The officer raised his voice so we could all hear him. He practically ignored Steven and Tadd who were standing a foot away from him. "You men all go home, except for your leaders. You forget whatever plans you're dressed up like that for. If you do, we'll forget you were ever here. We won't record your names and we won't charge you with anything. Even though you're carrying assault weapons on public grounds and could go to jail for just that action."

The Governor stepped out from behind a police car to face us, "I am the person duly elected by citizens of the Commonwealth of Kentucky to administer their state. I work with a variety of elected and civilian employees to accomplish projects to benefit you and your families. I am sorry there is confusion about who I serve, but I promise you I do serve you. You and your families."

There were some disgruntled comments, but mostly silence around me.

The governor turned to Steven. "Gentlemen, are you ready to follow the officer so the rest of these men — and woman — can go on home?"

Steven looked at Tadd. I had the feeling he was about to throw Tadd under the bus. Everyone waited. Then surprise of all surprises, Steven waved a dismissal of Tadd and the rest of us. "I'm the leader. I'll go with you and the rest of our men will return to our camp so they can dismantle it and return to their homes."

I heard a few yelps of delight, but mostly sounds of relief. Steven allowed himself to be taken into custody and all official cars and personnel left the lot. They remained within striking distance, however. The rest of us returned to our cars and drove away. All along, I was wondering what sneaky move Steven was planning. I just knew he wouldn't stay in jail for very long. Nor did he have any intention of giving up the fight to gain more personal power — for the good of the country.

It was late in the afternoon when we rode down the road that fronted the farm, a parade of great racing motors. No sooner were the engines off than men hopped out and scurried around in the barn — some of them packed up to leave and quickly disappeared through the gate and down the country road. Some rode motorcycles, but most were on foot.

When Tadd noticed the exodus, he bellowed for all troops to assemble in the barn. When the retreating men did not turn back, he barked that we were not really going to disband and for them to double time back to quarters. When instead, they jogged farther down the country road, he added that we would only move to another location. This time he screamed the command to return to quarters. Not one of the guys turned back to the barn.

He added that we were only doing what we had to do to convince the officials that we were disbanding. That Steven staying in custody was only giving us time to plan the move. By this time about a dozen men had disappeared and another half dozen were running toward the gate with duffel bags of their possessions bouncing around them.

I suddenly felt the need to hide because I didn't trust what Steven would do next. Or Tadd, for that matter. He liked me even less than Steven did. Since Steven wasn't here to control Tadd, I didn't feel safe.

Tadd tried to round up the departing men as though they were errant horses escaped from his herd. In the confusion of his futile attempt to keep men in camp, I ran behind the barn and into the tree line. I was more familiar with this area of the farm than with any other. And my unease pushed me farther. I climbed over the fence and fell face down into the dirt on the other side. I dusted myself off and listened for a moment as Tadd roared commands into the chaos of running escapees.

CHAPTER TWENTY-ONE

Within minutes, I heard the twap, twap of helicopter blades passing overhead. I pressed farther under the trees along the fence. The sounds moved over the barn and soon I heard what I thought was the machine itself settling into the grass on the far side of the structure.

I continued my run around the field, all the while keeping close to the tree line. The noise of the helicopter subsided. It was replaced by the noise of men yelling.

Now on the side of the field, I started looking for better shelter. Somewhere near the barn, a rough male voice demanded, "Where is she? This woman who has directed operations for you for all these months? You said we could interview her."

Another voice joined in the demand. "We got you out of jail so you could take us to this leader of yours. You said that only she knew the goals of the paramilitary group. We laid our reputations on the line for this interview."

Steven's voice was shrill, almost hysterical, "We'll find her. Tadd, how could you let her get away?"

Tadd's voice was a deep growl and his words were lost in the confusion in the distance.

The other male voice asked. "What do you mean, let her get away? You sound like she doesn't want to stay with this group of yours. Is she really your leader or not?"

"You made promises to us and we made promises to others."

Buddy's calm voice answered them, "Let me look for her. I know her favorite haunts."

I continued to run the perimeter of the corn, sometimes having to crouch to be stay hidden. I was looking for a place from which I could see without being seen.

Now, Buddy's voice came to me clearly from between the barn and the fence.

There were warning prickles on my back, up and down my spine. Was this what happened if you made friends with someone you weren't absolutely certain was friend material? And so, I continued my run along the far edge of the field until I was in a place from which I had the best view. Of the barn. Of the training areas. I reminded myself that although I might not be able to see through those trees, there was no guarantee that someone standing on the other side of this field couldn't see through them to see me.

I stayed against the fence on this side of the field hiding behind the trees obscuring it from view. The corn was so high that it hid me. In my state of anxiety, I didn't want to take any risks so I wedged myself between two trees that would shelter me from prying eyes in both fields. Shortly, I saw Buddy push through the tree line behind the barn to stand at the fence there.

Several men crowded in the space with him and he shooed them back to the barn, "Captain Marlowe, this is a dead end. You won't find her here. She's only come this far. She would never go into that field because I explained how many animals might be hiding in there to eat the corn. She's more afraid of snakes than of being charged with murder as the leader of men who have way too many guns. Steven doesn't know where she goes when she's not in the barn. I walk with her sometimes."

Was Buddy trying to warn me that Steven had thrown me under the bus? Was he saying I was to be charged with murder because of the troop's activities in the area — all those raids in the cities around this camp? All those innocent bystanders killed in their homes by stray bullets?

Didn't I see the glint of a metal badge as they jostled each other behind the fence line? That might be my imagination, but the fact that Buddy's voice was unusually loud was not my imagination. Was he trying to warn me? Was Steven trading me for his own safety? Was that the reason he held me here against my wishes? And yes, he is a snake!

I stayed in my hiding place until dusk. The very real possibility of being stuck out here all night was frightening. Besides, my stomach was making preamble noises to warn me that it was empty and expected soon to be filled. I might have been prisoner all this time, but I was not a hungry prisoner. I strained my eyes to look for any movement anywhere. I pulled myself out from between the trees and dropped to my knees. The row of corn that cut the field in two was a more direct route than the path around the field. And besides, it was getting dark and I didn't want to risk stepping on a snake among the corn plants by waiting until after sunset.

Buddy had not ever warned me of snakes. Never. Tonight, I was hoping Steven was the only snake he was talking about.

Slowly and crouched well below the tops of the stalks, I half ran through the field. It took a lot less time than traveling around the perimeter. By the time I got to the other fence line, it was dark and I was sore and tired. Not to mention hungry. I searched for any movement on the other side of the fence, after all, I would have to climb the fence and would be caught in a very awkward position if someone decided to inspect the corn at the exact minute I was straddling the fence.

I was on my way to another face plant when strong arms stopped me. Buddy. "How did you know I was here?"

He leaned over the fence to point to a shallow, body-sized hole in the dirt on the other side. "You were not very good at covering your tracks."

"Was that why you spoke more loudly?"

Buddy nodded and held his hand to silence me as he turned to search behind him. "Shh! I thought I heard something."

Minutes later, there was a shuffling and the smell of food. An arm came through the underbrush holding a plate loaded with things to eat. A rough voice followed it, "I thought you'd be hungry. I'm going to make sure I wasn't followed. Those reporters are still prowling around, waiting for you."

"Ah, you are my hero! You must have heard the call of my stomach from far away." The arm and its owner disappeared into the brush and left Buddy and me alone.

"Those guys seem really determined to meet me."

He nodded. "I think Steven exchanged you for his own release from jail. Since they went out on such a limb for the bargain, they aren't about to leave without at least talking to you. I got the idea they'd like to take you back to take his place in jail. Oddly, there are a couple of guys in there making friendly with the strangers. They might be doing it to get under Tadd's skin, though."

I giggled. "Is it working?"

He laughed. "You bet it is. And it's getting under Steven's skin, too. But Tadd is the one in full-bark."

I heard him chuckle again softly as he moved away from me. He slipped away as quietly as he'd come — through the trees and along the barn. I followed with less agility.

He held up his hand to stop our progress. We listened for other sounds but only heard quiet mumbling from someone on the far side of the building.

Buddy pulled me out of the thicket and led me along the tree line toward a door in the opposite end of the barn. He whispered, "I unlocked the door from the troops' quarters in case we needed a different way into the building."

Cautiously, he threaded his way among the trees as we walked. I had to eat on the move, all the while dodging branches, because Buddy didn't stand still long enough for me to empty the plate. I was too hungry to wait for him to get the idea to stop for dinner. And, I wanted to get the plate out of my hands to free them, just in case.

I had never been in that back portion of the barn and had

no idea how it was configured. When we were even with the door, he tugged me farther into the trees again.

As he pulled me, I almost lost my balance and, heaven forbid, dropped the rest of the food. "What in the bloody hell is going on?"

"You eat and I'll explain. I tried to talk them out of it, but Tadd and Steven got the idea in their heads that because the election didn't going so well for our side that we should attack the state capitol in Frankfort. Make a splash — reenergize the cause."

I groaned. "Yeah, and that didn't go so well."

"Well or not well, depends upon your point of view. We got into the building and after we separated, we didn't find a soul at any of the desks."

"I was there."

"You were in the front and I'd like to hear your experience, but first let me paint the picture of the pandemonium among the grunts."

I nodded and was delighted for the time to continue eating.

"They put me in charge of searching the different levels of the building and instructed me to take anyone we found as a hostage."

"Not a good move. That's a much higher crime, isn't it? No longer just a demonstration, then."

I could hear the rustle of his head nodding. "I guessed the military personnel Steven is so high on are actually not so competent. This was proof. These guys are not tacticians but they didn't want any input from mere civilians like me. Turns out they're all grunts, not an officer or high-ranking NCO among them. This fiasco was evidence they didn't have the skill necessary to plan strategy. In fact, they didn't even seem to appreciate it requires higher level knowledge. They know how to fight a battle, but not how to win a war. They don't seem to have any idea what to do after that."

Between bits of food I whispered, "But we did occupy the building."

Buddy sniggered. "Oh, yes, we did that. We essentially stood around with our thumbs up our . . . well, you know what I mean. I kept the troops with me from going into any files or any drawers. I wanted to avoid charges of vandalism or theft. There was a lot grumbling among the men. They thought it was wasted effort. Some pointed out security cameras and predicted we'd be identified from the photos. Most were ready to leave the minute we entered the building. It smelled like a trap."

I saw the gift from this assault on the state government. "Is that why so many of the men bolted the minute we arrived here?"

"They took the Governor at his word and when Steven agreed to disband the unit, they didn't wait for him to go back on his word — which we all knew he would."

"Of course."

Buddy's voice was close to laughter. "Another interesting outcome is that during this experience, the men around me didn't perceive the evil Cabal as Steven, Tadd, and the news always describe it. The police were polite and the Governor was nice."

"And they let us go free instead of charging us as they were in their rights to do because we were breaking the law. No Draco?"

Buddy shook his head. "You can pretty much tell when someone is acting and the guys didn't see any of that."

"So, they questioned the whole story?"

Buddy chuckled. "Yup! But some stuck to the evil manipulator explanation even in the face of evidence that police and governor were just people. In fact, they seemed like nice people who were working for the good of the citizens of the state."

I was more hopeful than I had been in a long while. "I'm

sure they got the excuse that these people were well-trained puppets controlled by Draco."

Buddy nodded. "Some took the bait, but others avoided the hook."

"Well from my vantage point, the mission went similarly."

"You had a slightly different situation because you could have taken a secretary as hostage."

I giggled. "Actually, she was not a secretary, but the Lieutenant Governor. She had Steven and Tadd totally buffaloed! They ate up her story about being the poor woman toiling at her desk night and day. All the while, she was probably delaying our departure so police could set the trap!"

"They were obviously tipped off, but I wonder by whom?"

I shook my head, "Not me. There was a lot of mumbling between Tadd and Steven about blowing up the building, but the secretary pointed out that people were the government, not the building."

"Smart woman."

It was my turn to chuckle. "Yeah, they never wondered at the fact that she actually knew a lot about the law and subtly told us that we were in deep doo-doo if we held her against her will."

"Did she fast-talk Tadd and that was why we were beating a retreat with our tails between our legs?"

I thought back to our "attack" in Frankfort. "Yeah, about the security cameras and facial recognition." For some reason, I kept my private exchange with her — well, private. I considered the benefits of having friends in high places.

Buddy was quiet. "They never intended to live up to their agreement to disband. Who's the evil one now?"

"Another question is why did they agree to reveal the location of the camp?

Buddy chuckled again. "Oh, they gave the orders in front of officials, but said they wouldn't take us to the city and transportation home until tomorrow."

I saw the picture now. "Tomorrow they'll make it look real by moving the camp to another location."

I could hear the rustle of his nod in the dark.

"Then the helicopters won't find us if they fly over this barn a million times."

Buddy slapped a stinging bug, "Right. Steven thinks it will look as though he did disband the group as he told the governor he would."

"Will you stay with them? This is a losing cause, Buddy."

"I'm not convinced either way, yet. But if you're staying, I'll stay to make sure you're okay."

I thought about the possibility of "escape" and decided I might still make some difference. "I'll stay."

"Then I will, too."

CHAPTER TWENTY-TWO

Buddy's hand was set to turn the doorknob when I put my hand out to pull him back into the trees.

He whispered. "What? What are you doing?"

"I can't sneak around forever. These guys might hang around all night. I don't relish sleeping in the fields. There are too many people and too few places to hide in the barn. If I am going to stay, we might as well smoke Steven to find out how low he'll go to save his own neck."

Buddy whispered, "Those are some good points. Aren't you afraid they'll turn you over to the police?"

I thought about that possibility and about my ace in the hole, the Lt. Governor. "I'm not in any danger. I would love to see Steven and Tadd wriggle. I know absolutely nothing about the inner workings of this movement. I wonder just how they'll handle a meeting between me and people who want specific answers? The added feature is that Steven obviously told them that I'm the person with the answers. So when I actually show up, they'll have to do some fancy footwork."

Again, Buddy paused before answering. His voice was thoughtful, "Of course, you're right. Your hiding actually plays into Steven's hand. You remain the illusive leader, hiding along with your knowledge of secret things."

"You bring me in and you become the hero. You show more competence than Steven or Tadd who probably spent their time schmoozing with reporters instead of searching for me."

"Or it looks as though they were calm, certain their minion would do the job."

"Either way, it can't be helped. We enter the way we always do. We don't want them suspecting we've been out here talking for hours." I tucked the plate under the trees before we moved. It could stay there till morning. A critter of the night might like to lick the remains.

No welcoming committee greeted us when we entered the barn. In fact, we had to go to the common room to find anyone at all. Everyone there was huddled around the television watching scenes of devastation: 100-year floods wiped out whole communities and killed thousands more people in Europe. The worst were in Germany. I flashed on the documentary I'd seen about the neo-Nazis alive and growing more active in Germany. Was this part of the answer to my questions about resolving the conflicts? Drowned men were no danger to civilization.

People around the television were so concentrating on the video and the death toll that they didn't even turn to see who walked through the door to join them.

Buddy and I look at each other in amazement. Okay, was I old news now?

I looked down at my arms and legs covered with dirt and my clothes snagged here and ripped there. I definitely dressed the part! A napkin served to wipe dirt from my face. I worked my way down my arms and the rest of me. By the time I reached my legs, the report was over and our guests finally turned to see who was standing at the back of the room.

At least the reporters had the good grace to stand as they extended their hands in greeting. Steven was suddenly at my side, to control my every move. His expression was one of panic. "This is Sylver. That's all, just Sylver."

The guest asked, "No last name?"

Steven shook his head. "Sylver."

Tadd moved more slowly to take Buddy's place at my other side. He roughly pushed my friend out of the way. "We knew Buddy would find her no matter where she was hiding."

I was suddenly hit with a barrage of questions by the reporters. I waved the questions away before answering them. "Do you mind if we sit? I'm tired."

What happened when we sat would have been hilarious if I hadn't been so worried Steven or Tadd would end the interview with a bullet. The reporters ceremoniously placed phones on the table in front of me. "With your permission, of course,"

I nodded my agreement.

One by one, they went through their lists of questions. When I opened my mouth to say that I had no idea, Steven and Tadd alternated to give a safe answer. I finally decided to save energy by keeping my mouth shut.

Both reporters ceremoniously checked regularly to make certain their phones continued recording. They didn't want to miss one word from the fearless leader.

I watched their attention swing like a pendulum from Tadd to Steven and back. I felt exactly like a puppet whose mouth was operated in turns by the men on either side of me and so I watched. The reporters noted other questions as they developed from what was said, but not once did they ask why I was not answering for myself.

I couldn't help grinning at the scene. I would have laughed out loud if the two guys hadn't been standing right there.

Information given these reporters was the same I'd heard for years. The devils of the Cabal. They are evil, worshipers of Satan. They abuse children. In fact, they kill babies to eat them. Individual members were identified as being controlled by Draco. Steven beat his chest and announced proudly we the people were pushed too far with our backs against the wall. The Deep State has cornered us and now we are standing up for our rights. Finally. We are in a struggle against control by these people who use us as slaves to make more money. Our power grew over the past decades and now we stand up to these monsters. Especially the banksters. When we gain control, they will be arrested and eventually executed for their crimes. On and on with the same balderdash about the misappropriated system that our candidates will fix once elected. Some won their campaigns this time, but we will have more and more representatives. They will keep the invading hordes from ruining our country. Yada, yada, yada.

One of the reporters asked if it didn't anger us that our candidate for Senate had made a fortune paying illegals pennies on the dollar for working her farm. She is for reducing taxes for the very rich. She is a member of that group of the very rich with all sorts of advantages and yet she is trying to get more special treatment from the government. She is all for defunding public schools in order to provide more money to private schools her children attend.

I loved the fancy dance Steven did to turn these positions into positives. He started every answer with, "That is an absolute and total misrepresentation of her position."

Tadd was just barely reining in his anger. His fists balled and his arm muscles tensed, ready to attack — the reporters or anyone who had the misfortune of getting within striking range. He kept looking at Steven and it looked as though he was sending signals asking for the go-ahead to kill the reporters. Finally, he blurted out, "She's thinking about the common good. What's best for all of us. If you weren't so stupid, you could see that."

The reporter nodded to Tadd and smiled slightly. He tapped a rhythm on his tablet and the result was the replay of an interview he did with the candidate. Her answers were positively damning.

Steven tripped all over his tongue, "Well, well . . . she said these things to get elected. She had to. She really doesn't believe all of it. Not really."

"So, she's a liar? Or does she know that the majority doesn't agree with her positions on many of these issues? So, she says whatever she thinks will get her elected. Did she plan to renege on her promises if she'd won?"

More confusion. And more anger threatening to push Tadd over the edge. I looked for a place to hide when the shooting started. Tadd must have read my thoughts and squeezed my arm with all his strength. Wow. Big bruise on the way.

"One more question. What do you plan to do now that your candidate for president didn't win?"

Steven and Tadd glanced at each other. Then Steven answered, "He'll stay around. He has plans to shape programs as much as he can from behind the scenes."

Steven had been spouting the party lies for so long, he now believed them with all his heart and soul. He was doing as told without looking into the situation for the truth. About the election in general. The virus. Climate change. And laws passed by the current administration. And the laws passed by the last administration — all for the rich and powerful, nothing for the average man on the street. The men taking notes in front of me could see Steven for the uninformed man he was. I was certain of that.

Finally, Tadd jerked to a place between the reporters and me. He barked, "This interview is over. Sylver doesn't have any more to say."

Both reporters looked at me and smiled enigmatically. And shrugged slightly. They closed their tablets and notebooks and put everything into cases. They turned to me again. "Would you mind coming back to town with us to answer more questions as we think of them? You can state your case on camera, with no interruption."

I couldn't resist smiling at his emphasis on the term *without interruption*.

His partner added, "This would be an opportunity to tell your side of the story and explain what's behind all these attacks. Not only here but in other cities in the country."

I shook my head slightly to indicate the negative. Steven piped up before I could say anything. Not that I had anything to say. "What would we do without our fearless leader?"

"Ah, but you agreed to decamp and send your warriors home."

More blustering from my right and Steven finally told yet another lie. "Yes, what would a final send-off be without words of congratulations from the head honcho?"

Steven was so full of it. He didn't even see that our guests saw through his baloney. As Tadd and Steven swaggered ahead to the door, one of the reporters mouthed, "Are you safe?"

I nodded and glanced in Buddy's direction.

The reporters nodded understanding. Well, I think it was understanding, but when using sign language and head nods, you can't be sure. I was praying they didn't give Buddy's position away. That could be very bad for the both of us and then I would not be safe. Neither would he.

I stood to follow the others out of the common room, through the hallway, and into the chill night air. Buddy followed at a respectful distance, his face a dour blank. The reporters glanced in his direction a couple of times, but didn't draw attention to him.

Steven and Tadd returned to the barn patting each other on the back at having manipulated the visitors so thoroughly. Buddy and I stayed in the field watching until the helicopter disappeared into the night sky. I wondered if they were really media or if they were sent by someone in Frankfort. Steven and Tadd had been caught and filleted and fried. Well done, in fact. And they loved every minute of it. In fact, I would wager that they would invite the nice reporters back for a replay any time. Any time at all.

CHAPTER TWENTY-THREE

Back in my quarters, I gathered towel and pajamas on my way to the kitchen where we had the shower set up. I scrubbed dirt from my body and dressed for bed. All the while, fatigue threatened to overthrow me. It was beaten back by the urge to consult the cards. I wanted confirmation of the reality I stitched together of news from around the world.

I was taught that positive and negative, good and evil, remain in balance. Did the increase of evil in the world indicate an equal increase in the enlightenment of others? Could we ever expect a world filled with only love, with only positive? Would we never have a world governed according to the Partnership Model and "love thy neighbor"? Or would the enlightened people pass over the veil to become on-lookers to this battle between the denseness of evil and the light of enlightenment rather than upsetting this balance with too much good, too much love? Would they continue to cheer us on from the spirit world? Would the requirement for that balance result in the ever-increasing hate now spreading across the planet? Is that the reason so many democracies were falling to be replaced by tyrannies?

The death toll across the planet had climbed to well over a billion from all causes — civil unrest, pandemic, disappearances in authoritarian countries . . . plus, natural catastrophes like earthquakes, storms, and buildings that just collapsed into the sand in Florida. How many more would have to die? Those people, at least, were able to watch the show from the other side of the veil.

The tableau repeated the earlier message. All were Major Arcana — the outcome was out of my hands. The outcome was being worked out by forces higher than the human operators on this planet. Spirit will take care of things if we simply do our part to heal the people and things around us. I was to stay here — an island of peace in this sea of hate and anger. I would endeavor to untangle this web of lies into which was built so much violence. Or did the cards mean that ETs flying in our airspace would land and forever end the battle with their arch enemies? I imagined they had both technology and strength powered by determination to defeat the Draco.

It takes a lot of interpretation to get from specific cards in a layout to this understanding. My interpretation felt accurate and I had renewed hope that all would end well. I hated that so many people were dying. Some collateral damage was understandable if these events were taking at least some people with evil intentions off the playing field. Unfortunately, there seemed to be too much collateral damage. Would the population really get down to five hundred million as the Georgia guide stones predicted? I was heartsick at the number of deaths the subtraction would require . . . so many would die. So many.

I was exhausted after the day's adventures and slept soundly that night. *Tomorrow is another day.*

~*~

As soon as we were coffee-ed and fed in the morning, Steven yelled, "Load up. All your possessions. Everything."

Grumbles followed troops into their quarters.

One passed me, "Ya think we're going home?" He was asking his mate.

His buddy answered with excitement. "Nah. We're not giving up. This is a fight to the finish. We signed up to take our country away from those aliens that live in tunnels down there. We won't quit. Not ever. Just relocating."

I threw my meager possessions into a plastic bin from the kitchen and went into the space in the end of the barn where vehicles were parked. I was shoved toward an SUV. A strong hand made my stuff disappear. As I settled, the driver looked at me in his mirror. He looked a bit surprised to see a woman in the back seat, I think. I would use the advantage of surprise. "Where are we going?"

He shook his head. "Can't say. Orders."

I smirked. "Not even to your Supreme Commander?" I might as well benefit from the charade I was playing. Perhaps he had seen or heard of me.

His eyes twinkled in the rear view mirror. "Well, in that case, we're moving to another farm owned by the same guy." He waved to indicate the field. "Farther off the grid, from what I heard when Tadd and Steven were talking. They didn't actually tell me so I'm not breaking a confidence, just passing on a rumor, something I overheard. Besides, you'll find out soon enough. We'll all find out."

A guy walking past this SUV demonstrated his audacity by asking Steven, "Didn't you tell the Governor we'd disband?"

Tadd held the man's shoulder in what looked like a death grip. He yelled into the crowd as the man cowered in extreme pain, unable even to cry out. "Do any more of you jerks want to ask about failing? About retreating with our tails between our legs? Giving up is not an option! Retreat is not an option. Only winning. Winning is the only option."

The men slumped lower. They moved quickly and quietly into designated transport. Tadd no longer sounded rational or reasonable. He sounded like a mad dog ready to tear anyone apart. Anyone close would do. He didn't need a reason. The men around him looked as though they heard his insanity. They were right to skulk around him — carefully. I wanted to warn them, but only telepathy was safe.

Steven motioned for Tadd to calm. "These men deserve an explanation. They've a right to be curious. Everyone saw my exchange with the officials." His voice was calm and strong as he looked into the eyes of the first guy. "Son, I was talking with the enemy and some distortion of the truth is expected in such situations. We can never divulge our real plans to the enemy."

As he passed me, that fellow mumbled under his breath, "But the man you just called an enemy was the governor my parents voted for. They obviously thought he would be a good person to lead the State. They're smart, know more than I do, so who am I to contradict them?"

Tadd barked, "Did I hear a comment from anyone else? Any smart aleck trying to get himself a run around the training field? Or a run all the way to our new home?"

More slinking into vehicles. Throwing duffel bags. Slamming car doors.

More than half our numbers were gone, decamped and headed home. I saw some run through the gate as soon as they could jump out of our transportation from Frankfort. More must have left during the night. Had they left even after Tadd assured them that the "fight" would continue? How many more men were beginning to see the futility?

During the short ride, Steven described the poison contained in the vaccine. "The minute they want to reduce the population, anyone with that vaccine in their body will die. They activate the nanorobots to dump the poison into your body and *poof!* You're dead."

I interrupted him mid-rant. "A question, Steven."

I took his nod as permission to speak. "Suppose the Cabal is behind the story that the vaccine is tainted?"

He was in the front seat and turned his head to see me. "What are you saying?"

"You describe members of the Deep State as cunning. They aren't stupid or they wouldn't be in control, would they?"

He turned a bit more toward me.

I took that as permission to speak again. "Wouldn't they want to get rid of people resisting them?"

"And how would they do that?"

"Suppose the Cabal encourages their followers to take the vaccine. All the while, they spread lies about the evils of it to key people in your movement? Those people spread word of nanorobots around units of paramilitary working against the Cabal." I waved around us. "Within our ranks. And anyone else who supports this movement. Our big donors, for example."

His voice and expression were riddled with ridicule. "And then what, Sylver? Then what? How could they use it against us?"

"Well, once their people are all protected, they spread a new variant of the virus around the planet. You said they were the original developers. The unvaccinated get sick and die. The vaccinated live happily ever after."

Tadd mumbled, "That new variant is increasing infection rates all over the world. The Delta variant." He suddenly fell silent. I could almost smell the smoke coming out of his ears and hear the whirring of his brain! At least, I thought he might have a brain.

Steven was not so thoughtful. "Ah, shut up, Sylver, you're just trying to confuse us."

"Explain to me why the Cabal would kill people who are obedient to their demands. I just don't understand how doing that would benefit them. Wouldn't they want to kill the rebellion? Wouldn't they want to tilt the balance of power back in their direction? Especially if they found out your groups have gained in numbers and training. They would plot to kill people who want to unseat them. I'd estimate there are about forty to sixty million people who are resisting anything the government orders."

"Why does that matter?"

"I was trying to figure out how many of the enemy the Cabal could get rid of if they did manipulate the situation as I suggested. Don't the Georgia Guide Stones say that's one of their goals? Or, I forgot, is that one of your goals, Steven?"

Steven sent a menacing look in my direction before he turned to look forward.

Tadd grunted, "There are more like a hundred million people refusing the vaccine."

"Or wearing masks and otherwise being more careful?"

Steven harrumphed in disgust, but did not turn to look at me.

I couldn't let the idea go and looked at Tadd as I inserted his information. "So what you're telling me is that by playing this game with people's heads, the Deep State could get rid of about one-third of the population of this country? That one-third would all be people against their rule?"

Tadd nodded thoughtfully.

I looked from Steven to Tadd and then to the driver of our vehicle. The driver looked in the rear view mirror at me with eyes that spoke of a grin. I finally landed a decent shot, my best shot up to now. Time to let the seeds germinate quietly. I looked out the window to enjoy the beautiful countryside. Our state is truly beautiful.

Moments later we turned into another field. This one had no coded lock on the gate. Actually, it had no gate and no lock. The roadway was rutted and rough and was fenced in on both sides. The barn was set back in a second field. An overgrowth of trees and squat plants practically hid it. I hesitate to call them shrubs because they were obviously volunteers encroaching on the bit of civilization trying to maintain its toehold on this land. Nature was winning the battle, it seemed, but that win resulted in a much more sheltered living space. This location was a better choice for a clandestine operation than the last had been.

I looked skyward. Someone in a helicopter could see the expanse of the barn, but might think it had been abandoned. Actually, it looked as though it had been abandoned and was now being called back into service to hide a rag-tag bunch of rebels. One look at the inside confirmed that assessment. We would have to do a lot to make the place habitable. The first step would be to shoo out the animal squatters.

The men tumbled out of vehicles and swarmed into the building.

I stood just inside the door, not wanting to tangle with any of the current residents. The men raced to the end of the building and up ladders to the loft overhead. The humans were doing some swarming of their own. There was a barn door at the far end that had been left ajar. It banged shut as several men struggled to release it from the bowed wood holding it open. They yelled to each other about the repairs needed. I laughed. It must sort of be like camping to the men. A fun adventure.

Here, there were mostly horse stalls lining the side walls. As I stood at the entrance, I didn't see any place offering me quarters with privacy. I did not feature the prospect of sharing a dorm with twenty or more men. I was almost hoping that Steven would see the problems in our new home and send me to my own home. Maybe the decision to stay with this group of bandits was a rash decision that I should now reverse — if I still could. There was no lock on the gate. Hmmm.

"Hey, there's a tack room down here and a room for a stable hand on the other side."

I heard Buddy's voice. "I claim this room in the name of Sylver, our fearless leader!" There was laughter in response to his statement. When I finally got to the door, he had scratched a big S in the wood.

Steven looked in my direction and his shoulders fell in resignation that he lost the better room. He yelled, "All right, you guys, start cleaning this rat's nest. We need to make it home for humans." Apparently, he recognized our competition for the nests already in the straw.

Since I didn't hear anyone being attacked by a monster, I moved farther into the building to explore for myself. By the time I got to the far end, Buddy had cleared out the stable hand's abode and it actually looked to be in decent shape, probably because the door had been securely fastened most of the time the barn was not in use.

As I moved cautiously down the aisle between the stalls, I looked into each area. I saw no enclosed room to use as a common room and in fact, no enclosed spaces at all except for the tack room. There was very little open space at either end of the barn for parking the cars. Any that didn't fit inside would have to be parked under trees. To my surprise, I was thinking like the fearless leader of a group of renegades!

When Steven handed me a shovel, I looked at him with scorn, "I am the fearless leader, not some grunt to be ordered to engage in manual labor!" I blew on my grungy nails and polished them on my tee-shirt with the haughtiest look I could manage.

Red rage crept up his neck to his face, but he turned to hand that implement of construction to the poor slob passing him just then — at the wrong moment. In that instant, he looked as though he was intending to remove some of the guy's body parts in the process of handing the shovel to him.

Buddy brought the remainder of my possessions and I set about making this creepy place more home-like. All the while, I wondered just how long I would have to remain an essential prisoner. In truth, I was allowed to roam freely around our compound and if I really wanted to escape I could. In fact, just recently I had been offered assistance several times. The bars around my prison cell were the media waiting outside for me and men still to be reached inside.

CHAPTER TWENTY-FOUR

That night, things were just beginning to settle down after a dinner eaten from plates balanced on knees when the sounds of racing engines alerted the ensemble to intruders advancing on our refuge. I was just starting to lay out cards on my bed when I heard yelling and a mass of troops gathering at the barn door near my room. Were they going to escape into the trees beyond the barn? Retreat today to fight some other day? The anxious grumbling indicated that the men were not certain what to do and were waiting at the head of the escape route for orders.

I opened the door to my lair and was pushing my way into the crowd when Steven's voice rang through the barn, "Nothing to worry about. New recruits are arriving. These men replace the cowards that deserted after our invasion of the state capitol."

I laughed inside at Steven's proud description of that failed military operation. In my dual role of fearless leader and curious prisoner, I moved with the men to the other end of the barn to greet our new recruits. As the new men passed me, some looked surprised to see a woman.

I stuck out my hand to everyone that passed close to me, "Hi. I'm Sylver." The arrival of these fresh new faces dashed my hopes for a rapid end to this nonsense, but I worked to keep my disappointment under wraps. No need to give away my position before they got to know me.

Some only regarded me with suspicion. Others answered with a handshake and a comment about seeing me on television reports. "You're the woman they talk about so much. The one who leads this militia. It is an honor to meet you, Ma'am."

I heard familiar voices around me. "Sylver's also our resident psychic. She's available for card reading most days."

I couldn't help laughing at that comment, "I have little else to do here."

Those comments generated more suspicion on some new faces. Did they believe that passage in the Holy Bible was an indictment against anyone with a connection to the spirit world, and not just a warning against consulting charlatans? They would probably be wary of anything I uttered from here on out. After all, I might just be "of the devil."

Steven was all smiles and went through the group introducing himself and patting backs in greeting. "You guys hungry? I'll bet you are. Walt, see what you can rustle up for the new men to eat."

Dinner remains were resurrected and a second meal was laid out for the newcomers. I sat with them, but didn't want to add any more to my girth. I was hungry for news from the outside world, the world that must still exist outside this bubble of rebellion. My hope turned out to be pure fantasy. Some of the men joining us were refugees from other units recently disbanded. Mostly for the same reasons our men had deserted. So this addition of men was a consolidation of assets, so to speak. Still others were men who had suddenly learned about the plots out there "to rig the elections and cause the guy who looks and thinks like me to lose his bid for the seat in the government." Of course, there was no mention of the female candidates.

To many of these men, "Democracy is bad if it means that people NOT like me can vote on what becomes law." They voiced that sentiment in different words as they got to know our guys. I didn't hear every conversation, but I did see lots of heads nodding in agreement.

Buddy leaned over my shoulder to whisper, "And so it starts again."

I answered with a chuckle, "Another day, another

reading."

I heard his laugh as he moved through the area to join a different group of newbies.

Tadd waited until the new arrivals were all together in the dining area to make his appearance. He didn't make any effort to shake hands or to make the acquaintance of any of the men individually. He barked his greeting, "You will learn my name soon enough. I am your worst nightmare. We will start training at dawn. I wouldn't want to interrupt your beauty sleep until then." He glowered at the men and then turned on his heel to make a grand exit.

I heard a number of comments from the room around me, "Nice guy." "Is he serious? We train at dawn?" And another, "He's like the monster in the unit I just left. The very definition of sadistic. I was hoping to get a human in this unit."

Familiar voices answered, "He's so fit, he wears us into the ground. And he never even breaths hard." "Oh, yes, there is a lot of physical training here." "I hate it, but I've never been stronger." "I don't think I could ever be as fast as Tadd is, but I am getting faster and can run longer."

All this was news to me. I knew the men didn't much like Tadd, but it seemed he earned the respect of some of them.

Soon enough, talk in the groups reverted to normal conversations. I sat with one group, but tuned into the others from time to time. I was trying to take the measure of our newest members. Most discussions focused on untruths I'd heard for months. Even though the election was over and done, they refused to believe their candidates had lost in a fair election. Some even quoted the woman who had failed to win the Senate seat, "I have lost because this election was rigged to fall the way the Cabal wanted. You are the people who should determine the future of this great country. You and you alone."

From what I heard, the campaigns were perfectly designed to appeal to the particular preferences of these true believers. "There's no way she could have lost in a fair election because she spoke for the people. She supported the wall to keep out the criminals and funding all schools, not just the schools for the poor."

I started slowly, "Did you attend public schools or private?"

The new guy, Henry, looked at me defiantly. "I went to a good Christian school. What of it?"

I shrugged. "Just asking." I turned to another of my new friends. "How about you? What school did you attend?"

He shrugged. "I went to public schools all the way."

I looked from man to man and shrugged. "I went to public schools myself. We weren't particularly poor. At least I don't think we were. But I turned out pretty well." I pointed to the man standing next to me, Paul. "You look like you're surviving, too."

He nodded with a grin. "I finished college and got my degree in engineering. Got a job waiting for me when all this is over."

"So all that money spent to support public schools did pretty well by us." I looked at Henry again. "I guess you just want for your private school to get in on some of that free money? Take it away from Paul and me and give it to your friends."

Paul and some of the others in the group looked thoughtful.

Henry waved his dismissal of my experience and went on with his own thoughts. "All those elections are going to be challenged in the courts. New vote counts will prove how crooked they were."

I laughed inside. I just couldn't let that one go, either. "So, you think all the people who won were cheating? All of them?"

Henry nodded vigorously.

"Both Democrats and Republicans? The elections must be

part of the plot by the bad guys in the Deep State to keep a tight rein over this country. To keep the real people enslaved by debt and poor education. Do they think that by keeping the average American dumb and ignorant, it will be easier to control them?"

"Damn right. That's why we have to fight for freedom of the masses."

Agreement was expressed by several of the guys, but some others shook their heads in confusion. I wondered if they saw through my argument?

"But you just told us you're in favor of starving the public schools of money in order to give that money to the rich guys in private schools. Which way is it? You or the Deep State keeping American citizens stupid?"

He blustered a bit and then marched off to another group. Most of the others stayed to discuss other topics. While every one of the guys was opinionated, they differed on some of the finer points.

Any defeat of those radical candidates must have been part of the plot by the bad guys, regardless of the winning candidate claiming they wanted to help the average man. *But they must be lying because they are not me and they don't want what I want!*

I listened to men rehashing predictions of the podcasters and other Internet heroes. I heard of them encouraging the militia to go out to "support the Constitution," translated into a call for more deadly clashes. More us against them. Riots that were futile attempts to rid the planet of the damned do-gooders and of people who claimed they wanted equality. But we know they just want to take over our country. We want to fight for freedom except for that group of people over there. As I looked around the group of new faces about half of them were nodding with energy. They were here to save our country. Filled with the zeal of the convert and the true believer. I sighed and started a slide toward despair. Did no one actually check the facts spouted by the podcasters beating their chests and shouting out the TRUTH?

Breakfast was more of the same. We're good and they're not. "What do they believe in?" "Hunh, hunh, I don't rightly know, but it's not what I believe in." It was all I could do to stay long enough to finish eating because the palpable hate swirling around and growing with every comment made me physically ill. And yet, I did see some of the men I'd met the day before staying out of the rants. Some of them leaned back in their chairs and actually listened to the conversations and prognostications.

I stood outside the barn to study the field surrounding it.

One of the new recruits startled me by coming up behind me. He took me by the elbow and led me a little way from the door. "I hear you do Tarot readings."

I nodded while I searched his face to see if he was reading me or joking.

"I might like to get one from you—soon."

I didn't hear mocking or derision of any sort in his voice. "I can do that. We just moved here so I want to get my bearings first, but maybe tonight?"

He smiled, "I could even pay you."

I started to argue. "I don't usually charge anything. I'm not really a professional. . . ."

He grinned. "I know. And I'm not really an insurgent. I'm a doctor, Edward Tanner, with the skills to give vaccinations."

My head jerked around so fast I thought my eyeballs were going to shoot out the other side. I whispered. "A physician? Did you volunteer hoping to save these guys from gunshot wounds?"

He quirked his shoulder. "That and I brought you the defense against the virus."

I lowered my voice to a bare whisper now. "Don't let that

186

get out around here. You might get lynched. Them's fighting words around these here parts."

He laughed. "That's why I'm talking with you. You can direct people to me rather than my having to approach people I don't know."

I quipped in response. "There has to be some catch."

His expression was of mock shock. "Me, snare you with a catch? Never. You are respected and know these men."

"Yeah, I know most of them are rabidly loyal to the movement to return this country to the people who love it best. White males."

He looked earnest. "But you talk to them about more personal issues. Surely, you could slip this one in."

"Slip it in." I shook my head, fighting against the despair knocking at my door.

Suddenly, Tadd burst through the door followed close behind by Steven. The minute they saw us, they lowered their voices. I wondered what new plans they were concocting. I heard myself groan.

Just as suddenly, my new friend changed subjects. "Will you read for me? I heard you're the resident psychic."

I was flustered and didn't take time to think it through. "Tonight. Tonight I should feel more comfortable in our new home and will be able to make connections with my spirit guides."

Tanner nodded, "To your spirit guides, then." He quickly moved off toward the middle of the field, probably doing some exploring of his own. Or was this just a way to avoid the prying ears of the leaders?

He needn't have hurried off so quickly. Steven and Tadd turned to the left and disappeared into the trees. They seemed consumed with whatever they were discussing rather than being the least bit interested in what we were discussing.

Alone again, pondering my new life and my new surroundings. I still hadn't decided whether to take the shot myself. Of course, my next move was to return to my chambers to consult the cards. "Tell me, oh tell me, what should I do?"

As I had contemplated this question earlier, it was a purely academic exercise. At the time, I had no real opportunity to get a vaccination. Now, the question had become real. Here was a man offering to provide me with the best protection man could provide against the virus at this time in history. What should I choose? What would I choose?

I meditated and asked that my surroundings be infused with energy of the spirits. I called on my favorites and waited until I felt comfortable. I opened my eyes and picked up the cards to seek the answer. I was surprised by what I saw. I would be fine either way.

I laid out another five cards, phrasing the question differently. "Will I be safe if I take the vaccine?"

The cards indicated a strong positive. I felt in my heart that getting the shot was a good move, especially since someone had gone through a lot of trouble to smuggle it in for me. And for the guys here. I wanted them to know I was grateful.

My solitude was interrupted by the twap-twap-twapping of a helicopter. There was the bustle of people running for the cover of the barn. Then silence. I slipped out of my room and joined the small group huddled around the back door. They watched through the crack, but when it was my turn to look I saw only trees, trees, and more trees. The helicopter didn't circle over the area as if it were looking for us. In minutes we were surrounded again by silence.

As I walked toward the common area, my new friend, Tanner, tapped me on the shoulder. "Does this happen much?"

I shook my head. "Not really. It is a curiosity." It crossed my mind that perhaps one of our new members was carrying a transmitter of some sort to alert the authorities of our location — and that we had not disbanded as Steven guaranteed we would. I also wondered if Steven had vetted these new members in any way. Wouldn't that be more important, since he was going against orders from a higher source and now actually doing something that should be considered illegal? But then, that was Sylver thinking like the fearless leader of these fighting men.

When I entered the common area, I was shocked to see make-shift tables all around. The common area had morphed into a real eating space. Where had they gotten such wonderful conveniences? They looked to be made of wooden pallets from some long-past delivery. Thank goodness some worker discarded them in the woods around here rather than burning them or returning them to the store. I looked all around the room, but didn't see anyone anxious to take credit for the improvement.

During lunch, I was proved wrong in my assessment of our new recruits' reactions to my "fortune-telling." So much for being psychic. Three men asked to have their cards read and we set up times during the afternoon. My dance card was beginning to fill. The only space offering any privacy for readings was my own quarters, with cards laid out on my bed. I would have to find another space with a table. I would have time for that later.

As always, I was not simply reading the cards, I was reading the men. First, we talked about romantic hopes and families. When the time was right and the recipient ready, I talked about Partnership versus Dominator models. The light of understanding sparkled in some eyes, but the darkness of ignorance clouded over others. No matter, I planted the seeds. Always hoping they would grow. I knew that some would need more water and food, but others. . . .

By the time dinner rolled around, I was tired and determined not to do so many readings in one day in the future. I could never be a professional psychic who had to see one person every hour or so! And yet I had one more planned for that night.

I was surprised to see Buddy come in for dinner, his arm draped over the shoulder of a new guy and they sat down at a table of other newbies. They laughed and yucked it up like long-lost buddies. I wondered if they were from the same small town in this state of small towns.

My hope of any conversation with a new acquaintance was ruined when Steven and Tadd sat next to me.

I was immediately curious. "The two of you look as though you're two cats full to the brim with canaries. What great feats have you planned for us?"

They only answered with enigmatic smiles, inscrutable.

I shrugged dismissively. "Well, if that's the way you want it. Far be it from me, your fearless leader, to complain of being left out of the good stuff."

Steven's expression got even smugger, if that was possible. He was chuckling as he answered, "You'll see it soon enough, our fearless leader."

Tadd turned on me with a vengeance. An unprovoked anger. "Did you tell anyone where we are?"

"How could I do that?" I waved my hands in the air. "No cell phone, no phone, no telegraph, nothing at all. How would I have gotten this message out? Smoke signals?"

Tadd looked at Steven, but neither said anything.

"Why do you ask?"

Tadd snarled. "Where did that helicopter get our location?"

I leaned back in my chair. "They flew over and then moved on. Why do you think they were looking for us?" This is precisely what I had wondered myself, but I didn't offer that up for discussion.

Steven's voice took on an oily tone. "What do you talk about with all those guys who come to your quarters?"

"Why do you ask? I entertain both them and myself by doing Tarot reading. I tell them about romances gone right and all sorts of other things important to the normal human."

Tadd spat out, "It's those other things that worry me."

I shook my head. "Professional guarantee of privacy, psychic-client privilege."

He looked confused for a sec and then started down another path. "I'm here at the behest of the *real* fearless leader. I'm here to make certain the men are properly trained and that nothing prevents us, this unit, from doing our part in this war. Nothing, and that includes you."

"I can't tell you because it's private and personal exchanges between them and me. I repeat private . . . personal."

Steven leaned forward into the table and for some reason that motion reminded me of our last dinner in the Ethiopian restaurant. That dinner seemed have taken place decades ago. He had been correct when he predicted that it was our last calm meal, eaten in peace. Funny, but he didn't seem half as scary now as he had then. The man raised his voice, "You are not a professional here. You're just here to serve our purposes at any time we have them."

Oops. I glanced around to see if anyone had mistaken that to mean sexual favors. No, I didn't think so. Most of the men had averted their eyes to leave us in a virtual privacy if that was possible for people seated four feet away.

Tadd added to the volume as he continued, "Our purpose right now is to find out if any of these new guys is a spy."

I laughed hysterically, so hard, in fact, I almost fell off my stool. I raised my voice, too, as much for the benefit of the audience as for the other players at my table. "You think a perfect stranger would confess to me they're here to spy on you for the other side? Why would they? I am the fearless leader, after all. Or are you saying these men are stupid?"

Steven was getting angry now and yelling. "You know that's a ridiculous joke. You are not the fearless leader. You're my prisoner."

I was afraid to look around the room to see who was listening, but I did hear a lull in conversations at adjacent tables. Rumor had now been confirmed. I was a prisoner held among them. How would they react to having a woman held against her will in their midst? Especially since her prison-guard was constantly beating his chest about how we were fighting for the freedom of the masses? Fighting for everyone's freedom but Sylver's?

Silence at my table. No answer. Tadd and Steven were obviously so furious they were ready to do me bodily harm, but they didn't say anything. The volume of talk around the room picked up. Was it my imagination, or were the people around me tittering nervously? They spoke in spurts rather than smoothly, as they had.

How would this revelation effect my reputation among the men? I was, after all, a prisoner. One of the enemy. In this group I might be considered a political dissident. It would help them understand the dynamics between Steven and me. No wonder we had it out from time to time.

CHAPTER TWENTY-FIVE

I got my vaccination and so did a number of others.

Sometimes I saw men looking toward the gate and the road. Toward home and freedom. Were they rethinking this fiasco? This treason? Or were they merely tired of the grueling physical training and being verbally abused by Tadd every day? After all, they were volunteers and not being paid for their time. Add to that, the accommodations seriously lacked and the food was no better. So, the question remained, just why did they submit to this abuse?

Although they may have contemplated deserting, no one actually left the compound. No one spoke up against the grueling physical training or the lack of sleep, abuses Tadd excused because they were now in "preparation for the big offensive." To the contrary, they all seemed to throw themselves more heartily into the "war effort."

Now, despair was constantly nipping at my heels, depression close behind. As Steven became more excited about the plan, I became more deflated. Would this never end?

Steven tuned into the news and we gathered to watch what I called propaganda. The constant repetition of the same old inaccurate negative information was like brainwashing and I was succumbing to it myself, regardless of understanding the process. The constant barrage of negative was difficult to resist. I was on the slippery slope.

The news reporters dutifully detailed devastation due to the different virus variants. There were numerous discussions about the someone who must be releasing this new killer into our struggle. No conclusions were drawn.

Steven raised his fist and yelled, "It's the Cabal, the Deep State."

I couldn't help but try to inject some sanity and reason into the discussion, "I thought they were going to kill through the vaccine. With nanorobots?"

Tadd yelled loudly, "It's all part of their plan. We have to kill them before they kill more of us."

I lowered my voice in response to their angry outbursts. "Why do unvaccinated people get sick at a greater rate? Aren't they the true believers and aren't they listening to podcasts telling them the vaccine is the killer?"

No response.

I continued. "Why are the people who support this monster — the one who demands that you kill your neighbor and who rails against the medical system — why are they the ones getting sick?"

Again, no response.

"Is he Draco? If the virus was spread by the Cabal, maybe the vaccine is used to protect their supporters against it? Wouldn't they want to kill only the resistance?"

No response.

"And that leads to the conclusion when you encourage people to avoid the shot, aren't you working for the Cabal? Perhaps that shot really works and you condemn your followers to sickness by convincing them to not get vaccinated?"

I cut off the blustering from the chair next to me with a loud accusation, "Well, if you're not working for the Cabal, at the very minimum you're helping meet their goals."

These were sentiments I'd voiced on numerous occasions, but for some reason they struck a dangerous chord tonight. Both men were red in the face and had trembling fists when they stood. They stood so fast that my chair tipped dangerously. An invisible hand righted me.

Tadd raised a fist to strike me, but another hand stopped his in the middle of the arc.

Later, I realized I might have been seriously hurt if they hadn't left when they did.

As the terrible twosome stormed out, the room filled with a babble of confusion. Steven stopped at the door to yell. "Turn off the television and go to your quarters. Now."

The noise ceased immediately, as though that invisible hand had activated the mute switch on a stereo. The room emptied quickly as the men followed the orders of their commander. Soldiers. Perhaps the mutiny of protecting me was the most they could reconcile in brains that had been broken by physical and mental abuse during daylight hours, coupled with the brainwashing at night. Actually, the brainwashing went on all day, every day.

Days later, the virus hit our encampment. Had some new recruit brought it with him? Dr. Tanner did what he could for the sick, given the lack of facilities and medicines. Finally, one day he dragged me into Steven's lair.

Tanner slammed his fist on the make-shift desk. "We have to take these men to the hospital. I — we — have done what we can for them here. They need more than I can give them. You're killing your own men if you keep them here without proper care."

Steven folded and slipped a paper under a notebook. "These new recruits must have brought that cold virus in with them. I knew I shouldn't accept them into the unit. Tadd also tells me they're not properly trained. No stamina. No fighting skills." He picked up a notebook and waved us out of his room. "Go back to your patients and help them get over these colds."

Tanner looked at me in desperation.

I leaned closer to Steven. "Tanner has done the best he can. We have no materials to help them. I've been helping care for the sick and they are very, very ill. They don't just have colds. Doctor Tanner is one of those new people and I don't know what we would have done without him. But he just can't do it all alone without the necessary equipment and drugs."

Tanner added, "She's right. If they don't get medical treatment, they will surely die."

Steven stood menacingly. "How do I know you didn't bring it in?"

This whole discussion was ringing some far distant bell in my memory. "Steven, have you been hanging around the stable hands lately?"

My doctor friend looked at me. "The stable hands? The guys working the horses in barns down the road?"

I nodded. "He's placing bets they suggest. I guess you call them tips, hot tips."

Tanner turned his laser vision on Steven. "Haven't you heard? There's an outbreak of COVID-19 on that farm. Too many of the workers there couldn't get the vaccine and. . . ."

I turned to look at Steven again, "These deaths are due to your greed!"

"I'm not sick."

"Not with COVID. But you are sick." I yelled at Steven, "You're letting your ego kill good men here. Have you no shame? And they all believed you, your every word. That was the only thing they did wrong. Well, mostly."

I stormed out of his room and was livid about the men sick and dying and about Steven's blithe reaction to the situation. And about my feeling of helplessness. Mostly about feeling helpless.

Within minutes, Steven emerged from his den. "Walt, get the van ready. You're going to take the sick men to the hospital."

The man looked around in confusion and fear. The other men backed away as though he had suddenly contracted the black plague. Was this the Army's form of volunteering?

Steven pointed at him, "NOW! Take them to the nearest hospital then return immediately."

Tanner's expression brightened. He took control of the situation with an impressive strength.

"Most of you should go far from this area while we bring

the sick through to the van. Anyone who will even come near the sick men should wash their hands and arms very well after they do. Walt, you make a mask out of something. A shirt or a towel or anything that can be washed later."

Buddy appeared in a long, loose shirt, constructed a makeshift stretcher out of pallets, and helped carry the men to the van. When the job was finished, he ceremoniously threw the shirt into a bucket of hot, soapy water.

Tanner worked alongside Buddy and then got into the van to ride with the sick. When I tried to follow him into the vehicle, he shooed me away. "Someone needs to be here in case we have more. . . . You know what to do."

I watched them drive away along with the other men who had helped with the operation. "Go wash right now before you forget it." I washed, too, right alongside the others. I sang the alphabet song to ensure a long enough scrub. They looked at me oddly but followed my lead and scrubbed for as long as I did.

Tanner returned hours later to report that several of our patients died in transit, even as short as the trip to the hospital had been. Others were admitted immediately and were intubated. His prognosis for them was not very hopeful. The two that remained strong enough to avoid being intubated had more hopeful prognoses.

And, still, Steven took no responsibility for this tiny epidemic in our home territory.

During the news that night, I looked around at the men sitting near me in front of the television. Who else would come down with the virus? Who of them would die? I had lived among them for so long, they were my friends and almost like family. I didn't want them to die, not from any cause. I didn't want them to shoot or get shot. And I certainly didn't want them to suffocate as I'd been told COVID sufferers did. At least in the hospital, the sick could be drugged to keep them more comfortable.

Why in the world did these men think fighting was noble? War is not noble. It is stupid and a waste of resources and of human life. I don't believe it actually changes very much, anyway. According to history I'd read, it only exchanged one dictator for another or one oligarchy for another. Did these men think they'd found some magic to change the outcome?

The men sitting around me were mesmerized by stories on the news of blood and suffering. Even though I had different values than they, even though I saw flaws in their thinking, they deserved better than to be used as pawns in someone else's game. Too many were dying of disease, why add to the body count with bullets?

They were being manipulated by someone I could not see from my vantage point. I felt it in my heart. Someone was playing on their fears and their desire to blame someone else for their problems. Hopefully, with better guidance and more accurate information, they could be redirected. And maybe they would listen to me to learn war was never good. Certainly, taking someone else's freedoms was never a way to ensure your own for the long haul.

Too many thoughts, too many. They were racing around my mind and none of them went anywhere productive. I escaped into the television news to listen to the reporter now in front of the camera.

The pretty girl on the screen reported, "The worldwide death toll has risen to a billion, five hundred thousand people dead from all causes during this year of the pandemic. It makes more sense to talk about the death toll during the last eighteen months during the pandemic that has swept the planet mixed in with the political unrest and ethnic cleansing. Add to that deaths from natural catastrophes and there have a total of over two billion people killed."

Her face was placid, with no hint of sadness for the dead or for their families, the people now mourning those dead. I saw no hint of any residual humanity behind the pretty face and the blank smile. None. To her these were just numbers. These were words on a teleprompter to read into the camera. Read and tilt your head to appear earnest, more believable.

The guy who replaced her center stage had the same deadpan expression, an expression that spoke only of his desire to present a pleasant image on the screen to please the viewing audience. And still, the news was filled with death. Was it the only thing selling air time?

He smiled blandly at us through the camera. No discernible human emotion. "New reports out from the CDC have noted that some survivors of the disease caused by the novel coronavirus have reported permanent organ damage. Even after recovering from COVID, significant numbers have died from such complications."

What they didn't say was that our former president had suffered from COVID. He played down the illness itself and the vaccine. Again and again, he repeated the falsehood that the disease was nothing and the treatments are very effective. What he did not say is that because of his position, he was treated much better than the average man on the street. He was given the best and most recently developed drugs and watched over constantly in a private room. Doctors and nurses danced around him night and day, answering his every call and meeting his every need.

His experiences did not compare well with the hospital scenes on the news of sick people on gurneys left in hallways because there was no room available for them. The doctors and nurses going from patient to patient doing the best they could with diminishing resources. No, the men who had left this morning would not receive the same treatment as the men and women in governmental positions who were deemed crucial for the continuation of our government. I could see how the rumor might spread that there was a group of evil reptilian agents controlling these members of a governing elite. There must be some explanation for their insensitivity to the rights and needs of other citizens of the country. After all, weren't they elected to help those very people, the citizens who elected them? Some of whom were now dying on gurneys in hospital hallways?

But how could I convince the men around me that although there might be some group of people working against the good of the people, law-makers proposing healthcare for all are not a part of that gang. Providing for the health of all citizens is really for the common good. Hadn't they heard the whole is only as strong as its weakest link? According to the Partnership model, helping your neighbor was not giving up your freedom, it was ensuring those freedoms for the future. I looked around and felt the sinking in my chest of despair and hopelessness. How would this end? When would it?

The Senators who introduced laws to limit the freedoms of other groups could just as easily turn on this group for the same purpose. Perhaps later, when they were no longer needed to upset the status quo. Again, I asked myself, who is behind this rebellion? Who would benefit most from the violence being promoted?

Most of all, who could stop this gallop down the path of destruction? I could talk to the people around me, but who would talk to the people of the world? Who was the Magician? We certainly need him to work some magic to get the human race out of this trap of one-on-one destruction.

CHAPTER TWENTY-SIX

I walked as far as I dared through the trees and into the field beyond them. No clouds — the sky was absolutely clear. I picked out Orion and Sirius and then the Pleiades. Those were the only constellations I knew. The barn door must face due east because the belt of the archer was right there in front of me.

A voice rasped suddenly out of the dark. I jerked in reaction. "There's a group of meditators praying for peace. . . . Oh, I'm sorry. I didn't mean to startle you. I thought you heard me coming through the underbrush."

I worked to slow my breathing and my heart. "No. I didn't hear you. I was concentrating on the sky."

Tanner laughed. "Are you asking for help from our extraterrestrial buddies? You've been looking a bit down-in-the-mouth these days. Giving up hope?"

I nodded and then turned my eyes back to the archer. "I hadn't thought of that, but perhaps intervention from the guys in space ships is exactly what we need."

Tanner snickered. "Well, they are our best allies in the fight to defeat the Draco who are destroying our country and our planet."

"You, too?"

I felt his hand on my shoulder. "No, but I did learn the lingo. And the story." He pointed to the clearing we were facing. "This would be the perfect landing place, wouldn't it?"

The clearing was approximately round and the grass was only as high as my shin. "Maybe they've used this area to set down before. I mean, maybe they've been providing guidance to the movement all this time and we didn't know."

"Maybe."

I turned to look up into his face. "You were saying something a few minutes ago as you tried to frighten me out of my skin?"

He nodded but his head remained tilted back, looking toward the sky. "You left pretty suddenly after the news ended, so I figured you didn't hear the little blurb from the other station I found."

"They let you tune in another station? How daring!"

"Yeah. Most of the guys were already out the door before they realized what I was doing, but Tadd turned the set off as soon as he could get to it."

"And?"

"Apparently, there's a gathering of a large number of spiritual leaders and their followers meditating on the subject of peace."

"The Maharishi Effect."

He nodded and turned to look at me. "That's what the commentator called it. I'm not familiar with the term. Will it change anything?"

I looked to the sky again to add my own prayer to the gathering. "The Maharishi Effect is what they called the influence of a large group meditating. Years ago, a spiritual guru and thousands of his followers gathered to work for peace. They met in a tent from what I remember, and meditated together. They were actually doing a study to determine if meditating for peace really had any effect. They analyzed measures of violence before, during, and after the period of the meeting. Data indicated an appreciable decline in killings of all sorts, from human actions as well as natural events."

"Appreciable? Like 50%?"

"As I remember, there was a 25% decline in violence during their meditation."

"Powerful."

I walked around in the grass in front of him. "Powerful. Unfortunately, the effect only lasted as long as they were meditating. When they left the tent, the measures of violence returned to their previous levels."

"How long were they in the tent? Days?"

"Frankly, I don't remember. It might have been only hours or a day. Did you also catch a call for help from other meditators across the planet?"

Tanner was quiet for a bit. "I think that's what they were saying just as the television was turned off. Seems as though Tadd didn't want this kind of news to circulate."

"No surprise there." I suddenly felt a lot more hopeful than I'd felt in a long while. "Did you catch a specific time? If people meditate, or pray, for an hour at a specific hour, their time, then the whole day is covered with meditators. I think that was the problem in that first attempt to bring peace. They did demonstrate the power of prayer. When the meditators left the tent there wasn't anyone to take their places. If people are meditating all over the world, then the effect should last much longer, maybe forever."

Tanner shifted on his feet. "I'd like to think you're right, but I'm not there."

"Who sent you?"

The man swayed as if my question were a slap across his face. Once he recovered, he paced in a narrow oval beside me. "I came on my own. No one sent me. I want to do what I can to save our country."

I reached out to stop him as he neared me. I drew him closer and lowered my voice to the lowest level I could and still be heard. "Tanner? Tanner. I have a sense about these things and I think someone went to a lot of trouble to embed you here in this group. My hunch is that whoever it was had concern about me. I am the lone woman in a mob of men on a testosterone high. I am essentially a prisoner, held here against my will."

He stood looking into the clearing. His voice was only a notch above a whisper. "I don't think you're actually here against your will. Maybe at first, but now you think this is somehow your mission. I'm not certain what you hope to accomplish, but you have something on your mind. From what I know of you, once you set your mind on a goal you wouldn't let any man dissuade you."

"What am I doing here?" The question was as much for myself as it was for the man standing next to me.

"I don't know, but I do know that you have become a sort of beacon of peace for some of the guys. I hear them talk about their meetings with you and how you help them understand life's situations. So many seek you out to talk. What do you say to them?"

Steven had just asked me this same question and I hadn't answered him honestly. I would try for honesty with Tanner. "Tanner, I try to explain the difference between the different models of relationship and hope they learn to discriminate between the two in the people around them. They have to decide for themselves the kind of family or marriage they would feel best in. Or the kind of country."

He shook his head. "You're trying to reach this bunch of guys who have been fed a constant diet of hate and teach them about brotherly love?"

"I know. Right? It's crazy. Most of them have spent years wallowing in the rhetoric of 'Us against Them.' I don't know why I think I can break through those barriers. But I have become the Grandmother."

"And the Grandmother has a certain power that no other human being has."

I thought about his words for a few minutes. They partly described what I was doing. "In Native American cultures, women have real power. Respect and power. And the Grandmother is a special woman with knowledge that few others in the tribe have."

Tanner nodded in understanding. "That knowledge and the way they use it magnifies the special powers they have as women."

I looked to Orion again. My heart resonated with his explanation. "I think so. And that must be why I'm here. Why I stay even when I was offered escape routes to the outside. All men are raised by women. Just think about the special place your mother has in your life."

We stood in silence for some minutes.

"Steven and I used to be friends. He and his wife and Bob and I used to go to dinner or to movies together. Then he shot Helen and Bob. He killed them because he said the Draco had possessed them. They were trying to stop him from accomplishing his mission."

"His mission?"

I gestured around and to the barn. "This must be what he believes is his mission. He's planning to take over the government. He and some of his friends are ready to take responsible jobs in the government to be set up after this one falls."

Just then I heard twigs snap and leaves rustle and crunch underfoot, under someone's foot. I stared into the clearing trying to stay calm and remember what I had said during the time anyone might have heard me. I didn't think I'd said anything incriminating. Besides, I'd kept my voice low and was faced away from the door.

Steven thrust himself between Tanner and me. "Are you telling this newby our secrets, my dear?"

I turned to look Steven directly in the face. "We have no secrets, Steven. You've already told a large audience I'm your mascot, your decoy. Then you told them I'm your prisoner. But when the bullet comes for the leader of this insurrection, you want for it to kill me instead of you."

Steven laughed deep in his chest. "I'm hurt, Sylver. I explained that I brought you along to protect you. I only said that you're a prisoner around members of our unit. And I only did that when you made me mad. That was your fault because you made me mad. I didn't say anything of the sort to people outside this compound . . . to them you *are* our fearless leader. You have importance . . . both now and when we win."

I couldn't let it go. "Protect me, Steven? I don't even know what you told the police about the murders. Did you tell them I killed Helen and Bob? Is that why I need your protection?"

He kicked at the grass and then flattened the growth to form a path extending about a foot into the clearing. When he returned to us, he stopped six inches from my face. There was something soft in his eyes that I hadn't seen for months. "No, I didn't tell them you killed my wife or Bob. I told them the truth."

"That they were taken over by Draco?"

He nodded. "I was sorry about killing Helen. She was a good person and a good wife, but she threatened to have them put me away if I continued to work toward the revolution. She lacked vision. I believed her threats. I couldn't lead this group from inside a prison or a psycho ward."

I saw a glimmer of the old friend I had known for years peeking out from the facade of *the leader of insurrection*. "But, Steven, where are the millions of people you thought would join the fight? The authors of those posts you sent me told their readers — us — millions of citizens would rush out to join the fight. Doesn't the lack of general support tell you this small group is alone in its fight against authority? Doesn't it tell you that most people in this country are satisfied with things as they are? They see no need to overthrow the government."

"They drank the Kool-aid. They're victims of debt enslavement. They're afraid, but when we show them how strong we are, they'll come out of their hiding places in their homes and in their quiet neighborhoods and join us. When they see how close we are to winning." As he spoke, his eyes took on the look of intensity that lit them most of the time lately. "It's my job to help save our country. How could I let her stop me? He was going to help her. I couldn't let that happen. They both had to die."

"You sent me dozens of articles enumerating groups owning guns in this country. The authors predicted all those people would join this fight and the units of men storming the ramparts would be so numerous that the bad guys would throw their arms in the air and surrender at the very sight of so many against them."

Steven backed a foot away from me, "And your point?"

I waved my hands to take in the area. "Where are they, Steven? Doesn't the lack of reinforcements indicate this is not a popular uprising? It's a battle being fought by a minority of men playing war. Their child-like enthusiasm was co-opted by you and some small faction who are pulling even your strings." Oops! Had I gone too far?

Anger flashed from Steven's eyes. "I am in charge. You'll see. When we take over Washington, you'll see exactly who is pulling whose strings. When I sit on the seat of power, you will regret that we didn't get there together. That you didn't help me. I hoped that you would realize how great we are together. We could achieve great things as partners."

I could feel Tanner's head jerk to look in my direction and so must have the man standing so close in front of me. Steven turned his head slowly to look at Tanner as though he had forgotten we were not alone. "Ah. Tanner. You're my witness. Sylver here is withdrawing as our fearless leader. I wanted to use her as our mascot to place her in the limelight and make her important in the warriors' eyes, but she's a traitor to the cause. You are my witness here. You are my witness." His voice was filled with emotion.

Tanner whispered. "You didn't mean to set her up as a target? But that's exactly what you have done. Made her a surrogate target. Someone to take the bullet for you. This isn't the way you treat someone you want to spend more time with. That's the way you treat someone you wouldn't mind losing."

I was suddenly frightened by the intensity of my old friend's emotions. "Will you shoot me now? Or put me center stage so the 'enemy' can do the job for you?"

Steven sighed and searched the sky. For reinforcements? From the little green men in space ships? "I hadn't thought of that when I made you our leader, but you do make an excellent point, Sylver. And an excellent target. Our fearless leader."

His gaze shifted to the barn. He suddenly stormed off in that direction. It was as if he were responding to some bugle calling to action. If I hadn't moved out of his way he might have bowled me over in his sudden march forward. I had this really bad feeling in my chest and almost ran after him to repair some of the rift just torn in our relationship, whatever imaginary relationship Steven had thought we had or would have. I felt Tanner's hand on my arm to quell that reaction.

My encounter with Steven had drained me emotionally. Again, I wondered why I was here and if I was truly as safe as I had assured Tanner. Maybe he was right. Maybe I should take any exit I saw the instant I saw it.

Tanner's hand remained on my arm, gentle and reassuring. He whispered into my ear, "You have a lot of friends here, Sylver. There are a lot of us to protect you. After all, you are the Grandmother."

I whispered my fears for the first time, "But Steven and Tadd control the guns. Tadd has never liked me and now Steven won't protect me. Not after this showdown at the not-so-ok corral."

"It was bound to happen. You're no good at hiding your feelings or your opinions."

I chuckled. "What an understatement. And you don't even know me very well."

Tanner squeezed my arm. "That trait is partly what makes

you who you are. That's why people want to talk with you. That's why people actually listen to you. They do, you know, even when they act like they're ignoring you."

I was grateful for his kind words. "But when he puts me in front of the other side's guns? Then what?"

I waited for more reassuring words, but Tanner was suddenly quiet. His hand dropped from my arm. His gaze returned to the constellations above us. The stars had moved a little along their trek across the night sky. "Are you looking for reinforcements? Somehow, I think you might look all night without seeing anyone."

Tanner stood still. "Have you read any of the reports the governments of developed countries have released listing the numbers and kinds of sightings of UFOs over the years, over the decades?"

I shook my head and turned my eyes to study the stars overhead. "I've been a bit busy lately, Tanner. Besides, I don't have access to a newspaper or computer or any source of information from the outside."

He snorted in amusement. "Well, they don't call them UFOs any more, but UAPs. I guess that makes it sound as though it's a new thing and they haven't been lying to us all this time."

"I guess."

"Now would be a really great time for some of them to come down to help."

I felt myself chuckle down low in my body. "Wouldn't it just. I would settle for any kind of help, really. They don't have to land right here in this clearing." I raised my voice to project toward the watchers who were supposed to be making sure we didn't annihilate our entire species or our planet. "I've always thought of the universe as a symphony and the whole composition would be terrible with even one instrument missing. Planet Earth would be missed in that musical ensemble. So come help us regain peace. Help us learn to live in harmony."

Tanner whispered. "Interesting concept, Sylver. Very interesting." He turned toward the sky and raised his own voice, "Ditto, you guys. Ditto. This woman has a good way of looking at the situation."

That's when I knew I could not leave yet. Not yet.

CHAPTER TWENTY-SEVEN

By the time I made it into the common area the next morning, everybody was gone. In fact, the barn was absolutely devoid of humans. Silent as a tomb, as they say. I fixed my own breakfast and cleaned my own dishes. Then I left to search outside the barn for someone, anyone at all. Maybe they'd gone on the big offensive and left me here since I was no longer a part of the In Crowd. I didn't have to walk far before I heard the sounds of men grunting through the physical training and firing on the shooting range or yelling as a part of maneuvers. Tadd's voice was louder and more brutal than ever. He yelled abuse at the men grunting in effort to move faster and hit harder. He called them lazy and slackers. Still, they worked hard to please the man who could not be pleased.

Once assured I was not alone, I turned back toward the safety of the barn. After all, I didn't want to be a target. Nor did I enjoy hearing good men being yelled at for nothing. It was emotional abuse and no one deserved to be treated that way.

Hours later I heard Buddy's voice calling cadence as they jogged back to the barn. They had to slow when they got into the trees. No sound of greeting came from any person in the unit as they passed me sitting in the woods. I was leaning against a tree sending thoughts of peace out to the plants around me. Out to the local communities. To all of Kentucky. To the world.

I listened to men huffing and puffing as they talked to each other. "I wonder what this major offensive is we're training for. Tadd's been pushing us like we were machines. I don't know how much more of this training I can take before I collapse."

"That A-hole never seems to get tired no matter how much PT he does. He's an animal."

"Or a machine. I don't know how he does it. He never slows down. He never seems to get tired and he's a maniac for training."

"Yeah, you would be, too, if you didn't ever get tired no matter how much you did."

"Tadd has some rod up his butt over this mission."

"Tadd has a rod up his butt. Period."

Lunch was big and conversation stifled. Tadd called for commanders to meet in the "briefing room" ASAP! "One more day. We have one more day to get ready, gentlemen."

Three men disappeared, grumbling. Buddy was among them.

The rest returned to "training" as soon as they finished eating. Tanner and the rest of the newbies were with that group. They all looked miserable. Tired and miserable. I wondered if they had trained at all before joining our ranks. They certainly did not seem to blend into the group of fit men who'd been with us all this time. I guess all that running and climbing over obstacles really did work to turn men into hard bodies. But how effective would a fighting group be if they were too tired to fight? I could see one benefit of exhaustion in that they were too tired to think or object. They turned into zombies mindlessly following any orders of the commander. Clever strategy. A form of brainwashing.

After dinner, we watched the news and I heard the requisite cheers when reporters described rebellions in other countries and suppression of "those left-wing radicals trying to destroy our country." More cheers at the introduction of laws to "discourage the poor and illiterate illegal aliens from voting in our elections." There didn't seem to be recognition that those very laws also suppressed the voting of the poor citizens from this country. Besides, only citizens could vote anyway. As I looked around the room, I didn't see many among us who would qualify for a PhD. I said nothing. I looked for hints about the building tensions. How and where would they be vented?

Somehow I expected an explosion instead of a gentle release.

In my mind's eye this assemblage looked as though they were doing the last grunting cheer a football team might do just before the first ball was kicked into play.

The men went into their quarters early and I heard the sounds of deep sleep very soon after. They were beyond tired. How much more abuse could their bodies take before getting sick or injured? Tadd seemed to be pushing them to the absolute limit of their physical capacity.

I was jerked awake by banging on my door the next morning before the sun was up. I was told to pack — quickly — and soon after was unceremoniously shoved into an SUV. We were on the road before the sun could dry dew on the grass. Finally, we were heading to that big offensive. Steven occupied his first-class seat in the front.

"Steven, where are we going?"

No answer.

"Lots of guns were packed, too. Everything."

No answer.

Soon I heard sounds of sleep from other passengers. Snuffling and snoring. The effects of so much physical activity. They could sleep anywhere, any time. And in any position, including standing up. One of the benefits of extreme fatigue. No energy for thought or questioning. No energy for wondering what our destination might be. No energy.

No one inside the car was going to answer my questions. In the absence of input from other humans, I asked the cards for guidance. The answer was — Tower, Magician, Sun, Ace of Wands, World. We would suffer a great change in understanding . . . a great change in our worldview. As long as you go with the changes instead of fighting them, you would be safe and all would end well for you. Someone would come with skills to bring the energies of heaven and earth together. They would help bring peace, for there would be peace and victory and joy at the end. Success. I asked, again, who was the Magician?

I turned over several more cards seeking clarification, but nothing was made clear. Nothing. Frustrated by the lack of explanation, I gave up trying to understand for now. I figured the answers would be revealed soon enough. We were barreling at high speed toward those very answers. No sense in agonizing over an issue that wouldn't be a question soon. I abandoned the search and tried to join the men around me in dreamland.

Along the route, we stopped for burgers and fries. Sometimes we stopped to unwind and walk in rest areas. Each vehicle had two drivers that switched off so we could make the best progress.

Eight hours later, we were in a rural part of Maryland. I only knew that from the road signs. I didn't quite understand why we were in Maryland, but there it was. The line of vehicles careened along country roads with twists and turns like any other country road. The land was beautiful. At yet another farm gate, we entered yet another code and drove to yet another barn. This barn was well-maintained. There were no critters, wild or domesticated, to shoo away and no spider webs to clear out of door frames. We didn't ever see the owner or actually anyone from the local area. The doors were unlocked and opened onto a space to park cars out of view. Once out of the vehicles, we each found ourselves enough personal space to stow our bags and to sleep. Tanner made certain my space had a solid door. I didn't see Buddy. Sometimes I imagined I heard his voice barking orders.

Finally, I got Steven alone and pretty much cornered, "Where are we going? I've heard murmurs about some big offensive, and since we're so close to DC, I imagine it's a show of force in the national capitol itself. Tell me what you're planning."

He looked at me, his eyes shaded by menace. This man was no longer the friend I had known for years. Had he been invaded by Draco? "It's on a need-to-know basis, Sylver, and you no longer have the required security clearance." He turned on his heel and disappeared around the other end of our new lodgings.

I explored the area, but there didn't seem to be a large enough space on this part of the farm to hold field maneuvers or to construct a shooting range . . . so "this must be the big one, Elizabeth!"

Tadd and Steven and sometimes only Tadd moved a reasonable distance from the unit to talk in private on a phone. He lowered his voice and if anyone dared walk close to him, he would wave them away and even yell, "Beat it!"

Buddy led his men in exercises, but no shooting or crawling through the dirt. There was no room for a decent run without using the road.

All personnel were busy with their assigned tasks. No one had time to talk with Sylver! So I remained in the dark about exactly where we were and what we were doing here. From the road signs on the way here, I knew we were fairly close to DC. That knowledge didn't encourage any calm in my mental activity, in fact, the very opposite.

The next morning, I was roused out of a deep slumber to dress in the "uniform" Steven got for me to play the fearless leader. I added a heavy jacket for warmth in the frozen north. We ate and were given something to tuck away for lunch. Finally, all personnel and weapons crammed into transport. After another two-hour highway drive and time meandering through the gridlock of Washington streets we were on Capitol Hill.

CHAPTER TWENTY-EIGHT

Our national capitol would be the scene of the Big Offensive. I got a sinking feeling things would not go well for us here. Mostly, I got the feeling things would not go well for *me* here. I should have run away from Steven when I had the chance. And now I was in Maryland on a collision course with a destiny I could not stop.

Hopefully, Tanner and I didn't give Steven the idea to use me as a target for the other side to practice on. As a shield for himself or Tadd. Men defending this city would be crack shots, professionals. They would take their responsibilities seriously. After all, their job is to protect the law-makers and the buildings in the capitol city of the most powerful democracy on the planet. This form of government, this democracy, was the experiment that succeeded. It was the form of government people all over the world hoped to duplicate in their own countries. The job of her defenders was to make sure it lasted for hundreds of years longer.

We mingled with the crowd gathered in the plaza in front of the capitol building. More and more people pushed into the area while we stood in a little knot of military-looking men in camouflage with black face goo obscuring their identities. I alone was actually visible, recognizable. All around us was a crowd gathering in energy like a gale-force wind slowly twisting itself into a tornado. I listened. I watched.

Reporters tried to interview Tadd but he pushed them away. "I have more important things to do here today than talk to you."

Then they turned to Steven. "What are you and these men doing here today?"

Steven smoothed his hair and smiled into the camera. His face was the picture of self-importance. "We are here to take back our country. There are evil people who have infiltrated the government. They work for the Cabal that keeps us enslaved with debt. They don't pass laws to help us, the citizens of this great country. They work for the rich and help them to become richer. You'll see, at the end of the day, I will be called a hero for winning back our freedoms, the freedoms guaranteed by the Constitution."

The reporter thanked Steven but moved away quickly before he could start another speech. Her comment was something about how wonderful it was to see such patriotic people ready to support the country.

People around us were agitated by a speech they had just heard. They were angry and determined to get their due. Here. Now. In that speech the former president had claimed that the win was stolen from him — again — and he commanded them to retake his office for him. "This is your country. Show them what you want, by force if they won't listen to your demands."

Unbelievable. The loser of this election was encouraging revolution. This was a scenario more familiar to citizens of countries run by tyrants. It was common in dictatorships where deposing a leader was only accomplished by force, by armed rebellion. I searched the faces of people milling around the space and saw anger in each of them. Righteous anger. Their voices were raised in hateful taunts and in threatening chants. Death to the VP. Death to the Speaker. In my mind I heard death to the democracy.

I watched Steven. He waved to other paramilitary groups I could see in clusters positioned around the building. He looked as though he was attending a party, a picnic to which he had brought some of the food. He laughed and smiled and waved. Having the time of his life, as they say. Was he seeing himself already on the seat of power as he had described the next phase to me? Was he already feeling the power, the control of the country he thought was his due? I shook my head sadly to see his growing madness.

Tadd was on the phone. His frown was etched so deeply into his face that I didn't know if he would ever be able to smile again, if he ever had smiled. He was apparently coordinating with the leaders of those units stationed around the building. Hundreds of men dressed in military-style clothes just like us and carrying assault weapons just like us. Suddenly something changed. We started moving. Steven motioned us forward. But Tadd yelled orders. His voice was loud and harsh. We snaked through the crowd and the men on the edges of our phalanx encouraged everyone they passed to join us. "We're going to take back what's ours." They repeated it as though it were a mantra.

Our numbers grew as we pushed toward the building. It seemed as though thousands of people, mostly ordinary citizens, surged forward. There was chanting, "Take it back." "Kill the criminals." "Hang the VP."

The flow of humans slowed as we climbed steps and forcefully pushed aside police protecting the building. Panic rose like bile in my throat. This was a federal offense and I knew this ragtag group of armed insurrectionists would not win. They could not win. Surely the real military would come to protect the government officials if not the building. Were they in front of us, ready to stop us before we could get too far?

The mob around us was not organized or trained as we were to fight the regular army. The men with me would not be enough to fight the numbers of soldiers that surely were on their way to defend this building. Didn't they see this was an impossible battle? The rebels had already lost before the fight began. They should retreat while they still could. We should retreat. I tried to scream the word as I pushed toward the edge of our group to escape. I would retreat even if I couldn't get anyone to join me. I was hemmed in by troops moving closely around me. I tried to strike out, but the muscled male bodies wouldn't let me pass. *Damn all that training.*

I did not want to be a part of this. I tried to hang back, but Tadd grabbed me by the arm with such force my arm was almost wrenched out of its socket. I had to follow him and closely to avoid pain from his grip. He pulled me along with him at the head of the unit. Up steps and more steps. We were followed by the men in a narrow line like the wake of a snail.

We pushed past men in the crowd who were knocking down police officers. One man was beating an officer with a pole. Another was slamming an officer against the wall and the mob pressed against him with such fury he called out for help. Anger begat fury. Fury begat insanity. Insanity begat violence against anyone within reach. And the mob pressed onward, rolling over anyone who didn't join in the forward movement.

Tadd growled at anyone in our way. Once he looked down at me with satisfaction that all was going according to plan. His eyes were yellow slits and I saw what might have been ridged skin at his neck. Was he a Draco? I tried to wrest my arm from his grip, but it was no use. The grip got tighter. Were those claws digging into my arm? He was not going to let me go.

Once we were on the top step, our forward motion was stopped by a locked window. Tadd released his hold on my arm to free both hands to work with his men using weapons and anything else they had to break through the window. He rammed his gun into the glass several times until it finally broke. I took advantage of his change of focus to get away. I was free and slipped between the shoving crowd and the building to get as far away as I could from the crazies on the forward edge of the attack. I felt the pressure of so many people trying to get through the very wall itself. I was trapped in the crush and was about to scream.

Suddenly a hand closed around my arm so tightly the circulation was cut off. I was afraid to look for fear that Tadd had caught up with me and was dragging me back to the window. He probably planned to push me through the opening and into the building. I would surely become a shield for the two of them. The shoving, yelling mass of people pressed close around me and pushed the air out of my lungs. Still, the strong arm pulled me against the current of human bodies and I felt like a battering ram against the wall of flesh.

I was dragged through the crowds. Down steps and away from the breach of the building. Going down the steps, I stumbled often, but the strong hand kept me upright. Inch by inch we progressed toward the square in front of the capitol. I wanted to cry from the relief of escaping my prisoners. Now there were two other bodies putting themselves between me and the on-coming mob, then more. Like a knife, they sliced a path through the mass of people. We moved faster in this formation. I was freer to move behind my protectors. Finally, I felt fresh air in my lungs as we broke free of the mass of insurrectionists. Finally, I was sure there was life after attack. Finally, I could follow without having to be dragged through the mob.

Gun shots shattered the air close to us. I heard a second shot followed by a volley. I wondered if Steven had killed another Draco. But my mind was muddled now from the stress of the moment and fear of being crushed by the crowd. That's when I saw Buddy leading his men down the steps away from the fight. Some of the men looked uncertain, but most of them looked relieved to be traveling in the opposite direction of the flow of the frenzied mob intent on joining the attack.

As one of our members had spoken up in the state capitol in Kentucky, "My parents voted to elect this Governor. They must've thought he'd do a good job."

I imagine some of the men had realized this government was elected to lead this country by the majority of US citizens. What right had this small group to interfere with the process described in the Constitution? The very Constitution they resolved to defend?

Yes, some of the people, regular citizens untrained by Tadd, gathering in the grounds had joined the paramilitary attack. They must have understood the meaning of this attack when they did. They shouted while moving up the steps, "Take back our country." But did they think about the reason? Did they remember this was to give power to a man who had failed to get enough votes in the election to win fair and square? This was a man who did not have the support of most of the voters in this country he hoped to control. Or had they simply gotten caught up in the emotion of this frenzied moment? Did they realize they were definitely a minority in this fight and had not been joined by millions of others? In fact, those millions of others were probably sitting at home watching the events on television, horrified by the actions of their friends and neighbors.

I looked around me to see the faces of so many who espoused the Dominator model and were willing to take power by the use of force. They shouted threats about killing Congresspeople . . . and anyone who served the country here in this stately old building symbolizing the power of this nation.

The sight of so many hateful people horrified me. The true believers would not give up this fight. I knew from the discussions in our camp. I could almost understand the brainwashing that had convinced so many of our members and the fatigue that made them so easy to lead. This was a fight to the death according to them. I wondered if these others marching with us were simply misguided? Would they wake up tomorrow regretting the actions they'd taken today? Or were they similarly brainwashed? Filled to overflowing with the lies that had led this paramilitary group to assault the seat of the United States Government?

CHAPTER TWENTY-NINE

I followed wherever my saviors led. All my strength was sapped by the fight to get free of Tadd, and away from the frenzied mob. I was exhausted by the fear I lived with for hours, for days, for months. I was ready to follow mindlessly. I didn't want to understand or interpret — I just wanted to feel safe now. Safe. As a result, I followed the strong men who were taking care of me. As I thought of this turn of events, I thought how trite the situation had become with the weak woman being taken care of by ten men. This was an anathema to my core beliefs. But there it is. Sometimes we just have to compromise.

We walked on pavement, large buildings to left and right. They looked official, like federal office buildings. Our little group met several National Guard officers. Tanner was at the front of our group and he was the one who talked with the soldiers. They led us into a large office building several blocks from the insurrection. We entered a grand lobby and climbed several flights of stairs. Eleven of us ended up sitting in large leather seats spread around this office, exhausted and awaiting our fate. A woman brought us deli sandwiches, chips, and soft drinks. I wondered what was going on. Why are they so nice to people who were primary actors in the debacle on Capitol Hill? I was so tired I could sleep sitting up in this solid leather chair.

Someone brought a television into the room and set it up on a desk. It was tuned to a network station with continuous coverage of the fracas we'd left. There were constant live broadcasts from different locations at the scene. Some footage showed reporters attacked by the mob. They were saved by the distraction of a roar from people entering the building itself. The attackers turned to run for the window where the action was taking place. They didn't want to miss the excitement.

Cameras located in higher positions filmed activities at the front edge of the mob. Cameras inside the building recorded images from inside the chamber and from hallways. The mob was disorganized and raging throughout the building with seemingly no goals, no direction. Only destruction on their agenda. As Buddy had explained to me, they knew how to win in battle but had no idea what to do after the battlefield win.

Where was the new government that was to replace the government now in power? Or were these maniacs intent on finding people to kill? I shook my head. Would these angry citizens actually kill people once they stood toe-to-toe with them? Were they that insane? Or were they so brainwashed they had become armed and dangerous? Mindless drones in the control of some other with the controller in their hands?

National Guard units streamed into the building and the steps around it, herding sections of the mob down the steps. They moved people out into the square and away from the area. Corral the people. First to go were the ones on the outside of the mass of attackers. Then a systematic movement of people farther up the steps and closer to the front of the charging malcontents. Once turned around they were kept moving. Walk behind them shoulder to shoulder to prevent any strays. Move them out of the plaza around the building. Set up barricades to prevent newcomers from moving against this stream of humanity. Walk behind shields to protect themselves. A peaceful parade of citizens leaving the plaza. No anger, no violence. What a difference when they were moving away from the target. They morphed into normal people again.

For these past months Tadd assured us most members of the military, all branches, would join the insurrection. All the people with guns were in favor of this fight against the current government. Millions would join us in battle.

To the contrary, here they were helping the capitol police clear the building and grounds of invading mini-hordes. We were the rabble, not the coordinated thousands he pictured. He told us we would number in the thousands. He lied.

Tadd. Tadd. Tadd was a reptilian. I had seen his eyes turn into non-human eyes of brilliant iridescent orange with slitted irises. Or had I gone into a fugue for the moment, insanity due to the relentless fear? The never-ending threat of violence?

Images on the screen became quiet, more peaceful.

Buddy appeared at the door to our room. I ran to give him a big hug. "You're safe. I worried about you." Tanner followed me.

He laughed and hugged me back. He waved a greeting to the men with me. "Me and my men are down the hall in a meeting room. Just wanted to assure myself that you're safe. Tanner and I worked this out last night." He looked around the room. "Seems to have worked. Eh, Tanner?"

Tanner nodded, smiling.

I turned to look at Tanner. "You did? And you didn't let me know?"

Buddy grinned, "We didn't know how things would go today. We had several alternative plans to choose from depending on the exact circumstances."

Tanner slipped in beside me. "I was scared when I saw how tightly Tadd was holding you. But you did a great job of slipping away from him."

I didn't want to think any more about the day's events, but my friends needed to know. "He was digging claws into me until he needed both hands to break through the window. Tadd is a Draco, Buddy. He's one of the reptilians. One of the bad guys. And this group has been following him forever. The minute he let go I wiggled in the opposite direction as fast as I could go. In fact, when I felt your hand, I thought he might have caught up with me."

Tanner laughed, "Charlie's hand. Charlie was the one who got to you first. We were spread out in case you could get free. We wanted someone in any direction you might run. You landed in Charlie's quadrant. Once he had you, he was afraid to let you go. Afraid you would get lost in the crowd."

"I'll have to thank Charlie. Truly."

"He would appreciate that. He told me you had a pretty shaky introduction."

I remembered the time he and I had met and laughed. "True, very true. I had no clue he changed his mind about me."

Buddy nodded. "He watched. Soon enough he realized who the bad guy was in the situation."

I realized how much had gone on behind the scenes. There was so much I didn't know. "What if Tadd had dragged me into the building?"

Buddy laughed. "We had a plan. I told you, I'm pretty good playing games and part of that is learning to see multiple options."

"All this time, Tadd and Steven had you with them in the leadership group and didn't take advantage of your knowledge!"

He quirked his shoulder. "I offered, but they thought that leadership was about retaining all control in their own hands."

"Their loss."

I waved to take in the room. "So, what is all this about?"

Buddy looked at his feet. "When I got the movie, I hadn't really set out to get a movie. I went into town with Steven and the library was the only place within walking distance. I told Steven I wanted to get a movie for the unit. That's why he let me go to the library. I really needed to use their telephone to call a friend in the FBI. I outlined what I was doing and he made some suggestions."

I smiled. "One of the suggestions was for you to get closer to the leaders. Another was to use your new leadership position to gain the trust of the men."

Buddy nodded. "You taught me the words to use. They worked to show the men how wrong our leadership was. Steven and Tadd only thought of themselves and their goals, not what was good for the group. They held too tightly onto control and used force too often rather than trusting in the ability of the men in our unit. In fact, the entire movement was Dominator model. These men could see that. Well, most of them."

"So, you were the one who taught them the difference between Partnership and Dominator."

He nodded.

I laughed. "During the movie they were showing you they'd learned the lesson."

"And you. They were showing you, too."

"Buddy, are you working for the FBI?"

He shook his head and hesitated before answering. "Not really. Sometimes I help out old friends who are agents. But I don't actually work for them."

I turned to Tanner. "And are you really a doctor?"

Tanner laughed. "Oh, yes. I am a full-fledged MD, with all the papers and missed sleep to prove it. But I'm a surgeon and I brought some knives just in case."

"Who sent you?"

"The short answer is the Lieutenant Governor was concerned for your safety. Let's leave it at that."

I nodded. "I thought so. I'm beginning to see how complicated all this is."

Buddy jerked his head toward the door. "I gotta go back to my men. I just wanted to make sure with my own eyes that you made it here safely. Also, the FBI has footage showing we're not part of the problem, so we're not in trouble. They just want to find out what we know."

"They plan to interview all of us, even if we only have to tell the same story as you did?"

He nodded.

I had to ask. "Will I see you again?"

He laughed down to his toes. "Come to the track. I work there most days." And then he left to return to his men.

Would I see him again? I didn't have a feeling one way or the other.

Tanner and I sat down to watch the insurrection on the little screen . . . as it happened.

Later, on the news shows, we listened to talking heads about the events of the day. Some of it rang true, but they missed on a lot.

As we watched video of Buddy leading his men away from the fighting, the reporter explained, "You can see some of the armed militia must have realized how wrong their actions were. This young man is taking control of the situation and is leading two dozen or so men behind him away from the area of conflict. He has saved their lives and the lives of people they might have injured. He is a hero in our eyes. We don't know his name yet, but we will find out who he is and commend him for some kind of award."

Cameras were trained on other clusters of Power Men. As the attack was commanded, men close to the commanders often turned to retreat instead of charging forward. The commentators voiced questions about their sudden change of heart. I studied the video and suspected they saw their leaders as Draco in the minutes before they deserted. Did it take a lot of energy to stay in human form? When they got distracted by the energy required for the attack, maybe the shape-shifting could no longer be maintained. Returning to their reptilian forms allowed people around them to see the real men through their disguises. The Power Men didn't contribute as much to the overthrow of the government as Steven had predicted they would.

I was filmed as I escaped Tadd while he was breaking through the window. The cameras were really focused on Steven and Tadd, but they could see that as soon as I was released from Tadd's stranglehold, I ran the other way. The commentators concluded I was an unwilling participant in the insurrection. Furthermore, only about ten men from our unit actually entered the building. Tadd's expression of shock when he looked back to order the unit through the window was priceless. Only those ten still wore expressions of rage. Tadd turned back to Steven whose face became a picture of horror. My hunch is that he discovered Tadd was Draco and that he had been working for the enemy all along. I kept this idea to myself because I didn't want to fuel any more conjecture about the potential war of the worlds that might be unfolding before us.

Steven and Tadd were some of the first in the building, but Steven was shot and fell forward. The reporter announced that he was shot in the back and therefore the police suspected one of the rioters of killing their own man. Tadd was also shot soon after climbing through the window. His body was spirited away by his buddies and was never found. As a result, there was no physical evidence to judge how he was shot or where the bullet had come from — inside the building or from the invaders themselves.

Just desserts if you ask me. My hunch was that someone else who saw his reptilian self pulled the trigger. What stories they would tell when they finally got home! Although invading an American government building alongside an enemy operator was not something a person fighting for freedom would want known by his buddies.

An FBI agent was interviewed by a reporter at the scene. "We promise that no matter how long it takes these criminals will be apprehended and sent to jail. Breaking and entering a federal building is a federal crime and the perpetrators of this incident will be punished. There are cameras all over the building and those security tapes will be used to identify each and every one of these criminals."

I wondered if the people who just got caught up in the emotion of the moment would regret their actions even more when they were arrested for the federal crime of breaking into a federal building. I had seen the men in our unit working to excite the people who were just standing around as we passed. Some of those people were impressionable and lured into the attack. I knew that, but the audience viewing the video didn't. I decided to tell the FBI as much as I could. I didn't want for all these people to end up in jail. A question popped into my head: why not?

Footage was shown of the losing candidate and his entourage watching the attack on the capitol as though it were a football match. Some of them were celebrating with singing and dancing and proclaiming a victory well before it was, in fact, a victory. They made videos on their telephones and posted them immediately on the Internet. Big mistake, because plenty of the remaining law-abiding citizens were witness to these shameful actions. The gang of losing politicos were celebrating the attack on our country.

Instantly, those videos went viral and were circulated among the various social media as well as the regular television news programs.

Over half the comments in response to these posts were people irate that our American principles were being threatened by these people who had lost in their bid to regain power. Some viewers actually posted that THEY were the people of the United States and their loyalty was to the nation and the Constitution. They were against anyone who would have the gall to attack their country. Some even said they were sick and tired of the lies and all the effort spent to mislead the gullible who believed every word.

The true believers in the audience cheered the campaign and agreed to continue to support the movement in every activity. That support would take the form of financial donations and hours worked in renewed campaign efforts.

The news reporters went into communities across the country to interview a large number of people who'd watched this day of televised rioting and insurrection. Some were in bars, eating chicken wings and drinking beer with friends. Between bites of chicken, they answered her question, "I think all those people ought to be put in jail. That building belongs to all of us. They destroyed our property. I elected some of those members of Congress. They work for me. They should be protected from lawless people who are willing to hurt others."

Some were caught as they came out of restaurants. "I might not like everything they do, but killing them is no answer. We're a democracy here, not a dictatorship where the only way to get five minutes in the spotlight is to attack members of our government."

In another restaurant. "I am tired of seeing all this hate and killing. When are we going to compromise and work together? And not just here in this country, there's fighting all over the world. We're like three-year-olds fighting over a favorite toy."

The reporter asked, "What would you say to these people?"

"When are you going to grow up? Adults talk things out. They sometimes have to compromise and don't always get their ways. We want a leader to bring the people together. Kennedy did that with the space race."

His wife added. "We used to pull together during the Olympics. We all cheered for athletes representing the United States. It didn't matter which state they were from. We just wanted them to cross the finish line first. To win the honor for us, for the whole country."

A man sitting with the same group added his two cents, "We're sick of hate and killing. If our leaders can't grow up and negotiate like adults, perhaps we should fire all of them and hire a new batch that can. But we do that by electing them, not by killing them."

I was amazed at the adamant calls for peace and working together. Here was the sign of enlightenment I was hoping would come as a result of all the hate.

Then I heard an alarm. It was insistent and went on and

on. Was there a fire or some other emergency in the building? Why was this alarm sounding? I looked around me, but didn't find anything amiss. I seemed to be the only one hearing the sound.

Suddenly, the building started shaking and I wondered if we were in the middle of a massive earthquake. The reporters on the television made no mention of seismic activity in the area. Or were the space ships landing? Were the watchers coming to help us in our hour of need? A foggy mist settled over my brain. Was the extreme emotion finally getting to me? I had done so well to hold it together for all these many months and now that I was safe, I felt as though I was falling apart. Falling apart.

Strange thoughts were careening around inside my brain. I couldn't see any pattern. Yes, space ships landing on the lawn of the capitol? Finally, they were coming to help. Space ships? Would I feel them this far into a big building? The shaking got stronger and my whole body was shaking. I looked up to see if the walls had begun to crumble yet. Shaking, stronger and more violent with every second.

CHAPTER THIRTY

A male voice cut through the fog of my mind. It was familiar. It was Bob.

"Sylver. Sylver. Wake up."

Was I dead? No, the voice said I was asleep. Bob's voice finally made its way through the confusion in my head. Bob's voice?

I was numb with sleep paralysis. Not one part of me would move. Not legs, not even eye lids. It took total concentration to force them open. Once my eyes opened, I worked feeling into the rest of me, piece by part.

"Sylver, wake up. You must've been really tired, but you have to get up now. Sylver. Sylver? We're supposed to be at Steven's house for the dinner soon."

"Steven's?"

"Steven and Helen. Remember? We're going for dinner and then to watch the primary results."

I focused my eyes on the source of the voice. Bob leaned over me. I wanted to prove to myself it was really Bob. Bob? I reached up to touch his face. I touched a real face and not some phantom.

"Bob? The primary? The election — who won the election?"

Bob laughed. "You must have had a doozy of a dream. No, no winner yet. The elections are months away. Today is June twenty-third. The democratic primary was held today to see who the voters want to represent the party. We're all going to watch the results."

I smiled and hesitantly moved my arms and legs, stretching

out the kinks and working life back into them. "A dream? Yes, the dream was — well, exhausting. Mentally and physically exhausting. I'm too tired to be with other people tonight." I closed my eyes again and could feel the pull of slumber. Should I risk going back to sleep? What kind of dream would I have if I did allow myself to fall asleep again?

Bob shook my shoulder. "Sylver, wake up. We're supposed to be at Helen's in an hour and you know how long it takes you to get ready."

I opened my eyes again, "Really? Helen's?"

"We promised Helen we'd be her support group. She's afraid to watch the primary results with Steven and his conspiracy theory buddies."

"She should be. He might shoot her." *Warn Helen. Warn Helen. . . .*

"Not with witnesses there." He laughed at what he thought was the joke. "Our job is to keep him from shooting her."

My heart and lungs remembered what to do. They worked together to send energy to all my body parts and I pulled myself out of bed. I managed to shower and dress. No bruises on my arms or anywhere on my body. A closet filled with real female clothes. I would wear a dress. I felt it had been ages since I had. I even remembered how to apply make-up. Polish on my nails was perfect. Not a chip. No dirt under them. Wonder of wonders.

I was more alert by the time we got to Steven and Helen's house. Still, I felt the hangover from sleep paralysis. Helen answered the door. She smiled and hugged us both. The same Helen, my friend. She pulled me into the living room. It was the same midnight blue. Stunning. I remembered the white lamp in the corner. I had always loved the way the white of the lamp was set off by the dark walls. She had positioned white vases filled with white flowers around the room. It was the same as I remembered.

As we moved farther into the house, I took a deep breath, inhaling the aromas coming from the kitchen. "Is that Ethiopian food I smell, Helen?"

"You know your smells, Sylver. Yes. Steven loves it — it's his favorite. So, I learned to cook a couple of recipes. Just for my honey."

I snapped into the fight or flight reaction when we stepped through the arch into the television room. The walls were covered with glass cases filled with shooting trophies, silver and shining. Proof of Steven's skill with a gun, any weapon really. But my attention was riveted on the people sitting there.

Helen smiled. "Meet our friends, Tadd, Rick, and Tanner and his wife, Georgia."

I shook Tanner's hand and then his wife's. "Dr. Edward Tanner and Georgia. Nice to meet you."

Georgia looked confused, but Tanner grinned. "Just Tanner. People call me Tanner, but you know that."

I hesitated as I extended my hand to Tadd and then to Rick. "Pleased to meet you. Where's Dereck?"

Tadd and Rick looked shocked. "He's — he's out of town." They looked at Steven quizzically. "But, how? Did you set this up, you rascal? Steven, what all did you tell her?"

Steven laughed. "I told you she was psychic. After a while you get used to it. It's unnerving at first." He turned to me. "Did I tell you anything about my friends here?"

I shook my head and stared at Tadd. I could almost envision a tee-shirt with the picture of a reptilian covering the front. I tore my eyes from the two of them to look at Tanner again. He knows Tadd?

Tanner turned to Georgia and nodded. She took a package out of her bag and handed it to me.

"Tanner saw this and thought you might like it."

I opened the package. A tee-shirt with the Magician card imprinted on it slipped into my hands. I looked at Tanner and quirked my head, "But how?"

"Steven said you read the Tarot."

I smiled and wondered who Tanner was. Who was he really? "Thank you so very much. I think all of us are part of the Magician. All of us meditating for peace."

Out of the corner of my eye I saw Tadd and Rick shifting nervously in their seats.

Tanner grinned. Georgia patted his knee proudly.

Bob wrapped his arm around my shoulder.

Helen walked to the dining room door. In her bright, happy voice, she announced, "Time for dinner. Everyone, follow me."

www.ingramcontent.com/pod-product-compliance
Lightning Source LLC
Chambersburg PA
CBHW071431260626
47170CB00008B/2668